Gravewriter

Gravewriter

Mark Arsenault

THOMAS DUNNE BOOKS

St. Martin's Minotaur ♒ New York

This is a work of fiction. All of the characters, organizations, and events portrayed in this novel are either products of the author's imagination or are used fictitiously.

THOMAS DUNNE BOOKS.
An imprint of St. Martin's Press.

www.thomasdunnebooks.com

www.minotaurbooks.com

Library of Congress Cataloging-in-Publication Data

Arsenault, Mark.
    Gravewriter / Mark Arsenault.—1st ed.
        p. cm.
    ISBN-13: 978-0-312-33596-0
    ISBN-10: 0-312-33596-2
    1. Gamblers—Rhode Island—Fiction. 2. Revenge—Fiction. I. Title.

PS3601.R75 G73 2006
813'.6—dc22   2006042920

First Edition: December 2006

10 9 8 7 6 5 4 3 2 1

For Joseph P. Arsenault,
my father

Gravewriter

one

That ain't piss down my pants, thought the old convict. *That's blood.*

He reached a hand around, fingered the wet tear in his shirt-tail, stuck a pinkie in the hot, sopping sinkhole in his lower back, gasped at the pain.

He ran on, cradling the package, wrapped in a garbage bag and a newspaper, like a football in his left arm.

I ain't been shot for twenty years.

Garrett had been shot two times before, and shot *at* two dozen times. None of those bullets had brought him down. He doubted that the small-bore pistol that had drilled this new peephole onto his kidneys would take him down, either. Nobody was going to snuff Garrett Nickel—the outlaw the papers liked to call "Nickel-Plated"—with a single pop of a .22-caliber Ruger.

Garrett grinned as he ran, impressed with the double-crossing son of a bitch who had taken Garrett's own gun and shot him when his back was turned.

Garrett's first whiff of the betrayal had been the gunpowder. That son of a bitch had colder blood than Garrett had ever figured. To conceal a killer's soul from Garrett Nickel was a trick; Garrett usually recognized a kinsman the moment he looked into his eyes.

He ran along a deserted street in a failing industrial park, toward the pink horizon to the east, and the flickering yellow glimmer of the harbor.

Garrett ran with a loping stride, still graceful after nine years in an eleven-by-seven cell. He ran on toes that lightly tapped the asphalt. He had been starving himself by necessity the past two months, yet he felt no fatigue as he ran. Garrett was juiced on adrenaline and two lines of coke. He switched the package to his other arm and pumped his legs harder.

To his left, a thin railing of iron pipe ran between the street and a narrow canal of swamp water flowing from a bog, toward the bay. Straight ahead, single-story manufacturing buildings, dark and shuttered at this hour, were silhouetted black against the sunrise. He heard the distant groan of heavy machinery at the docks, where the work of unloading cargo ships took no notice of night or day. To his right, a sagging chain fence surrounded a construction site on three sides. The side that fronted the road was open. Dusty tire tracks curled from the site into the street.

Garrett needed a place to hide, to regroup, to stuff a wad of cloth in the hole in his back, and to plot his revenge. Garrett's vengeance would be slow and bloody.

His spiteful side, which was most of him, wanted to run to the police station, bust through the front door, and spike the package, like a running back in the end zone, right on the blue-and-gold Rhode Island state seal embedded in the floor. That would teach the son of a bitch to double-cross him. He chuckled at the fantasy. Visiting the cops would not be in Garrett's best interest, and Garrett Nickel was a slave to that which was best for Garrett.

He heard a car.

He dived left, toward a billowing bush on the side of the street, at the base of a utility pole. He tucked up against a newspaper vending box, flinched at the wave of pain, gritted his teeth, and held his breath as the worst of the agony passed. He panted. Burning vomit rose in his throat to the back of his tongue. He choked it back down.

The car sped away.

The bullet hole felt like somebody was slowly turning a hot screw into Garrett's back.

Hiding beside the vending box, he rested. The telephone pole smelled like tar.

On the front page, in the newspaper machine's window, Garrett saw his own face and laughed aloud.

"Lookie there. They printed a late-night extra—just for me," he said out loud.

The picture was a courtroom photo from before he got his life bid, before his hairline had started its retreat. Even after nine years in max, Garrett was still a front-page headline:

"NICKEL-PLATED" OUTLAW ESCAPES
Killer of three, Garrett Nickel,
in prison break with 2 armed robbers

Killer of three? If they only knew . . .

Garrett was impressed he had made that day's paper; they had only been free for one night.

Beneath Garrett's photo, the paper had printed police mugs of two other convicts: a scarred street thug with a bulging Adam's apple, and a kid, half Garrett's age—big-eyed, sunken-cheeked, smooth-skinned. *They call him an armed robber?* A junkie punk, that's what he was. The kid had tried to look tough in the picture—eyes narrow, head cocked to the side, lips in a half pucker—but to Garrett, he looked like a frightened bunny. Garrett hacked up phlegm from the back of his throat and spat on the image.

The goop that oozed down the glass was dark brown.

Motherfuck.

Must have been blood in his vomit—the bullet had reached deeper than Garrett had thought.

Fear passed over him like a cold breeze, and he felt his bladder release.

"Goddamn it," he cursed, wiping the front of his pants. Even after a lifetime as a predator, and nine years locked up with men eager to jam a pencil in your neck for spitting in the shower, the Nickel-Plated Outlaw was still afraid to die.

He had rested long enough; the double-crosser would be looking for him. They would meet again, Garrett swore, as soon as Garrett found a weapon. He also decided to find a doctor, for a house call—at the doctor's house. Garrett would do the calling; the doctor would do the healing at the point of a gun.

But first—the package; it was slowing him down and he had to stash it.

Garrett tugged the door of the vending box. Locked. He didn't have four bits. The stream? No. The package was his insurance.

Across the road, at the construction site, a wall of cinder blocks climbed a squared-off steel frame. New offices, probably. Maybe a bank. Garrett peeked around the vending box, saw nobody, pulled himself up with a groan and a grimace, and jogged across the street.

The artists of the night had tagged the unfinished walls of the construction site with graffiti and cast their empty paint cans to the ground. Over a background of baby blue, a twisting green snake spelled out "Isaiah" in script.

Isaiah? I know Isaiah.

On impulse, Garrett picked up a spray can and shook it. The shaker ball clacked inside. This can still had a little color in it.

The can hissed at the wall.

Garrett smiled at his own cleverness as he sprayed two-foot-high balloon letters in ruby red, spelling out a fragment of Scripture he had committed to memory, to remind himself of where he had hidden the package.

He stood back, admired his work, and tossed the can aside.

Behind him, somebody cocked a gun.

Garrett froze.

"Quoting the Old Testament?" the double-crosser said. "The line I like best is, 'Eye for eye, tooth for tooth, hand for hand, foot for foot.'"

Garrett smirked. He continued the verse: " 'Burning for burning, wound for wound, stripe for stripe.'"

"Turn around, Garrett."

Hot piss dribbled down Garrett's right leg. He bit his bottom lip in anger. "Why don't you shoot me in the back again?"

"You're empty-handed, I see. Where is it?"

"Fuck you."

"I want it," the double-crosser said. "I want the picture back, too."

Garrett said nothing.

The double-crosser clicked his tongue. "Turn around, Garrett."

Garrett bent at the knees and rose up on the balls of his feet. He rolled his head lazily around his shoulders.

"Did you hear me?" the double-crosser barked. "I said, Turn around."

Garrett lit fire to his rage and exploded at the double-crosser in a sudden bull rush—mouth open, teeth bared, his huge hands clenched into claws, Garrett hissed like a wildcat and sprayed a dragon's breath of bloody drool at the son of a bitch who had shot him.

The double-crosser reared back in shock and raised an arm on instinct as Garrett pounced.

The gun fired once.

Garrett wheezed. His chest tightened, as if all the air in the world had been suddenly sucked out into the vacuum of space.

Son of a bitch knocked the wind out of me.

He staggered past the double-crosser, toward the street. Garrett couldn't inhale; he felt like he was breathing through a pillow. His right palm pounded his own chest to loosen whatever had gotten stuck in there. The thump against his chest echoed through him.

His hand came away smeared red.

The gun fired twice more. It sounded far away.

Garrett made for the river. It came unsteadily toward him.

He reached for the railing at the river's edge to brace himself, and then heard the gunfire again; it sounded muffled to Garrett, like it was underwater. He heard the crack of splintering bone, and then suddenly Garrett went blind and deaf, as if deep beneath a silent black sea. *Don't be afraid of the water,* he told himself. He remembered his Scripture.

What manner of man is this, that even the winds and the sea obey him?

He felt himself roll over the rail.

Fearing nothing, Garrett plunged into the river.

two

If you're going to get me killed, at least you can let me watch."

Billy Povich smacked the twelve-inch television. The silverware on the table jumped. The TV's vertical hold snapped awake, grabbed the picture and held it steady, though for some reason every object on the field was now being shadowed by an identical twin. Billy had forty-four players and two footballs to worry about.

"Who's getting killed, Billy?" asked Bo brightly. He was seven.

"Eat your cereal."

"I don't like this kinda milk," Bo said. "Who's getting killed?"

"Michigan State, by the looks of it," sniped the old man. "What kind of line did you get, boy?"

Billy reached both arms to the TV. His fingertips lightly touched the sides of the television as if it were a lover's face. He gazed into the screen. Down by eleven with four minutes to play, this was no time for a lecture from his father.

Billy lied: "Seven points."

The Las Vegas line in the paper had been seven; Billy's bookie had offered only six and a half, and Billy had taken the bet.

"Christ Almighty, boy," the old man scoffed. "Just seven goddamn points?"

"Don't swear in front of Bo."

"State's defense is banged up—they ain't stopped nobody in a month. How much is riding on these seven points?"

"Two hundred," Billy said, lying again.

"Billy!" cried Bo. "The milk is gone bad." He whapped his spoon three times on his milk-logged Count Chocula. And then he pointed his toy pistol at the bowl. "Pow! Pow!"

"What do you think you are?" the old man asked. "A cereal killer?"

Billy was too busy to commit parenting. "Pa?" he said, passing the buck.

"It ain't spoiled," the old man gently informed his grandson. "It's skim—it's just a different kind of milk. They took the fat out."

"Can we put it back in?" Bo asked.

"Huh," the old man said. "I don't see why not. Add some butter if you don't like it."

"Jesus Christ!" Billy screamed. He clutched his head in disbelief. "That pass was right in your hands!"

"Jesus Christ!" Bo echoed happily as he crunched a breakfast carrot and stirred a tablespoon of margarine into his cereal.

"Hush that language, boy," the old man said sharply. "Save it for church."

Bo drew an invisible zipper over his mouth. The kid respected his grandfather. On rare occasions, it seemed like the old man *could* raise the boy, if Billy wasn't around.

State's offense trotted off the field as the kicker trotted on.

Billy closed his eyes, exhaled some stress. Then he looked at the old man.

His father had parked his wheelchair at a short side of the rectangular kitchen table. Billy watched the old man peering over his glasses as his quaking hand reached a knife to the margarine. The glasses had heavy black frames, as they did in Billy's childhood recollections of his father. He remembered his father wearing those glasses at parties—there had always been a party when William Povich, Sr., visited the Providence flat where Billy grew up. Only in adulthood did Billy realize his father had come only on the holidays.

Now, the old man reminded Billy of a dehydrated version of himself—sunken chest, shriveled cheeks. The muscles over his shoulders had long ago evaporated to the bone. What was left of his hair was oily and limp. He wore three days' worth of white whiskers.

How does he shave without slicing off his wrinkles?

His coffee-stained teeth had drifted slightly apart. He had a bulbous, swollen, old-man nose with immense dark pores, and oversized ears, through which the sunlight shone red. He was just seventy-one, but the stroke had aged him. His worthless legs were like bone china wrapped in rice paper; he could walk on his own no more than a step or two.

The old man looked ancient all over—except his eyes, still a pellucid pale blue on immaculate white. Back when William Povich, Sr., was a young man, the women who peered into those eyes would see their reflections undressing for him.

Billy's mother had been one of those women, though not nearly the last.

The old man's mind was younger than his body, though his attitudes had not aged at all; his worldview was forty years out of date.

Could the old man raise Bo?

If he had to?

Michigan State had too many men on the field and called time-out.

Billy smacked the TV again to clear up the picture—and to punish State for wasting their last time-out. The blow knocked out the color, and Billy stopped hitting before he made it worse. The network went to a commercial.

Billy grabbed an open bottle of aspirin from the table and shook four tablets into his mouth. He chewed them like candy. Billy liked the taste of aspirin. He didn't mind the smell of skunks and was never bothered by fingernails on a blackboard.

He grabbed a breakfast carrot from the table and crunched it. Then he rested his head lightly on the TV screen, chewed the carrot, and looked at his son.

For thirteen months, the boy had been living in Providence with Billy and the old man. The kid still mystified Billy.

Why does he like me so much?

Bo's birth certificate said that he was legally William Roger Povich III, though Billy wasn't sure if the kid even knew his full name. He had been born with thick brown hair, like monkey fur, which a nurse had tied atop his head with a little green bow, so that he had looked like an onion.

The new mom had loved that green bow. The boy became "Bo" before he came home from the hospital.

Has it really been seven years?

The boy's dark mane had quickly fallen out; in its place was a golden patch of cowlicks, like misbehaved yellow crabgrass, which Billy, wielding kitchen shears, had unevenly mowed into a long crew cut. The blue eyes had skipped a generation after the old man—Billy had been stuck with brown; Bo had the blue. The eyes were unusually big for a little face, and they made him look smart and curious and sad. The boy was skinny—all three Williams in the Povich household were slim. Bo had his mother's fair skin and button nose, and Billy's pointed chin and long, lean limbs. Bo's bottom jaw was missing a tooth, which he kept on the table in a shot glass from the Bellagio hotel and casino. The tooth was soaking in Windex, which Bo believed might polish it and increase its value.

Since Bo had moved in with Billy, he had saved every dime he earned. The kid was good with money.

He's nothing like me.

In addition to the name, Billy could think of just one trait shared by the three generations of Povich men living in his three-bedroom apartment in an old Victorian: They all loved breakfast. They ate breakfast food all day: waffles for lunch, johnnycakes and scrambled egg for dinner, bacon and orange juice during *The Tonight Show*. Bo had never touched vegetables before Billy had invented the "breakfast carrot."

Michigan State lined up for a field goal, but then Wisconsin called time-out to jinx the kicker.

Billy muttered under his breath, "Up by eleven, can't you just give them the fucking points?"

"Whachu say?" the old man asked.

"I said I have an ulcer the size of France."

Organ music—slow, low, and somber—suddenly rose through the kitchen's red-flecked black linoleum.

"Funeral today?" the old man said, incredulous. "It's three o'-clock."

Billy stepped to the window. Outside, the vast green parade field across the street was dotted with sunbathers and families unpacking picnic baskets. Joggers shared a walkway around the field with kids on bikes and people pushing strollers. At the far end of the green, the Cranston Street Armory sat like King Arthur's summer palace, a gigantic castle of walls and turrets, trimmed with rough-cut granite and tarnished copper. The armory was a pale pottery color in bright sun, and it turned golden when the light softened near sunset. It had been built for the National Guard a hundred years ago, but the guard had left and the armory had become Rhode Island's largest and most attractive pigeon coop.

The city's well-to-do, and its funky cool people, lived on the East Side of Providence; Billy, the old man, and the boy lived on the West Side. Their neighborhood was a cluster of Victorian apartment houses along the squared-off blocks surrounding the armory, populated by people who couldn't afford East Side rents, and by those who wouldn't pay East Side prices on principle. The Armory District had gentrified over the past twenty years, though it remained a little rough. The neighborhood would never live down the time the police came upon a man shot dead in his car, somehow missed seeing the body—and wrote him a parking ticket.

Two dozen parked cars jammed the street below Billy's window. Couples dressed in black hugged and murmured and clung to one another on the sidewalk, on their way to Metts & Son Funeral Home, on the first floor of Billy's building.

"It's a funeral," Billy confirmed. "Not on the schedule, far as I remember."

"You got time to get the mail?" the old man asked.

"Once the music starts, it's too late."

"Awww," the old man moaned, "I got something coming in the mail today. Why do we gotta stay out of sight?"

"Because that's what it says on the lease," Billy said, grimly looking down on the mourners. "We can't use the stairs during a funeral unless the building's on fire. They'll be done in an hour."

"I'll be napping in an hour."

"Then you won't be missing the mail."

"I can get the mail," Bo offered. He pointed down a narrow hallway, toward his bedroom. "Out the window and down the tree."

The old man raised his eyebrows and looked with hope at Billy. "The boy can go down the tree!" he echoed.

Billy looked from his father to his son. They both had the same pleading look, waiting for Billy's permission. Some vague paternal instinct told Billy not to allow his seven-year-old to climb out the second-floor window, into the skinny upper branches of the red maple in the backyard, then down to the mailbox. But Billy never gave edicts without reasons, and he couldn't think of *why not*—the boy was the best climber of the three of them.

Billy shook a finger at Bo. "Stay out of sight."

"Yay!" cheered the old man. He saluted Billy with a breakfast carrot.

Bo pushed his cereal away and shot from the table. "Thanks, Billy!" he called out, pattering down the hall. "I won't let you down."

"Mm-hm," Billy said, his attention back to the game.

The old man waited until Bo was out of sight. He scolded, "You're his *father*. The boy shouldn't be calling you 'Billy.' "

Billy watched Michigan State break its huddle. Sarcasm was his favorite weapon against his father's nagging—the old man had no ear for it. Billy deadpanned, "Wouldn't 'William' be too formal between father and son?"

"That would be worse!" the old man cried.

"Yes!" Billy shouted as the football tumbled through the uprights. He pumped his fist. "Time for one of those fantastic finishes. It's comeback time!"

The old man stared slack-jawed at Billy.

"What?" Billy said. He sighed. "Bo has *always* called me 'Billy.' I couldn't change that now if I wanted to, which I don't. 'Pa' and 'Dad' make me nervous—those are names for *you*."

"You're forty years old," the old man said. "And still going by 'Billy.' "

"My byline in the paper was 'William,' " Billy reminded him.

The old man scrunched his face, like he had just inhaled sewer gas. "Now you write more than anybody and you never have a byline."

"They don't byline obituaries," Billy said. "That's the paper's policy."

"Why can't you go back to real writing?"

Michigan State kicked off to a pipsqueak return man, who

squirted through the first wave of tacklers. Billy screamed, "Get him! Get him! GET HIM!" Somebody finally did. "Thank you!" he called sarcastically to the television. "Somebody on kick coverage needs to have his scholarship yanked."

"When are you going to get back to real news reporting?" he father nagged

"Eh," Billy said.

"I was in newspapers all my life—it's in my blood, and your blood, too."

"You were a printer, not a reporter."

The old man set his jaw. "The best goddamn printer they ever had." He passed a hand over the newspaper on the table. "I touch this and I still smell hot lead." He smiled, losing himself for a moment in old memories. "You can stay off the police beat and go back to covering politics, if you don't want to write about any accidents."

"Angie didn't die in an *accident*," Billy told him sharply. "It was a crash—and a crime."

The old man held up quivering palms. "I didn't mean that she did," he said, suddenly retreating to a gentler tone. "It's been thirteen months, Billy." He fidgeted in his chair, grunted, and wheezed—old man noises that hinted of an inner struggle. Finally, he said what he was thinking. "She wasn't even your wife when she died."

Billy would not look at him. "That was just temporary."

Wisconsin ran up the middle for nine yards. "Come on," Billy moaned to the Michigan State defense. "You're gonna get my legs broken."

" 'Temporary'?" the old man said. "It sounded pretty permanent in divorce court." He waited for Billy to answer. Billy said nothing. The old man pleaded, "Why won't you go back to work?"

Billy turned to his father. The old man stared, lips slightly parted. He wheezed through his mouth, a downcast cloud about him. Billy looked into the old man's perfect blue eyes, hunting for some sign of the wisdom that should come with seven decades of living.

The organ music stopped downstairs; the praying began.

Billy wanted to confess.

He wanted to tell his father about the darker part of himself that Angie's crash had uncovered—it was a new perspective, exposed by Billy's pain and his guilt, or perhaps created by it. In his ever-more-violent dreams, Billy had seen how an unspeakable act could also be righteous, how sin and justice could intersect. Billy was aware that this dark perspective was pulling him down, moving him closer to action against the man he blamed for Angie's death, yet he couldn't do anything to stop himself. It was like one of Billy's credit-card and casino jags—he knew it could only end badly, yet he could not help but ride the bomb.

Wisconsin muffed the center snap and the quarterback had to fall on the fumble.

Billy imagined himself in black and white, straddling a nuke with Slim Pickens at the end of *Dr. Strangelove*. Could the old man understand any of this? Billy's father was at the same time a child and a sage.

"Pop," he began.

"Billy! Billy!" came the cry from down the hall. "I got the mail!"

The old man's head whirled. "Take your time, boy!"

Bo pounded down the hall, carrying a brown cardboard cube about one-foot high, bound in packing tape, and half a dozen white envelopes.

"Anybody see you?" Billy asked.

The kid beamed, and shouted, "Nobody!"

The old man reached for the box. Bo pulled it away and said slyly, "Twenty-five cents?"

"Bo, stop extorting your grandfather," Billy said. "What are you saving all that money for, anyway?"

"I'll give ya a dime," the old man offered.

"Fifteen!" Bo countered.

"Deal," the old man agreed. "Can you bill me?"

Bo smiled and handed him the box. The old man could expect an invoice printed in purple crayon by the end of the day. He had a hundred of them.

Blood oozed from a fresh scrape the size of a postage stamp on Bo's left elbow. The kid didn't seem to notice the wound from his adventure out the window; the sight of the boy's blood weakened Billy's knees.

The old man tore at the package like a raccoon trying to open a bag of bread.

Billy had to look away. His father's incompetence with the simplest physical task disgusted him. Billy felt shame, too, for the stroke was not the old man's fault.

"Help your grandpa," he ordered Bo.

On third down, Wisconsin ran around the left end for no gain. Time to punt.

Together, the old man and the boy sawed the packing tape with a butter knife. They spilled Styrofoam peanuts on the floor and the old man fished out a white ceramic head with a handle. The piece seemed slightly too large to be a coffee mug. He held it to the dangling ceiling lamp for an inspection. "No chips," he said. "A little glaze crazing around the nose. Not bad. Another treasure of the past from almighty eBay."

"I can't believe the money you blow on junk," Billy said. Realizing he had just set a trap for himself, he tried to sidestep. "Though I guess you earned your pension and the right to spend it."

The old man pounced. "I could blow my dough on junk, or on the greyhounds, like you, but at least I still got the junk."

Ouch. Billy smiled. The stroke had taken much from the old man, but not the razor tongue.

"That's a big nose on that guy," Bo said, reaching to feel the smooth ceramic.

"This is George Washington's head," the old man explained. "This is a souvenir from the World's Fair in New York, way back in 1939. Put some black coffee in there for your grandpa, okay?"

Bo took the head, looked inside, and frowned. "It's dusty inside."

"Aw, dust can't hurt an old Polack like me," the old man said. "Go fill it."

The old man flipped through the envelopes that had come in the mail, classifying them: "Overdue bill. Overdue bill. Junk. Junk. Hey, Billy, here's a bill that ain't overdue. Somebody has a lot of nerve, sending this. Ha!"

The Wisconsin punter hit a low line drive, which Michigan State fielded at the twenty-three-yard line, with twenty seconds left in the game. Billy held an open hand over the television, like a faith healer.

"Billy?" the old man said, sounding grave. "Did you get arrested and not tell me?"

"Mmmm!" Billy said to silence him. To the TV, he preached, "Block that guy! And that guy! Run! Cut it back! Good!"

"Because this letter is from the superior court," the old man said. "Addressed to you."

"Hallelujah!" Billy screamed. "He broke it! Run! Run! Yes! Score!"

Billy threw up his arms, jumped in celebration, and jammed his fingers on the yellowing stucco ceiling. *"Son of a bitch,"* he muttered. He stuffed his hands under his armpits and watched the Michigan State players pile onto their kick returner in the end zone. Billy had no joy in victory, only relief: The money he had just won from a Federal Hill bookmaker would cover his debt to a loan shark in South Providence. Michigan State had just saved Billy from another broken nose.

"Fine, fine—you won," the old man said, not sounding too happy about it. "What about this letter from the court?"

Billy snatched the envelope and ripped it open. There was a sheet of blue paper inside.

"Aw, goddamn," he said. "I got jury duty."

Billy looked up, to see his father sipping from George Washington's head, and his son, with tight-lipped determination, stirring margarine into his chocolate cereal with the barrel of his toy gun.

The old man said, "You'll probably just hang around in the jury pool for a day, and then come home."

"Probably," Billy agreed, barely listening. He felt a quick flutter in his chest. He had never before been called to duty by the court. To sit on a jury would be good, he thought, in case one day he had to face one.

three

The frosted glass rattled in the door. From the hallway outside the law office came a muffled muttering, "I'll sue that goddamn locksmith."

Inside the office, Carol dog-eared the page to mark her place in the ten-year-old decision from the first circuit court of appeals, and then called, "Martin? It's not locked."

The door rattled more violently. "I'll take his house!"

"Martin?"

"His car, his boat, his wife, children—and his cocker spaniel!"

"Turn the knob to the left."

The door burst open and Martin Smothers stumbled into the one-room office, clutching together in one hand a McDonald's bag, a sheet of white paper, and a battered silver briefcase. The other hand still held the doorknob for balance as Martin's slippery fake-leather vegan shoes skidded on the buffed tile. With the door open, Carol could read the black stenciling on the glass: MARTIN J. SMOTHERS, ATTORNEY AT LAW. The letters had been painted in a curve, like a giant frown, which seemed right for the moment.

"What the hell did they do to my goddamn door?" Martin shrieked.

"They fixed it," Carol said, but Martin didn't seem to want an answer. He blew into the office, let the door slam, slapped his briefcase and his lunch on his steel desk, and sent loose papers fluttering.

Martin Smothers was sixty years old, slim-shouldered, and potbellied, with dark, puffy bags beneath his eyes, a shiny bare forehead, and long, wiry white hair bound by a rubber band into a ponytail, which had been threaded through the back of a Providence Steam Roller cap. The 1928 National Football League champions went out of business before Smothers was born, but he liked their logo, which looked like a drunken border collie sticking out its tongue.

Martin dressed in a tan linen suit, as he did every day, in all seasons. He wore natural-fiber red suspenders and an organic silk necktie blandly colored with vegetable dye—special ordered by his wife.

"Why is it so goddamn dark in here?" he said, jerking open the blinds to reveal the vista of a brick wall five feet away.

"Lovely," Carol cooed. "And if you look down the alley, you can see the gleaming new Dumpster. It's Caribbean blue."

Martin wasn't listening. "Look at this letter I got," he shouted. He had a thin voice that cracked when he raised it, like a bad cellphone connection. Why juries would trust that voice had been a mystery to Carol, until she realized that Martin's desperate voice made him sound like the underdog. And everybody roots for the underdog.

Carol reached a hand out for the letter, but Martin had decided to perform it.

" 'Dear Attorney Smothers,' " Martin called out, reading dramatically from the paper. " 'It never fails to amaze me how low some people of your so-called profession will stoop. Congratulations—you have sunk to a record low, either to get rich or to glorify your own ego—I don't know which.' "

He clapped the letter between his hands and growled.

"Considering what you're paying me," Carol deadpanned, "I'd say it's for ego."

Holding the letter in two fists, Martin read more. " 'That animal Garrett Nickel got what he deserved a year ago—a death sentence on the night he escaped. Too bad it happened quickly and relatively painlessly, which is more consideration than Nickel ever gave any of his victims.' "

"If you consider bullets and drowning to be painless," Carol offered.

" 'That punk Peter Shadd, who escaped prison with Nickel and then shot him, deserves two things,' " Martin read on, " 'a medal for ridding the earth of subhuman scum, and a noose. The only thing he did wrong was not turning the gun on himself after shooting his partner. Why are you trying to get him off? This was a case of scum killing scum. Shadd is a junkie, a thief, an escapee, and a killer. Why are you defending him? Why can't you just let him rot? You talk in the papers about his rights—don't you know that nobody cares about his rights?' "

Martin crumbled the letter and hurled it with a grunt toward the open window. It sailed high, bounced off the glass, and rolled into a corner near a mousetrap baited with petrified peanut butter, an abandoned spiderweb, and a dozen other paper balls.

"How can you respond if you throw it away?" Carol asked.

"I have the return address," Martin huffed. "Take a letter down for me. Please?"

Carol smiled. Martin had never said "please" for anything before Carol had entered law school, six months ago. With her legal pad and a sharp no. 2 pencil, she wheeled her chair to the center of the small office, sat, and crossed her legs. She saw Martin's eyes flicker for an instant to her coffee brown thighs as she casually pulled at her skirt and flipped it down over her knee. She looked away and smiled again. Martin had been married longer than Carol had been alive. She readied the pad and pencil.

Martin rubbed his chin, looked off toward Saturn, and dictated.

" 'Dear Dickhead,' " he began. " 'In response to your rant, there's a little document I like to refer to from time to time, known as the fucking U.S. Constitution. I suggest you read it, or'—strike that—'I suggest you have somebody *read it to you*. I hope you can understand it, though I realize it was written a long time ago on old-fashioned crinkly paper, and there has never been a sitcom or a reality TV show based on the Bill of Rights.' "

Martin stuck his thumbs in his waistband and paced, dictating off into space. " 'Idiots, such as yourself, may find the Constitution an inconvenient document, especially the parts about getting a speedy and fair trial, and the right to speak your mind in the newspapers. Well, fuck you. I will defend Peter Shadd because he is *a man,* a human being, presumed innocent, with rights of equal weight, in the eyes of the court, to you or me or the goddamn *Pope*'—uh, Carol, don't put 'goddamn' before '*Pope*.' "

"Mm-hm," she said, scribbling.

" 'So in conclusion,' " Martin said, " 'take a civics class and then kiss my ass.' "

"Short and sweet," Carol said.

"Signed 'Martin J. Smothers,' blah, blah, blah—you know the rest."

"Mm-hm."

"Oh, and add a postscript. 'When I say kiss my ass, I *don't* mean the smooth white outer regions.' "

"Of course not."

Martin plopped hard on his desk chair and tore open his McDonald's bag. He bit into his burger and squirted shredded lettuce onto his blotter. "Uhhhhh!" he moaned in delight.

"You sound like an addict getting a fix."

"Read back to me what you got," Martin said, grease shining on his chin. "Please."

" 'Dear sir,' " Carol said, reading her shorthand. " 'Thank you for expressing your opinion to me. What a delight it is to engage in robust debate. As a private defense attorney and a former public defender, I believe in the value of providing all citizens charged in a crime with a vigorous defense, as prescribed by the United States Constitution. Though you and I may disagree on the matter at hand, be assured that I respect your opinion and will take your comments to heart. Sincerely, Martin J. Smothers.' "

The telephone rang on Carol's desk.

Martin grumbled, "At least you got the Constitution in there."

Carol grinned as she stepped to the phone. "Martin Smothers, attorney at law," she said, using her polite but icy professional voice. Her eyes turned hard to Martin. "Oh—hi, Nicki," she said, suddenly sounding breezy.

Martin gagged and spit cow into the trash.

"I'll check," Carol said, and then put the call on hold.

"How does that woman *know* every time I'm eating meat?" Martin cried.

"Because she's been your wife for thirty-five years."

"I'll be sleeping alone on the sofa for a month."

Carol laughed. "Your own fault for marrying into PETA."

"Tell her I'm having a salad—no, too obvious and unspecific. A falafel! Extra humus! And I'm not here. I already ate and you found the wrapper on my desk. Please!"

"You know I don't like to lie."

Martin stiffened, indignant. "Who says you gotta like everything you do to work here? I defend killers and rapists. Do you think I goddamn *like* it?"

four

"Povich! You brilliant son of a bitch! I'm glad I found you at work."

Billy could almost smell the whiskey through the telephone.

"Phil?" he asked, checking his desk clock. "It's almost two in the morning. Are you hammered?"

"There are *anvils* that don't get as hammered as I am right now," admitted Phil Nussel, the paper's lead investigative reporter, sounding like he had a mouthful of Novocain.

Billy laughed.

Nussel explained: "So I'm sitting here an hour past deadline with the Madam Vroom column, and I'm blocked, man. Fuckin' blocked." Billy heard a bottle hit the table. "Whoops! Hang on. . . . Anyway, I'm working on my column and I asked my buddy Jim Beam for some ideas and, goddamn it, he's fresh out, too. So I thought I'd call my old partner, Billy f'ing Povich. 'Cause there's nobody cleverer than him."

As an investigative reporter, a sober Phil Nussel—or even a slightly less hammered one—was the best, like an FBI agent working under the First Amendment.

Billy had no idea why Nussel had agreed to secretly author the paper's horoscope column while Madam Vroom was out with bunion surgery.

"What made you think you could write astrology?"

"Pfffft!" Nussel scoffed. "Anybody can do it, so long as you know your ass from Uranus. Help me!"

"I always try. What's the sign?"

"Capricorn," Nussel slurred. "My nephew's a Capricorn, so I was thinking of writing something to pick up his spirits. He threw six interceptions in his junior varsity game last Friday."

"How about 'Try, try again—but after six times, give the hell up and join track,'" Billy joked.

"Hmmm," Nussel said, sounding interested.

"No—you freakin' drunk, don't write that!" Billy shouted. "Lemme think. . . . Um, try this. 'Capricorn—troubles today feel like life or death? They're much more important than that—they're about life. Live through them, and don't back down.'"

Billy heard typing over the phone. "Oh, yeah, that's beautiful," Nussel said. "You should have this job. How do you do it every time?"

"I'm a Capricorn."

"You, plus Alexander Hamilton, Martin Luther King, Jr., and Jesus."

"That would be a hell of a poker game."

Nussel laughed, then suddenly became quiet and serious, the way drunken people do when they have something to tell you they think is so important, it could change the world.

"Look, Povich," he began. "When are you gonna get off the obituary desk? It's below you, man. You're a good reporter."

"Was."

"Still," he insisted. "You think you don't care about journalism, or the truth, anymore, but you're wrong. I can still see it, even in those obits you write. Look, I got some political yank around this place. . . . I could sober up and put in the good word for you, maybe get your old beat back."

"Sober up," Billy said. "You can do that much for me. Otherwise, I'm cool here for now. Look, man, the fax machine is spitting out another dead body, so I gotta go."

"When you're ready," Nussel said. He hung up.

The obituary department's fax machine ground out the dead all night long.

Billy was amazed that a life of seventy, eighty, ninety years could be condensed to a single sheet of paper, faxed from a funeral home. *We should teach kids in preschool,* Billy thought, *to grow up ambitious enough to deserve a second page.*

The continuous flow of obits reminded Billy of visiting Niagara Falls as a young man. He had looked up from the deck of the *Maid of the Mist* tour boat and wondered how so much water could come so fast, for so long, without running empty. How many people lived in this puny state? How many people could die in one night before Rhode Island ran out?

Billy worked the late shift in the newsroom annex. The building was a converted train depot in a forgotten part of downtown Providence, isolated four decades ago by highway construction. The *Daily Pen* had taken over the depot and then divided the soaring space with a second floor to make two levels. The old redbrick walls had been covered with Sheetrock and painted a two-toned dirty yellow and avocado. Fluorescent tube lights hung from a web of stainless-steel conduit bolted to the timber-beam ceiling.

A television was tuned to a twenty-four-hour sports channel. Billy kept the sound off. During the day, the dozen people who worked at the annex processed community news—graduations, military promotions, wedding and birth announcements, real estate transactions—the least glamorous parts of the paper.

Billy Povich worked the obit desk alone at night, 7:00 P.M. to 2:30 A.M. He was generally undisturbed, except for when the security guard ambled through, smelling like pot.

The obituaries Billy processed would be printed in the paper's noon edition, which the editors put to bed every morning at ten o'clock. It was an inviolable deadline, controlled by the delivery drivers' contract, so the late obits had to be in the can when the first editor arrived at 5:00 A.M.

Billy liked the solitude. It spared him the looks from the paper's city-side reporters and editors, who looked on Billy with pity and with contempt, for how far he had fallen.

The depot's wall clock, some six feet across, had stopped decades ago at six minutes to midnight. The giant clock face, with its black iron hands and fancy Roman numerals, reminded Billy of the Doomsday Clock, invented by the *Bulletin of the Atomic Scientists* in 1947 to symbolize how near mankind had flirted with atomic destruction. If the Doomsday Clock ever struck twelve, the world would fizzle in a blizzard of hydrogen bombs.

Billy had come to imagine that the depot's clock measured his own doomsday.

Six minutes to midnight.

Seemed about right.

The fax groaned and clacked and spit another dead soul into its tray.

Billy snatched it up.

A woman, seventy-eight years old. She had been born in Providence, gone to Providence schools. She'd lived here, worked and retired here, and died here yesterday. She'd be buried here tomorrow. She'd had her church and her garden club. No husband, no children. Two nephews in Colorado listed as survivors.

Is that it?

Billy sighed. He punched the information into his ancient computer, touch-typing a ten-pound keyboard so old that the letters on the keys had worn off, except for *X* and *Q*. When he had finished typing, he measured the obituary electronically.

In the paper, it would be three inches of text, less than half the length of most obits.

Billy was outraged. Goddamn lazy funeral director couldn't get more information than this?

This will be the shortest obituary in the paper . . .

What to do?

No editor would say a word to Billy if the obit ran in the paper the way it was. Nobody would even notice it—that was the problem.

There had to be more to Ms. Margaret Eleanor Drew.

He dialed the funeral home that had gathered the raw information for the obit. An answering machine picked up. Billy slammed down the phone, looked up the undertaker's home number in the paper's database, and dialed it.

He waited.

Billy let the phone ring thirty times. He hung up and snarled out loud, "I hope I at least woke the bastard up."

Billy ran the name of Margaret Drew's church through the paper's computer archives of past news stories and found the name of the parish priest. Yanking open his bottom desk drawer, he fished through a strata of racing forms and losing lottery scratch tickets and hauled out a Providence telephone book nearly five inches thick.

The brass plaque Billy had won for investigative journalism was under the book.

The award was seven years old.

Billy frowned at it and slammed the drawer.

The rectory's answering service picked up after six rings. "I need Father Conley," Billy said.

"Is this an emergency, sir?"

"It's life and death," he said. Not a lie—not really. Billy felt no need to explain any more.

The service rang the call through to the priest, who got on the phone, sleepy and startled.

Billy introduced himself.

"A little late to be calling for a quote, Mr. Povich," the priest said, now fully awake and peeved at being bothered by the newspaper at two o'clock in the morning.

"Margaret Drew," Billy said, in no mood for a snippy priest. This guy could sleep anytime; Margaret Drew had one shot on the obit page.

"Yes, a parishioner of mine—she passed away."

"I'm working on her obituary and I need to know more about her."

"I thought the funeral home—"

"That home sucks," Billy said, cutting him off. "They gave me nothing. She's got a three-inch obit and she's going to look like a god-damned *loser* who never did a thing with her life . . . and I can't be-lieve somebody like that could live to seventy-eight. I'm not running this bullshit obit the way it is. So tell me something more about her. Or tell me who else I need to wake up."

The phone was silent a moment. Then the priest said, "She went by 'Maggie.'"

"Good," Billy said, typing. "More."

"Uh . . . for years she was part of a crew of ladies who hosted the church coffee hour, after eight o'clock Mass on the first Sunday of every month." He chuckled. "Maggie was in charge of the coffee for a while, until she got voted out of the job for making it too strong."

" 'Too strong,' " Billy echoed as he typed.

"So they put her in charge of doughnuts. She took it in good hu-mor."

"Mm-hm."

"Never married, of course. And she didn't have much beside Social Security and a tiny pension from that jewelry factory where she had worked. But she had inherited her little house and didn't have a lot of bills, which is why she could sponsor so many people."

" 'Sponsor'?"

"The church's sponsorship program," he explained. "Somebody in America pays eighteen dollars a month to sponsor a hungry person in Kenya."

"That's not much money."

"It goes a long way over there. It's enough to make sure a person gets three squares a day, vaccinations, and some basic health care."

"And Maggie sponsored someone?"

"Oh, no, she sponsored a whole enclave—something like thirty people. She got letters from them all the time and drawings from the children. In fact, the main path through the village over there is named for her. It took nearly every cent she had each month. Toward the end of her life, when her own medical bills went up, she would skip lunch and sometimes dinner to keep her commitments. Not many people knew about it, but those who did have already volunteered to take over her sponsorships in her memory. Um, what else can I tell you?"

They chatted a few minutes more about the sponsorship program, how the money was collected and distributed. Billy thanked him and hung up.

He thought for a moment and then typed.

PROVIDENCE—Margaret E. "Maggie" Drew, 78, of 11 Quentin Parkway, died Thursday at home of natural causes.

She had been a hero to impoverished African villagers she never met, for she gave them all that she had, took away their hunger, and suffered it herself. . . .

He read over what he had written. Tears blurred the gray block letters on his screen. *Now this was a life. . . .*

———

The fog had drifted up the bay, into the mouth of the Providence River, and then into the city. It had spread through downtown like delicate snow twenty stories deep, through which rose only the tops of the tallest buildings in the city's financial district. Waves of fog splashed in slow motion against the truncated towers and then curled back down into the white. To the north, the fog thinned at the base of the Rhode Island State House, the state's grand cathedral to politics, done entirely in glossy white Georgia marble.

After work, Billy had planned to drive past the cop's house—nothing more—early this morning.

The swirling fog had stopped him. He slid the van's transmission into park on College Hill, one of the city's seven hills, overlooking downtown. He had decided to wait maybe twenty minutes or so, to watch the rising sun shoo the fog back into the bay.

Behind Billy, empty streets zigzagged up the hill to the gates of the Ivy League Brown University. Below him, pristine Colonial-era homes crowded streets barely wide enough for two horse carts to pass between the brick sidewalks, which rose swollen around the trunks of sugar maples; it was the most expensive real estate in Rhode Island. From here, the tenements of South Providence were invisible, as if they did not even exist.

In a nearby park, a stone arch framed a statue of Roger Williams, who had founded Providence three hundred years ago, after the Puritans kicked him out of Massachusetts for shooting off his mouth about religious freedom, and being a pain in the ass. Nobody knows what Roger Williams might have looked like. The statue depicted Williams as Jesus, spreading his palms over his city as if to bless it, or to turn its two rivers into wine.

Billy watched the fog out the driver's side window, across the narrow park surrounded by a low fence of iron spikes. He caught himself absentmindedly stroking his fingers through the fake-fur steering wheel cover. The van's engine idled unevenly, seeming to work hard just to sit still. The headlights threw weak yellow beams against the morning gray.

He had not expected to see Maddox so early in the morning.

Billy's stomach twisted into a rope when Maddox hobbled into view. He had approached, unseen by Billy, up the hill from behind the van, on the far side of the street. Billy's neck tightened and his skull pressed back hard against the headrest.

He watched the injured cop's slow waltz with his cane.

Maddox paid the idling van no attention as he struggled up the street. He stepped with his left foot, paused, reached out deliberately and set the cane, paused, rolled forward on his bad right hoof, and then rested for two beats.

There was something graceful about Maddox, the rhythmic way he moved. Billy's thumb tapped the steering wheel, keeping time with the old cop.

Step. Pause. Reach. Pause. Step. Pause. Pause.

Step. Pause. Reach. Pause. Step. Pause. Pause.

In truth, Maddox was neither old nor a cop. He was maybe fifty, though the stringy mop of white hair added a decade. He was no longer on the police force, having retired as a sergeant on a disability pension, forty-eight hours after the crash that had crippled him.

Maddox was a soft-shouldered bear of six three, with a Neanderthal brow atop a big square head. His fists were like cobblestones. Maddox reminded Billy of the plastic boxers standing toe-to-toe in Bo's Rockin' Sockin' Robots game.

There was something odd about seeing such an imposing physical specimen struggle with something as simple as walking, something Billy could do all day. Billy noticed that Maddox had withered below the waist. Where were the cannon legs?

This was a rehabilitation walk for Maddox, of course. He was get ting over the crash, getting on with his life, thirteen months after he had been mangled.

Billy's eyes stung. He refused to cry, but he allowed his eyes to flood. Through tears, he watched Maddox's sloping shoulders from behind as he shuffled. His torso was shaped like a tombstone.

Billy tasted blood and realized he had been chewing the inside of his cheek.

He thought about his father, who, at this hour, was probably fighting to get his own decrepit body into the bathroom, where his old-man weaknesses were most plain to him, and where he cursed the commandments and cried to himself and complained out loud to God or to nobody that old men had no dignity, and why did he have to sit to piss?

Billy thought about Bo, asleep in his twin bed. Bo's quilt was from the *Star Trek* exhibit at the Las Vegas Hilton, though the boy didn't know Kirk from Spock, because his mother had informed him that that sort of television was crap and had never let him watch it. Bo would leave the room out of guilt when Billy and the old man watched science fiction. Begging the boy to stay did nothing; it was as if his mother's ghost were dragging him from the television.

Billy wondered about free will. *Does a person* always *have free will? Or are there acts larger than ourselves, which we must do according to the way nature's rules are scratched into our souls?*

Seventy yards down the road, Maddox came to the curb, looked both ways for traffic.

Billy wiped his sleeve over his eyes and looked for traffic, too.

None. Nobody was around.

Nobody was working on this Sunday. It was still too early to leave for church.

With a wobble, Maddox stepped off the curb to cross the street.

Billy slid the gearshift into drive.

He would have to hide the van, of course. Maybe drive it straight to New York City later this morning. Then take the tags, abandon the old Ford on Seventh Avenue, with the windows down and the keys inside, and ride Amtrak back to Providence in the afternoon.

Pay cash for the train.

Billy eased his foot off the brake and let the van creep forward. It rolled on without Billy having to touch the gas, as if driving itself toward Maddox.

Maddox stopped unexpectedly in the road. With his weight on his good leg, he bent to the ground, facing his ass toward Billy.

What the hell is he doing? Mooning me? He doesn't even know who I am.

Billy's foot hovered over the gas pedal as the van rolled steadily forward.

If the damage was not too severe, Billy could keep the van in the driveway, with a tarp over the nose. He could tell Mr. Metts, the landlord, that he needed a few days to fix some old dents. Then he could remove the damaged panels, the grille, headlights—whatever—saw them up, stuff them in his kayak, and scatter the scraps over the bottom of the bay.

Maddox slowly stood, facing away from Billy, and paused against the cane to gather himself.

Billy's fingers dug deep into the fur over the steering wheel. His right foot lowered toward the gas; his left foot tapped on the high beams.

What the—

Two ghostly green dots appeared over Maddox's shoulder, boring at Billy like lasers.

Billy tapped the brake.

Cat's eyes . . .

Maddox had picked up a cat and thrown it over his shoulder. The eyes bounced Billy's headlights back at him.

It was Ziggy.

Angie's cat.

Billy hesitated.

Of course Maddox would have the cat. Angie had brought Bo when she had moved in with Maddox; she would have brought her cat.

Angie died, Bo went to Billy, and the cat had stayed.

Ziggy had to be ten years old by now. Billy recalled old Ziggs as a kitten, just gray fuzz, like a lump of dryer lint, small enough to nap in a coffee mug. He remembered how he had wrapped the cat in a Christmas box. He smiled, recalling the kitten whining from under the tree, and Angie cuffing Billy lovingly on the arm to scold him for wrapping a cat. He pictured her cuddling the kitten against her cheek that Christmas, both of them near sleep; it seemed neither could have been any happier.

Maddox gave Billy's van an uninterested glance and then plodded for the sidewalk.

Ziggy turned toward Billy and stared at him over Maddox's shoulder with those supernatural eyes.

Billy's foot pressed down on the brake.

five

Yellow pinpricks shone like stars through the screen of stretched silk that separated Billy Povich from the priest. In the confessional, silk was as strong as steel.

The priest cannot speak a word of this, Billy reminded himself as he absentmindedly traced the sign of the cross and then wiped wet palms on his blue jeans.

Through the beige screen, the priest was a shadow with blurred edges, the way he might have looked to a man who was nearly blind. "Father Capricchio?" Billy whispered, unsure. His foot found the kneeler; he lowered himself to it.

The shadow grew darker as the priest leaned closer to the screen. He replied, "Yes, my son." The voice was at the same time gentle and grave.

"Holy shit," Billy whispered in delight. "You padded the kneelers since last time I was here."

The priest chuckled. "Hello, Billy," he said. "No more kneeling on that pine board."

"Is this real velvet?"

"The thickest I could find," said Father Capricchio. He spoke in a deep, clear voice, enunciating each syllable as if announcing the words in a spelling bee. "The cushioning is a space-age gel, like they use in expensive running shoes. I passed the basket an extra time in April. You like?"

"So soft—I feel like I could confess all night."

The priest laughed in a happy, deep-bellied sputter. Billy had never seen the padre's face, but he imagined him with thinning blond hair chopped in a bowl cut, dark eyes cradled by sleepy lids, a set of floppy jowls and reddened cheeks, rough and windburned. Billy smelled coffee breath through the screen, and imagined gray teeth.

The priest had never seen Billy's face, either—Billy had made sure of that by driving into Massachusetts, just over the state line, into the border town of Fall River, to this little yellow-brick church on a dead-end street in a deforested neighborhood of asphalt and cinder block, where the priest would not know him.

"We're sinners on this side of the screen," Billy said, teasing the padre. "Should you be coddling us with luxuries?"

"We're sinners on this side, too," the priest reminded him. "And I have here for my comfort a bottle of coffee milk and some Skittles."

Billy imagined the priest smiling. He held the image in his mind a few seconds. When it faded, cold silence filled the confessional and Billy shook with a chill. "Well," he said finally, "I should probably get the show started with a prayer. I guess that's the rule."

"Eh," the priest said, sounding unimpressed with the idea. Eddie heard him sip coffee milk. "However you want to do it, my son. It's more of a guideline than a rule."

Billy's throat tightened. "But not the secrecy, right? That's a rule!"

The priest was nonchalant, "I'd die for your secrets."

Suddenly, Billy was hot. "What does that mean? You die if you tell?"

Billy heard a plastic bag crackle behind the screen. "What happens here stays here," the priest promised. "Like in Las Vegas—and I know you're familiar with Vegas."

Father Capricchio chewed candy. The scent of artificial fruit made Billy's mouth water.

Billy confessed: "I think I'm going to kill him."

I think I'm going to kill him.

The ring of certainty in the gambler's voice froze Father Capricchio in mid-chew; there was a confidence in the way he spoke. This was new. He had heard Billy's confession seven times before—well, they had been more like therapy sessions than confessions, which was all right with Father Capricchio; not everyone could afford two hundred dollars per hour for a professional to listen to their problems. And he liked talking to the gambler, who had introduced himself as Billy—if that was his real name. Billy was without pretension. All of the people who confessed on their knees with Father Capricchio said that they were sinners, unworthy of God's grace; Billy truly seemed to believe it.

Father Capricchio knew each of his 166 parishioners. This man, Billy, the gambler, was not one of them. Since Billy had first come to confession, Father Capricchio had been sure to introduce himself to every stranger who appeared in the pews of Saint Victor Romano Catholic Church.

He had still not met Billy the gambler.

The priest was sure that if he could look Billy in the eye, he would know in an instant if he were capable of murder in cold blood.

"How have your dreams been?" the priest asked, trying to sound breezy despite the trembling of concern in his chest. He chewed his soft candy to putty and swallowed it.

"My dreams are—ah—tense," Billy said. "I've been keeping a dream journal, and doing exercises before I sleep to give me some control over the content of my dreams."

"Does it work?"

He heard Billy shifting on the kneeler behind the silk screen. "Sometimes," he said. "When I become aware I'm in a dream, I can manipulate it—like I'm both the star and the director. It's called 'lucid dreaming.' Any first-year psychology textbook will tell you all about it."

Father Capricchio laughed and offered his own confession: "Lucid dreams are treasured by the celibate."

Billy snorted.

The priest let the lightness of the moment linger. Then he pried gently: "Are you still dreaming of committing violence?"

The gambler hissed out a long, noisy breath. He said, "Freud argued that every dream is a wish."

"What do you think?"

"Before I started doing my dream exercises, I used to think God was fucking with my head at night."

"Or the devil," Father Capricchio said. "That would be his realm."

"There's no such person."

The priest's bushy white eyebrows rose at the certainty in Billy's voice. "How can you know that?" he asked.

"Who needs him? I sin fine by myself."

The priest sipped coffee milk and thought about the answer. This man, Billy, never stopped impressing. He was an incongruous mix of street talk and philosophy; a Socrates who had grown up with the wise guys on Federal Hill, perhaps? Billy had claimed he used to be a writer, which Father Capricchio had dismissed first as a fantasy, and then as misdirection to hide his true identity. But maybe he *had* been a writer.

Who are you?

"Why do you want to kill this man?" the priest asked.

Billy was silent a moment. "More of a *need* than a want," he said softly. "I can deny myself what I want, but I've never had much control of my needs."

Father Capricchio realized Billy was being vague because he doubted the sanctity of the confessional. That was all right; they would get to the details eventually. The priest chuckled out loud to show Billy how silly his fears were, and then assured him: "I'm sixty-two years old and I have been listening to confessions since before you were born, I suspect."

"Close, probably. When did you start?"

"I entered the seminary right out of Brown University– as soon as I realized I wouldn't be drafted into the National Football League." He laughed. "Had I known that earlier, I'd have practiced less blocking and studied more philosophy."

"Did you wear leather helmets in those days?"

"Now, I'm old," the priest said, "but not older than plastic." He sipped his coffee milk. "The point is, Billy, I'm an *old pro* at the sacrament of confession. Not by word or deed may I reveal anything I hear in the confessional. I cannot let it affect my actions in even the slightest way. I have kept every secret I've ever gotten." Father Capricchio lowered his voice. "And I've heard some kinky shit."

The gambler laughed. "That's my irreverent reverend," he said. "That's why I like it here—you're different."

Father Capricchio felt his cheeks flush at the compliment. Maybe he *was* a little different. He paid little attention to the formalities of his office, to the annoyance of the bishop, who had banished Father Capricchio to this little church in a broken neighborhood on the outskirts of the diocese. He had survived his own crisis of confidence as a young seminarian by accepting that God—the concept, the person—could be pretty weird, and that there was no one right way to help a lost child find his path.

Billy's admission about wanting to commit murder had shaken the priest, but as Father Capricchio sipped coffee milk and spoke of the sacrament of confession, he felt his own confidence seep back. A human life was at stake—two, actually, for Billy's life was also at risk. And then there were the ripples—the families of a victim and a would-be killer.

Father Capricchio blessed himself and offered a silent prayer: *Smack me when I start to screw up.*

"What makes you a slave to your needs?" Father Capricchio asked. He thought about the question and sharpened it: "What makes you gamble, for instance?"

Billy thought for a moment, and then explained, speaking quickly, with excitement, "People who play sports say that losing feels worse than winning feels good. Gamblers see it the other way. We're used to losing 'cause we do so much of it, but *winning*—winning is more addictive than caffeinated cocaine. Losing crushes you. Winning pries the weight off for a little while, lets you breathe. I didn't gamble for money—at least not before I lost all that I had, and fell into debt to some gentlemen who, uh, probably don't go to confession too often. I gambled to feel the win. Losing was a side effect."

Father Capricchio said nothing as he processed the information. Then he urged him to say more. "Tell me how it relates to this man you want to kill."

Billy said, "Well, there's this other weight crushing me."

"What kind of weight?"

"I don't, uh—"

"Is it like the weight of losing?" Father Capricchio asked.

Silence.

"Is it?" the priest prodded. He waited. "Billy? What is it, Billy?"

Billy's fist pounded the wall in rage. The answer came strained through gritted teeth. *"The son of a bitch killed my wife and got away with it."* He bolted from the confessional and slammed the door.

Father Capricchio sat paralyzed and frightened. What had he done? His Skittles rained with tiny clicks onto the tile floor and bounced into the corners.

six

The hardest part about having no home was the logistics of daily life. The shelter in which Franklin D. Flagg spent most nights was in Cranston, a fifteen-minute bus ride from Providence. Every morning brought the same routine. The staff woke the "clients" from their cots by 7:30—to give them time to pack duffels and garbage bags with their hand-me-down clothes and their paperback romances and the tattered files they kept on the landlord who had screwed them out of a security deposit five years ago—before everyone got pushed out the doors by eight o'clock.

The bus to Providence was called "the Goose"—after nine months riding the thing, Flagg had never learned why they called it that. Maybe because it honked.

It dumped the riders at the Holy Gospel Church, just outside of downtown Providence, for breakfast. There, the lucky among the homeless—luck, Flagg had learned a hundred times since he had been paroled from prison, was relative—would meet up with the people who had spent the night on the street. Those folks looked like extras in a zombie movie, after a night under a bridge, or passed out stoned inside an ATM booth, or fighting for space on the heating grates behind the old civic center.

The short stack of flapjacks on Flagg's tin tray filled the hole in his stomach. The food was always fine, if you could stand the preaching.

From breakfast, the homeless filed across downtown, over to the Kennedy Plaza outdoor bus depot, where panhandlers pestered bankers for change with sad lies about car troubles or that somebody had stolen their bicycle and they needed cab fare to get to a job interview *right now*. People got so sick of those tired stories. Flagg once asked a guy for money to buy himself a beer. The guy laughed, clapped Flagg so hard on the shoulder, it hurt, then slipped him twenty just for being original.

Across the plaza, a dozen concrete steps brought homeless people down below the street, below the ground, like where dead people went—the day shelter.

The day shelter was a large windowless room with six rows of cafeteria tables. The place smelled like dirty hair. Along one side, doors led to offices, where the clients could meet with nurses or social workers, or to gripe to some volunteering law student about the mysterious settlement they were supposed to get umpteen years ago for the fender bender that had hurt their back.

The day shelter was lively, full of gabbing and laughing and the sounds of sickly people hacking wet phlegm.

Around the room, some people read books, and some filled out job applications. They chatted about winning the lottery, about the weather, the Red Sox, or the wisdom of taking their Social Security money to the Indian casino. They gossiped about the homeless guy they *thought* they knew, who might not really be homeless, because a friend of a friend had sworn he saw the guy dressed in a duck costume as the full-time mascot for the Quack-in-the-Box takeout joint.

The hookers staying at the shelter wore short shorts and shook their asses for people.

Crazy folk sat alone and grabbed at invisible flies.

There were some quiet, tidy people embarrassed to be there, and loud, stinky people who didn't know that they *were* there.

Mostly, the homeless just passed time. Funny thing about being homeless in Providence, Flagg had noticed: Time passed as slowly as it had in prison.

The staff who served the free sandwiches at noon—bologna, yellow cheese, and a smear of Miracle Whip on white Wonder bread— were all saints, of course. The executives who worked in the upper floors of the bank tower next door probably threw staff parties every month that cost more than these saints earned in a year.

Flagg pitied the saints of the day shelter.

He might have been a homeless ex-con, but he was not shackled to the shelter forever by any sense of Christian duty, unlike the saints. At least Flagg had a *chance* to get away from there and make some money someday.

From across the room, Flagg watched Mia, the little redheaded saint who dyed the tips of her spiked hair a different color every week. At the moment, her hair was teal blue. She was a teeny thing, dressed in black slacks and clunky black heels and a long, flowing silk shirt tied at the waist by a matching silk belt. From the patterned splotches over the shirt, Flagg thought it looked Far Eastern, like a tiny bathrobe from Japan.

Mia had coaxed Flagg into the shelter system.

Flagg remembered her walking without fear beneath the highway overpass under which he had settled in a nest of trash to ride out a cold night. The social services called what she did "outreach"—to go where the bums were and to bring them inside.

Flagg lusted for her.

He listened to her laugh louder than anybody else in the room and watched her ass swing side to side when she walked. *That would be a good time,* he thought. He wanted to strangle her, too. She had taken him off the street but had landed him in this cycle of shelters that kept him barely alive. He couldn't escape. Maybe Flagg would have been better off living without a net, on the street, where you either clawed yourself back into a normal way of life or died.

Flagg read a battered crime novel from the shelter's meager library. Every few pages were ripped or missing, and he had to guess at what he had missed. He kept close watch on the clock. Around four in the afternoon, the daily migration of homeless reversed—as people started scheming to get back to the overnight shelters. The Goose bus would take you back for free, but it was slow. By the time you got to where you wanted to sleep, the place could be full and your ass would be on the street. The city bus was faster, but it cost money. The homeless traded bus passes like their own legal tender.

At three minutes past two, a tall man in dark slacks and a white shirt descended the concrete steps and entered the shelter. He balanced a pizza box on one hand, like a waiter carrying a tray. The deliveryman looked close to fifty, which seemed too old to be driving pizza for tips.

"Yo, pizza guy, over here," beckoned a hoarse voice from the back of the room.

The deliveryman ignored the cry and spoke to a clique of homeless women, each in matching red caps they had scavenged from the pile of free clothes at the day shelter. The women glanced at one another and shrugged, and the deliveryman moved on.

Flagg watched him bounce from table to table, working his way around the room, obviously looking for somebody. He spoke to the fat man whom Flagg had taken for two bus passes in a tense game of cribbage a few weeks before. The fat man rubbed his bottom chin and jerked his thumb in Flagg's direction.

The pizza guy thanked him and walked the pizza box to Flagg.

"Franklin?" the deliveryman asked.

Ten years in the slammer had taught Flagg to trust nobody. But the scent of the pizza pie overpowered his wariness. Maybe the delivery was a lucky mistake.

"Yeah." He put his hands out for the pizza.

"Franklin Delano Flagg?" the deliveryman asked.

"You got him."

The deliveryman reached to his back pocket, drew out a sheet of paper folded into thirds, and gave it to Flagg.

Flagg unfolded it.

A court summons.

Flagg had been had. "You're a fucking process server," he muttered, irked at himself for falling for the pizza gag. The summons ordered to him appear as a witness in a murder trial—for the kid on the hook for killing Garrett Nickel.

A swirl of hot rage stirred in Flagg's belly as he recalled what Garrett Nickel had done to him in prison, the way that son of a bitch had humiliated him. He caught himself grinding his teeth, and then reminded himself that Nickel was dead.

Dead in the stinking river.

Flagg smiled at the thought.

The process server left the pie on a table and started to leave.

"Wait," Flagg said, suddenly remembering the rules of the court. "I'm supposed to get, like, eighteen bucks in travel money to get to trial."

"I spent it," the guy said, "on the pizza."

seven

Martin Smothers stared at a speck of dirt on the wall ten inches from his face and tried to concentrate on the critical business of the moment, despite the prosecutor whining in his ear.

"Come on, Martin, take the deal."

"I'm busy, Ethan."

"Don't bother holding out on me," the prosecutor said, his voice echoing faintly in the tiny white-tiled bathroom. "I can't go any lower than manslaughter for Peter Shadd."

"Can you see that I'm trying to take a piss?"

Assistant Attorney General Ethan J. Dillingham stood back, rested an elbow on the neighboring urinal, looked Martin up and down, and frowned. "Yeah, what's taking so long? Stage fright?" He laughed through his sinuses, an annoying hiss-hiss-hissing. *Goddamn that laugh* . . . "I know I intimidate defense lawyers in the courtroom, Marty, but the courthouse men's room, too?"

"We're not taking any deal."

"Thirty years on paper, he's out in ten."

"Oh bullshit," Martin muttered. "He's already got thirteen years left on his original bid for the armed robberies, plus the three additional he'll get for escaping. He has to serve that time before he'll even start a new sentence."

"I won't ask for the three."

"Who gives a crap? There's no way he's taking the offer. With Peter's record, his file would be delivered to the Parole Board in a steel box with a biohazard sticker. He'd do the full thirty years."

Ethan paused a moment, then gave a disapproving cluck. He held up his hands—Yankee hands that were calloused only from gripping the silver spoon he'd been born with, hands that had never touched a rake or a mop, hands as soft as a virgin's thigh. He touched lightly on Martin's shoulder and said gravely, "The case is a slam dunk. If we go to trial, Shadd will leave prison in a hearse, however long that takes."

Martin stared at him. Ethan was forty-seven, handsome, even striking at first glance, but slightly unreal when you looked a little closer; it was hard to pinpoint, but maybe it was the orange-tinted salon tan. Or the colored contact lenses, too pure a shade of ocean blue. Or the impossible perfection of his chemically whitened teeth. At least the hair was real, unless Ethan had somehow dyed it salt-and-pepper. The prosecutor was six three, slim and fit. The tan suit Ethan had worn to court probably cost more than the car Martin had driven there.

Oh hell. When the two lawyers stood side by side, Ethan would remind the jury of an anchorman, somebody they trusted by habit. As for Martin? He'd look like Ethan's reflection in a fun-house mirror. Oh well, at least Martin knew it—lots of potbellied, dumpy guys enjoyed the delusion of being studs, but not Martin Smothers. He was aware he could pass for a porked-out, hippied-up Colonel Sanders.

Martin finished his business and zipped up.

Ethan stared down at Martin, lips pressed tight enough to squeeze the pink out of them. "The kid is *twenty-two* years old," Ethan said. He let Martin digest the number a moment. "To be convicted at that age of murder one? If he's unlucky enough to stay healthy, he could do *sixty years.*" He repeated at a whisper, "Sixty years, Marty." He turned his palms up, then made fists and gently shook them in the air, saying, "Why not take the deal and at least give him some hope of one day seeing a sunrise over Conimicut Point?"

Martin breathed deep, looked up into those Pacific blue eyes, and replied, "You are so full of shit, you should be pumped clean twice a year."

Ethan's hands covered his heart. "Marty!"

"Why do you need a deal so bad?" Martin glared up at him. "Is it because the Yankees are at Fenway this week?"

"That has nothing to do with it."

"Or maybe you're afraid of this case."

Ethan's face wrinkled. "What rubbish," he said, his tone hardening. He folded his arms, leaned against the wall, and gave Martin a blank face. "You won a minor skirmish in pretrial—because of your motion, I can't mention the hack job your guy did on that other junkie. Big deal."

"Nothing connected Peter to *that* body—no blood, no evidence, no nothing," Martin reminded him. "That's why I won the motion to suppress, remember?"

"It's hardly going to matter, with the case I've assembled," Dillingham said. He gave an awkward grin that might have been intended as a menacing grimace. "I will swat that bug Peter Shadd with a polo mallet."

Martin smiled. Was there anything funnier than blue-blooded bravado?

"You're scared," Martin said with a snicker. "Everybody knows you hired a pollster to test the electorate for a run for governor. How's your name recognition? Did you top the magic fifty percent barrier? You obviously can't afford a loss in court before the election.

Especially with this case—like you said, it's a slam dunk." He needled Ethan with a cheerful grin.

"Okay, you've been right all along," Ethan said dryly. "I have Yankees tickets."

Martin laughed. He had gotten to the unflappable Ethan Dillingham. For a defense lawyer, that was difficult—and fun. "Put your tickets on eBay," he said, "because we're going to trial."

Ethan dropped the soft sell, put a finger in Martin's chest, and seethed. "I'll hang life without parole on that skinny son of a bitch."

Hiking up his pants, Martin rose to his tiptoes and leveled his eyes with Ethan's craterous chin dimple. The hair on Martin's neck rose to attention. He said, "Not if I beat you."

Ethan stared back, unblinking. He chuckled, just making the noise; there was no humor behind it. He said, "You think you can get him off?" and then paused, as if the question was not really rhetorical. When Martin said nothing, Ethan continued: "Nobody cares about this case—this was scumbag-on-scumbag crime. Garrett Nickel is dead and that's a blessing. We ought to give Peter Shadd a medal before we lock him away and weld shut the door. Two predators thinning their own ranks. Who gives a goddamn?"

Ethan laughed again through his nose; this time, it seemed he really did see some humor. "But I guess that's why they call you Saint Smothers—the patron lawyer of hopeless causes. You want to take this case to trial? Fine!" The word landed wet on Martin's face. "It's *your* reputation, what there is of it. . . ." He banged a fist on the chrome lever and brought water rushing into Martin's urinal. "You're free to flush it."

Martin watched the water pool around the disinfectant cake.

"Forgive me," Ethan added bitterly on his way out, "if I neglect to shake your hand at this moment."

Peter Shadd sat on the lower bunk, feet tucked against his bony ass, knees drawn up to his face, arms tightly wrapped around his legs. He rocked gently from side to side. His back was to a concrete wall streaked with black scuff marks from where somebody had tried to kick his way out of the holding cell. The top bunk blocked the bleak yellow light of the ceiling bulb and threw a sheet of shadow over Peter. He was in his court clothes, Martin was relieved to see: black denim jeans that looked dressier than they really were, a white cotton dress shirt—the long sleeves hid the needle scars—and sparkling maroon leather loafers. Martin frowned. He could see Peter's ankles where the pants rode up his legs. No socks. Some knucklehead juror might take that as a sign of disrespect.

Martin stepped into the cell. The door boomed shut. He had trained himself not to flinch at the noise, but he still felt a flutter whenever he heard his freedom being crushed, however briefly, in a steel door.

Peter stared a moment at Martin. The young convict's round brown eyes bulged from his face, as if one size too big for their sockets. Martin sighed. With those insect eyes, the sunken chest with two points of rib cage jabbing knifelike from under his shirt, those drawn cheeks that told a history of street fights through fading scars, and the long, hooked fingers that moved in a meticulous, buglike way that was graceful and creepy at the same time, Peter looked like a madman's dim-witted henchman.

That's how the jury would have to see him. A dimwit, a follower, a lamb.

Peter looked away, buried his face between his knees, and hugged his legs so hard that his skinny arms shook.

Martin watched Peter rock on the bunk. He said, "The jury can't see you this way."

You look too fucking guilty.

"I'll pull it together, man." Peter's voice was low and smooth, like the third-shift DJ on a slow-blues station; it was a fat man's voice, too deep and textured for such a thin face.

Martin stepped to the bunk, taking notice of the sharp click of his shoes on the unpainted concrete floor. He had worn his one pair of *real leather* cap-toe dress oxfords—his trial shoes, bought in secret with money he had cleverly laundered within his own household.

He sat next to Peter, leaned back, and stared at the underside of the upper bunk. After a minute of silence, he said: "Remember I told you they would offer a plea?"

"Don't want no deal."

"That's what I told them." Martin reached out an index finger to test if the little black spider under the upper bunk was alive. It reared back from his touch. He told Peter, "Their offer is a little better than I had expected."

"Unless it's an apology and a blow job, I ain't interested."

"Manslaughter. Thirty years, with a free pass on your escape."

Peter reared away from Martin, as the spider had. "What's that?" he cried. "Thirty? I already got thirteen."

"You're parole-eligible after doing one-third."

" 'Eligible'?" He looked away briefly, doing math. "Shoot, my parole officer ain't been *born* yet." Peter gaped at him. "Are you telling me to take it?"

Martin couldn't look at him. He turned away. "I'm telling you what they told me to tell you."

"What they told you to tell me?" Peter echoed. "Christ! Who's in charge of my case? You or them?"

"You're in charge, Peter—you. I just present the options."

"It's a shit deal, man."

The spider rappelled silently from the top bunk on an invisible web.

Martin spun around on the bunk, put his leather shoes to the wall, and lay on his back, his face directly below the spider. It levitated eighteen inches above his nose.

Peter warned, "He's gonna land on your head, man."

Martin blew gently at the spider and sent it swaying. "This case," he said, "is a son of a bitch. I can't tell you how it's going to go."

"It's all circumstantial, man."

"These spiders aren't poisonous, are they?"

"If they are, can I get a mistrial?" Peter said. "On the grounds that my attorney was too busy fighting paralysis to present my arguments."

Martin chuckled. "Ethan Dillingham doesn't need DNA to win a conviction," he said. "He's a master of drawing a logical picture from circumstantial evidence. The opportunity, the motive, the gunpowder residue on your hands—he'll make a good show. He's a prick in real life, but the jury won't know that. They'll like him."

The spider sank another six inches and held there. Martin could make out the teeny hairs on its legs.

"How come you never asked me if I was guilty or not?" Peter said.

Martin's stomach tightened. *Not this conversation, not now.* Their discussion was protected by attorney-client privilege, but Martin's conscience was not—and it was too late to pull out of the case if Peter admitted something.

"I never ask that question," Martin said. He shot Peter a glance. They skinny young con had stopped rocking. He was rubbing his chin and studying Martin's face. "I wouldn't expect the truth, regardless," Martin explained. "Everybody in this county jug is innocent, right?"

"What if somebody was to tell you he was guilty of something?"

Don't say it, Peter.

"I'd have to quit as his lawyer."

Peter laughed and clapped his hands once. "You saying you never defended a guilty person in your life?"

"I assume," Martin said as the spider slowly dropped toward his face, "in a philosophical sense, that all my clients are guilty. That doesn't matter to me—every accused person deserves an intelligent and vigorous defense. But I can't argue that they're innocent if they tell me they're not."

"That spider's gonna bite you, man."

"This is a tough case to win, Peter. I'd say it's a long shot."

Peter laughed. "He's gonna wrap you up in a big cocoon. Then he'll eat like the King of the Spiders for the next hundred years."

"You could do life."

"Versus what?" Peter said. "Another thirty years?"

"I know, it seems like eternity now, but—"

"Fuck the thirty years, man," Peter shouted. He banged a fist on the thin foam mattress and sent up a puff of dust. He sighed, disgusted, and then suddenly spun around, put his feet to the wall, as Martin had, and lay on his back, mimicking his lawyer. Both men stared up at the top bunk.

"All I want," Peter said in a calm voice, "is for you to defend me as good as you would somebody with money. I'll take my chances with that."

He held out his hand for Martin, who took it and shook.

Martin closed his eyes. It hurt that a man with no money would think he couldn't afford a fair shake. "There are rich people in jail, too," he said.

"I never met one."

Martin looked at him. Peter had relaxed. He was far more presentable without the tension in his face. Maybe the jury could be taught to see a glint of innocence in Peter's bulging eyes. Martin drew from his pocket a pair of round glasses with silver rims. "Wear these at all times in front of the jury," he ordered.

Peter hesitated a moment and then took the glasses. He put them on and looked around to test his vision.

"Nothing but plain glass," Martin said. "They make you look as smart as you really are." And the size of the lenses distracted from Peter's bug eyes.

The spider sank lower. Martin pulled out his own eyeglass case, opened it, and held it below the spider for a gentle touchdown. He closed the case with the spider inside and slipped it back in his pocket.

"You taking him home?" Peter asked, astonished.

"I get inmates out of jail any way I can."

eight

The caller on the line, a woman with a sultry voice, wanted to tell Rhode Island and most of southern Massachusetts, including the Cape and the islands—if the weather was just right and the WGLX signal was carrying well—that radio host Pastor Abraham Guy was an inspiration, so why the heck didn't he run for political office?

"Like governor?" Adam, the producer, suggested.

"Oooh, he'd be the best governor ever," she said. "Can you get me on the air with him?"

"Maybe," Adam said, chuckling to himself. Pastor Guy would hang up on his own mother to speak to *this* fan. He got her name and hometown and put her on hold.

He typed, "Line 2 . . . Jennifer . . . Pawtuxet Village . . . wants to say you'd be a good gov."

Adam transmitted the message from his computer in the control room to the flat-screen monitor eight feet away in the broadcast booth.

Through the window that insulated the broadcast from the noise of producing the show, Adam saw Pastor Guy glance to the screen and then break into a broad smile. The pastor glanced to Adam and nodded, then craned his neck to look past Adam and give the thumbs-up to Victor Henshaw, his political consultant, in the waiting room.

Adam watched Victor through a glass wall. He didn't know what to make of the guy, and he couldn't imagine how he had hooked up with Pastor Guy. The pastor was a gregarious, rabble-rousing former stockbroker who had become a preacher at age thirty, and who now, as he approached fifty-five, was violently fanning the rumors he was going to run for governor. Victor Henshaw was everything Pastor Guy was not: young, muscled, tight-lipped, and brooding. As far as Adam could see, Victor had done nothing for the past month but sit quietly through Pastor Guy's shows, listen to the audio feed in the waiting room, and make notes in a leather binder.

Adam noticed another man in the waiting room, a stranger, about fifty, dressed in a gray sports jacket and jeans. He sat patiently with his legs crossed, his nose in this week's *Time.* There was a manila envelope on his lap. He was waiting for somebody. But who? The man casually checked his watch. Adam reflexively checked the clock. Sheesh! They were running out of time. He grabbed the cassette with Pastor Guy's exit music and set it on the counter, then slipped on his headphones so he could hear the action in the booth.

The on-air listener was rambling about the horror of bare breasts in R-rated movies.

The pastor flushed the caller, interrupting. "Thank you, Jim on the car phone. That gives us a lot to think about."

Pastor Guy paused to give his unseen audience a moment to refocus its attention on him.

Then he said, "Let's switch gears now to Jennifer in Pawtuxet Village, who wants to talk politics." He gave the hearty "heh-heh" chuckle that was his trademark, and added, "A subject of deep interest to all Rhode Islanders who give a darn about the shoddy manner in which their state is being run. Jennifer? You're next on GLX, your Galaxy AM talk station."

"Thank you for taking my call, Pastor Guy," she said.

"My pleasure. Let me tell you, Jennifer, the people who run this state have been trying for years to marginalize people like you and me—the people who have something to say about the crooked politics around here. You want to make a cockroach run? Shine a light on it. That's what we do on this show every afternoon from noon to four. What's on your mind, my dear?"

She laughed. "Well, I read the papers—"

"Good for you. Most people don't, and that's why they're ignorant."

"—and it seems to me that what we need is a governor with integrity."

"Amen to that."

"And, um, some humility."

"I hear you," Pastor Guy said, cheering her on. "Somebody who knows how many commandments there are, right? Somebody who can count to ten! Heh-heh. Somebody who respects the people's money and the people's property, and who respects his family enough to keep his fly zipped in the state house."

She giggled at the reference to the incumbent governor, E. Charles Rex, the white-haired Republican limping to the end of his first term after the newspaper had exposed his affair with a thirty-year-old lobbyist from the petroleum industry.

"You mean Governor E. REXtion," she said.

Pastor Guy laughed. "That's what some of my colleagues here on Galaxy AM have taken to calling his Excellency, the governor. Heh-heh. I try not to make politics so personal."

Adam thought, *Not personal? At least not on the air.* He mumbled aloud, "*You* thought the name up in the lunch room."

The caller said, "I saw that poll from Brown University."

"Oh, that little thing," the pastor said, with a wink to Victor.

"You should run for governor," the woman urged. "The poll said you could win."

"To be fair, it said I have better name recognition than the old hacks who everybody expects will go after the nomination. Not that I would necessarily win, because you know how hard it is for an honest man in politics. If you won't compromise your principles to pander to the special interests, what chance do you have of winning? Not much—unless *the people* decide they want you."

The caller cooed.

Pastor Guy looked to Victor again and then licked his index finger and drew a little line in the air to show that he had scored. Victor acknowledged him with the slightest nod.

"You got my vote," the caller promised.

Pastor Guy dodged the compliment with a chuckle. Adam jammed the exit music into the console. A stirring gospel chorus filled his headphones.

At the sound of the music, Pastor Guy frowned and checked his clock.

"It seems we're out of time today," the pastor said. "This is an interesting topic, heh-heh, and I'll have more to say about the governor's race pretty soon, don't you worry, Jennifer." He paused, expertly, as the choral music grew louder, then switched gears again. "Your early-rush traffic is up next on WGLX, Galaxy AM, and I'll be back tomorrow. Until then, remember that it's *your* government, heh-heh, so stay in tune, stay informed . . . and get involved."

Moments later, Pastor Guy emerged from the booth, grinning, on a self-balancing two-wheeled Segway scooter, which he drove everywhere, due to alleged back troubles. He was a sleepy-eyed, red-faced clergyman, whose shape reminded Adam of the letter *D*—straight along the backside, bending out like a bow in the front. Abraham Guy was a real preacher—or at least he had been before his radio gig—at a nondenominational Christian church in a storefront in Cranston, between a barber and a TV repair shop. He smelled of Cohiba cigars, and sometimes of Beefeater and Angostura bitters, though Adam had never seen him smashed.

The pastor let the scooter balance itself beneath him. He straightened his three-button vest, stuck his thumbs in the elastic waistband of his black preacher's pants, rocked onto his heels, and waited for his daily review.

"Good show, Pastor," Adam said dutifully.

"Heh-heh."

Victor entered from the waiting room, looking grim and bored, as if his life was nothing but funerals and study hall.

"Did you hear that last woman?" Pastor Guy cried. "That's not just a voter, my friend; that was a future campaign contributor!"

"Did you get her address?" Victor asked flatly.

Pastor Guy slapped his consultant on the shoulder. "Don't worry, my boy. She'll find us after we announce—" He noticed the stranger from the waiting room, now leaning in the door, and squinted at him. "Who are you?"

"Abraham Guy?" the man asked.

"You heard the show," the pastor said, sounding annoyed and suspicious. "Who the hell do you think?"

The man handed the pastor the manila envelope. "I'm a process server," he said. "That's a subpoena."

"Oh, you cocksucker," the pastor blurted. He stared at the envelope, which he had accepted in hand, and which, under the rules of process serving, he now owned.

"You're welcome," the man said. He tipped an invisible cap and left.

Pastor Guy sighed and then tore open the envelope. Inside he found eighteen dollars in travel money, and a command to testify.

"It's the Peter Shadd murder case," the pastor said. "The defense wants me as a character witness."

"You know that guy?" Adam asked.

"From my prison ministry," he explained. "I'll have my lawyer quash this thing tomorrow like the flea on the elephant's ass, as soon as Judge Palumbo slides on his black satin dress."

"This is Ethan Dillingham's case," Victor Henshaw said.

The pastor looked up from the paper, blinked hard a few times.

"Isn't he running against you for governor?" Adam asked.

"Nobody has announced yet," the pastor said.

"If you don't testify," said Victor, offering political analysis for the first time in Adam's presence, "it's going to look like you're avoiding him because of politics."

"God forbid," the pastor said dryly. He frowned and smoothed a bushy eyebrow with his thumb. "Of course, if I get the better of his cross-examination . . ."

Victor completed the thought: "You announce your candidacy on the courthouse steps."

nine

Billy rumbled down the steps to outdoors and then turned to wave to Bo in the window. The kid beamed, waving the nickel Billy had given him for putting his cereal bowl in the sink after breakfast, where it would soak until it was washed and dried by magic elves, or until there were no more cereal bowls in the cupboard and *Billy* had to wash it, whichever came first.

A shadow moved over Billy.

The shadow of a man as big as a bear left Billy light-headed and weak in the legs.

Capricorn: Well, it's finally payday—too bad you're the one writing the check. Empty your pockets and dig deep, dig until it hurts.

"Hey, Billy."

Billy kept smiling, kept waving to Bo. "Not in front of my kid," he said.

The bear, all six-seven of him, jerked around. "Well, whadda ya know," he said. He smiled at Bo in the window. Then he waved—a dainty side-to-side wave, like the royal family's wave, which seemed odd from a man with wrists as thick as fence posts. "Look at the little feller in the window," he said, and laughed. "He living with you now?"

"Since Angie died."

"We can go around the corner, Billy—I know you're not the running type."

"Thanks, Walt."

They stood and waved a while longer, big fake plastic smiles on their faces, and then Billy and Walter the collector walked away together, as if two old friends. Joggers circled the park on their right, in front of the giant sandstone armory. Billy looked at the castle and sighed. He imagined a dozen knights on horseback charging from the gates to help him.

They skirted a homeless man in a soiled Miami Dolphins sweatshirt, who had stopped to pick fresh cigarette butts left by mourners at a funeral the night before. The morning was cool, the sky perfect blue but for the expanding white streak of a jet heading north. Billy watched the jet with the irrational hope that it could take him north, too. Where? Bangor would have been far enough. Or New Brunswick. Iceland must have some nice neighborhoods.

Walter the collector hummed a cheerful little melody. For such a huge man, he had a gentle way about him. His size-fourteen shoes landed softly on the concrete. He placed his hand lightly against trees and telephone poles as he came to them, as if to guide his bulk around them without doing any damage. He was polite to people they passed, smiling and nodding.

"Notre Dame fucked me," Billy said.

"They were giving three points on the road, with a second-string quarterback," Walter said. He frowned. "Can't see what you were thinking."

"I thought Anderson was going to play."

"Not with a broken bone in his hand."

"Nonthrowing hand," Billy said in his own defense. It sounded ridiculous when he said it out loud. He kicked a rock down the sidewalk, disgusted with himself. "Yeah, you're right. I don't know what I was thinking."

The first punch to the belly folded Billy in half. He managed only a tiny squeal as his lungs emptied and felt as though they would collapse. His knees buckled and he started to sink to the ground. The second punch struck higher and rattled Billy's rib cage. He collapsed on his side in the alley, his face a twisted grimace as he strained for air. He saw a rat hole in a brick wall. He wanted to wiggle into it.

Walter lifted Billy's wallet from his back pocket and thumbed through it. "Fifty-eight dollars?" he said. "Christ, Billy, is this it?"

Billy tapped a fist on his chest and writhed meekly on the ground.

Walter lectured like a disappointed father reviewing a bad report card. "You gotta do better than fifty-eight bucks, Billy. Mr. C. told me not to settle for less than the hundred-dollar minimum. What am I supposed to tell him?"

Gasp! Air leaked back into Billy's lungs. He lay there on his side, hugging himself and trying to breathe normally and calm his frantic heart. Walter was the most decent of the collectors Billy had come to know over the past decade. Once Walt decided you had been properly punished for a late payment, he stopped punishing you; he never hit for fun, unlike the other leg breakers. Two cannonball shots to the gut must have seemed like enough, for Walter grabbed Billy by the lapel of his sports jacket, dragged him as effortlessly as he would Raggedy Andy, and propped Billy against the wall.

Billy flinched at a sharp poke of pain in his side. He rubbed a finger over the spot. Bruised ribs, maybe cracked. It hurt when he inhaled too deeply.

Walter squatted next to him, a hand gently on Billy's shoulder.

"The word's around that you hit a three-team teaser with Michigan State this week," he said.

Billy nodded, managed a tiny smile.

"Who made book for that bet? Mr. A.?"

Another nod from Billy.

"A man can get in a lot of trouble betting with two bookies," Walt said. "So where's the money?"

Billy wheezed a deep breath, felt the twinge in his ribs, and explained. "I used it to pay Garafino."

"The shark? You owe dough to that punk?"

"I borrowed from him a couple months ago to pay an old marker with Mr. A., but I made good on a nice part of that loan this week."

Walter waved his hands, as if to say, *Too much!* The tale was already getting too complicated. He summed up and reviewed. "You took the winnings from Mr. A. and paid on a loan to Garafino? Okay, Mr. C. is gonna want to know why you didn't pay *him*."

Billy shrugged. "I couldn't decide who to pay, so I flipped a coin."

Walter's eyes narrowed at the answer; Billy worried that the truth might have sounded flip. Then the big man's face softened, and he threw his head back and laughed. "You gambled over who you should pay?" he said. "That's my Billy Povich!" He clapped Billy on the shoulder. "Mr. C. will get a kick outta that." He took the money from Billy's wallet and flipped the billfold back to Billy. He stood over him. "We'll consider this an interest payment. You'll pay the principal next week, eh? The whole wad."

"Can I keep five for lunch?" Billy asked. "I got jury duty."

"That why you're all dressed up?" He stared at Billy for a moment. Then he held up a fiver and said, "I met this new girl, born the sixth of November. She's hot, but a little tight. . . . You see what I'm saying? She reads the Madam Vroom horoscope every day. Do you still have pull with that column?"

Billy thought for a second and then dictated a horoscope: " 'You've been cautious long enough, Scorpio. It's time to let loose in matters of romance. Just this once, follow your lust and let your new special someone penetrate, uh, that wall around your heart.' "

Walter laughed and flicked the five to Billy. "I got a date Saturday night," he said.

"I'll call my buddy to get the correction into Friday's column."

"You're okay, Billy," Walter said as he walked away. "I hope you got Mr. C.'s money next time I see you. I really do."

ten

Such a courtroom could never have been built today, not for what it would cost. Nobody wants to pay for grand public spaces anymore—the white marble Rhode Island State House, the U.S. Capitol, Grand Central Station. The architects of modern public buildings are often commanded by budgets to work with cinder blocks.

The courtroom was a cube, more than two stories high, the walls paneled floor to ceiling in mahogany, the sight lines broken up every few feet with decorative hand-carved columns. The floor was tiled in shiny gray Westerly granite, except for an eight-foot pink inlay below the judge's rostrum, in the shape of the State of Rhode Island and Providence Plantations, including Aquidneck Island, Jamestown, and the larger harbor islands.

A waist-high mahogany rail cut the courtroom in half, separating the spectators from the participants. A similar rail, higher and chunkier, penned in the jury, which sat in two rows of chairs.

The judge's elevated bench was to the jury's right. The bench had been made from a lighter-colored wood, and decorated with the state seal—a barbed anchor under the one-word state motto, Hope, and the date of the founding of Providence, 1636. The seal, as big as a manhole cover, had been fashioned from brass and polished like a mirror. The witness stand rode like a sidecar off the judge's rostrum.

The prosecutors and the defense team sat at heavy oaken tables, stained almost black, each with an antique desk lamp of brass and green glass.

Four rows of unpadded mahogany benches—like church pews, but less comfortable—were available to any citizen with an iron ass who wanted to see justice at work.

Billy's attention went to the chandelier, a wagon wheel suspended on a chain at the midpoint above the floor. From the rim dangled six miniature wagon wheels, each holding six silver spotlights. The light they threw seemed as bright and natural as the sun.

Back when he had been writing about trials for the newspaper, this courtroom, one of the most impressive public spaces in the state, had dazzled Billy. It was somehow more impressive from the back row of the jury box, the seat in the corner, farthest from the judge.

Billy imagined himself facing justice in such a room; what was impressive to a juror was probably intimidating to a defendant, especially a guilty one.

His fellow jurors fidgeted in their chairs, gazed around the courtroom, measuring their surroundings. The jury, including two alternates, was comprised of seven men and seven women. The youngest was a woman of barely eighteen; the oldest, a graybeard as ancient as Billy's old man. The jurors dressed in tailored suits; they dressed in blue jeans. They shopped at Nieman Marcus; they shopped at Old Navy. Billy had always been struck by the randomness of a jury trial. The lawyers dueled over excluding a handful of potential jurors, but those arguments generally took place in the margins, to eliminate extreme candidates who might have trouble being objective, such as former prosecutors and the people who could tell you exactly why the CIA killed Kennedy. For the most part, a jury came together by chance, names drawn by lot from a stovepipe hat.

What the hell am I doing here?

Billy's recollections of that morning seemed like fragments of a dream. He had come to the courthouse as if on autopilot, answered some questions, stewed in his own cold sweat, rubbing the bruise on his rib cage where Walter had whacked him, until his name had been called and he was seated as juror number twelve.

How could anyone think that Billy was qualified to sit in judgment?

Capricorn: He's a loving God, but beware His twisted sense of humor. Your choice today is to roll with it, or let it drive you drooling mad. The stars recommend the former.

Billy felt self-conscious and transparent, as if everyone in the courthouse knew he had been fantasizing about murder and so they had concocted this elaborate trial to torture him.

A jury trial is an impressive production, and since the jury is always last to come into the courtroom, all the other actors were already there.

The production started with Judge Palumbo. Billy knew the judge by reputation. He was a sawed-off former jarhead, who had left the softer side of his nature on the Khe Sanh plateau in Vietnam. Neither law school nor two terms in the state senate had wiped away Palumbo's tough-guy squint. The judge reminded Billy of an angry man who needed to pick a fight with the biggest guy in the bar.

Seated at a table in front of the judge was his clerk, a nameless three-chinned political hack, who guided tons of paper—motions, briefs, and court files—over the judge's desk.

Next to the clerk, at her own portable station, was the court stenographer, a trim woman in her late forties, who transcribed every word of the proceedings onto a strip of paper tape, which would eventually become the official court transcript. Perhaps two thousand pages, it would look and read like the world's longest and most tedious screenplay.

Throughout the courtroom roamed the sheriffs—black pants, blue shirts, no guns for any defendant to grab. They escorted the defendants from the holding cells and patrolled the gallery. This morning, the gallery was nearly empty. Just ten people had decided this trial was interesting enough to visit. Billy guessed that one was a reporter from the Associated Press and that another was from the local daily. Billy noticed a sketch artist but saw no TV news camera. Not surprising—trials could tie up a film crew all day without any guarantee of good film for the six o'clock broadcast. TV producers preferred to cover crime, not justice; crime was more photogenic. The other spectators were in their early twenties, and overdressed—probably law students on an assignment.

The stars of the production, the lawyers, sat side by side at their separate tables, surrounded by their props—legal pads, briefcases, and mounds of transcripts from depositions.

Seated at the defense table was the man for whom all this was taking place.

Billy was surprised at how skinny Peter Shadd looked, how feeble. Shadd rubbed his wrists. He was not handcuffed, but Billy knew from covering trials that defendants in custody arrived and left the courtroom in cuffs. Most judges agreed with defense lawyers that a jury must never see a defendant in chains—the image hurt the presumption of innocence.

Billy stared at Peter Shadd. He wanted to catch his attention, but the young man was engrossed in a legal pad dotted with scribbles.

What did Billy expect to see in the young man's eyes?

For the past thirteen mouths, Billy had not passed a mirror without looking into his own eyes to see what dark deeds he was capable of committing. If Billy could just look the kid in the eye . . .

He caught himself absentmindedly rubbing his own wrists.

eleven

So what does it mean when we hear that much of the evidence in this case is *circumstantial*?" asked the prosecutor, Ethan Dillingham. His voice echoed in the corners of the giant room. "It means that nobody saw the defendant commit the crime—that's all."

He paused in his opening statement to let the jurors digest the point.

"It means that this man"—he pointed to Peter Shadd—"was cunning enough to take a gun and shoot the victim multiple times when there was nobody around to identify him as the killer."

Billy and the other jurors looked at Peter Shadd, who hunched over and shrank in his seat.

"So when Mr. Smothers, the defense attorney, attacks the state's case as *circumstantial,* all that means is that there's no eyewitness. What the state wants you to consider are the *circumstances* suggested by the evidence. Add it all up. All the evidence points to one man, the defendant.

"Let me tell you what the evidence will show," Dillingham continued. He paced before the jury, his left hand resting inside his jacket pocket, as if he were modeling his suit in a Brooks Brothers catalog. "Let's start with the defendant himself."

Billy noted how he referred to Peter Shadd exclusively as "the defendant" to dehumanize him, a bit of subliminal psychology to undercut the jurors' instincts for compassion, and the natural reluctance of ordinary citizens to send another human being away for life.

"The defendant is a longtime heroin user," Dillingham said. "And we know he will do anything to get heroin, including robbing people at gunpoint. At the age of nineteen, he was convicted of four armed robberies, and he was rightly sent to prison for punishment and rehabilitation. Rhode Islanders thought they were safe from the defendant's reign of terror, at least while his sentence was running.

"While incarcerated—locked up, that is—the defendant met the victim in this case, Garrett Nickel, a killer of notorious reputation, who took the defendant under his wing, so to speak. The state is alleging that this unholy alliance between the defendant and his victim broke down, and turned into murder.

"And let us not hesitate to dispense justice in this case, even though the victim was also a brutal murderer, and not deserving of our compassion." Dillingham paused, stopped his pacing, and turned to the jury. "Because if this defendant is capable of murdering a cold-blooded killer like Garrett Nickel, imagine what he could do to you. Or to your family. Or to your neighbor." In a low voice, he informed the jury, "This is a very bad, very *dangerous* defendant."

Several jurors shifted in their seats, shooting glances at Peter Shadd. Dillingham might have been melodramatic, but he could be effective.

"The state will prove," he continued, "that Garrett Nickel, this defendant, and another inmate escaped together from prison. You will hear testimony from the defendant's former cell mate. You will hear how the defendant quickly returned to his old ways after their escape, and pulled a gun on his cell mate in Roger Williams Park, to rob him of money he had hidden there. That gun was the same caliber of weapon that was used to shoot the victim in this case.

"You will hear from the medical examiner, who will tell you that Garrett Nickel was shot first in the back, no doubt betrayed by a confidant." He pointed and his voice boomed. "Betrayed by *this* defendant." He paced again. "You will hear about the gunpowder residue on this defendant's hands, which could only have been there if he had fired a weapon. And you will hear about his arrest, in a drug-induced stupor, in the basement of an abandoned boathouse, with his veins stuffed full of heroin, and his pockets"—he paused a beat—"stuffed full of cash."

Dillingham looked silently to the floor for a few moments, gathering himself.

It had been an impressive opening statement.

Billy glanced to the defense table. Martin Smothers, the lawyer, was scribbling notes like a madman. His black felt-tip pen squeaked against the paper. What was he writing?

"When all the evidence is in," Dillingham said, projecting a sense of fatigue, as if there was so much evidence that it exhausted him just to talk about it, "I'm going to ask you to return a verdict of guilty of murder in the first degree." He scanned the two rows of seven jurors, looking each person briefly in the eye.

Then the prosecutor stepped to his chair, slowly pulled it out, and sat. The jury turned its attention to the defense table, and to Martin Smothers.

Martin had scribbled furiously on his legal pad, trying to distract the jury as Dillingham brought his opening statement to its big finish. His hand was on automatic, writing, "Ethan Dillingham is a self-absorbed prick. Ethan Dillingham is a . . ." His attention was tuned to the prosecutor's description of his case.

Dillingham intended to push hard on Peter's character and criminal history, which Martin had expected since the pretrial motions, when Judge Palumbo had ruled that Peter's full criminal record would be admissible at the trial. Painting Peter as a dangerous thug would camouflage the shortage of direct evidence in the case—if the jury believed Peter were *capable* of killing Garrett Nickel, well, who the hell else would have done it?

Damn, Martin thought, listening to Dillingham, *he's got his fastball today.*

If the jury had voted after Dillingham had finished, Peter would have been convicted on the spot. Martin's opening statement would have to do more than point out holes in the evidence; it would have to plant doubt about Dillingham's credibility, too.

Martin waited until Dillingham was seated before he rose to give his opening—so that the jury wouldn't see the taller prosecutor towering over him.

He stood. Mustering as much authority as he could, Martin addressed the jurors.

"When the witnesses get up on that stand to testify before you," he began gravely, pausing to gesture to the witness box, "the judge won't permit them even to say their *names* until each has raised a hand to pledge the court's solemn oath—that under penalties of perjury and even jail, they will tell you the *whole* truth, so help them God."

He pressed his lips closed and let them think about that setup, timing himself in his mind—*one one thousand, two one thousand . . .* at the fourth beat, Martin softened his stern face, and then gave them the punch line: "I'm pleased to say that we lawyers are not inconvenienced by such an onerous oath."

He smiled.

Chuckles echoed through Judge Palumbo's courtroom. Several jurors, still intimidated by the responsibility that none of them had asked for, hid smiles behind their hands. Two jurors laughed out-right, delighted at the break in the tension.

Martin downshifted into the "aw shucks" style of a country lawyer who's smarter than he looks, a character these jurors would recognize from TV.

"Sure as heck is easier to do this job when you don't have to tell the whole truth," Martin said. "Not that anybody's *lying* to you here, not really." He twisted a lock of beard and paced before the jury. "See, the thing with we lawyers—if there's a piece of evidence we don't like, well, we tend to ignore it. That's not lying, is it?"

He met eyes with a juror, who gave Martin a little shrug.

"I mean," Martin said, pacing faster and turning up the energy in his presentation, "take Mr. Dillingham's opening statement, for ex-ample." Martin didn't look at Dillingham, though he could feel the prosecutor's eyes boring through the back of his head. "If Mr. Dillingham had been required to tell you the whole truth about my client, Mr. Peter Shadd, he would have mentioned that Peter had been physically addicted to heroin *in the womb*."

A gasp escaped a juror in the front row.

Martin spoke directly to her, "That's right, ma'am. Peter was born addicted to the heroin his mother injected into her own veins throughout her pregnancy. But Mr. Dillingham didn't have to tell you that." He noticed jurors shooting glances at Dillingham.

"So when Mr. Dillingham refers to Peter as a heroin *user,* he ain't lying to you. But he neglects to mention that Peter has the disease of addiction. It's something each of us might have seen in our own families. Not with heroin, probably, but whether it's street drugs, single-malt scotch, or a half-decent pinot noir, addiction is all the same."

Martin paused a few moments, letting the jurors replay their own dark memories of the parent shamed by a drunken-driving bust, or the belligerent uncle who got plastered and started a screaming fight at the Thanksgiving table.

"So if you put an addict like Peter Shadd on the street, without supervision, without somebody to crack a stick over his knuckles, he's going to fall under the spell of those drugs. And he'll even steal to get them. He'll rob his own cell mate, and that's what happened in this case."

It hurt to acknowledge that Peter had played stickup man after he had escaped, but Martin had no choice. He couldn't accuse Dillingham of ignoring the whole truth and then ignore some of it himself. He had a few more inconvenient truths to get through; he plowed quickly past them, spinning the facts best he could.

"You'll hear from Mr. Dillingham about the gunpowder residue on Peter's hands, but he won't tell you that *any* weapon would have left that powder there. He neglected to mention that they don't have the gun that killed Garrett Nickel—they can't find it. He won't tell you that Peter has a reasonable explanation for the powder on his hands." The actual explanation, not as reasonable as Martin would have liked, could wait for later.

The tough part over, Martin attacked on his strongest point.

He stopped before the jury, stuck his hands on his hips, and said, "And because he doesn't have to tell you the *whole* truth, Mr. Dillingham can brag about his star witness, the cell mate, whom Peter allegedly robbed with a gun, but he doesn't have to tell you that his witness is a conniving con man and a violent felon, with a record as long as winter in Buffalo, who escaped from prison, too, and is being rewarded for his testimony with leniency. I wouldn't trust this witness to water my wife's geraniums, but Mr. Dillingham wants you to trust him enough to send another man to prison for life.

"The state's case is based on the premise that Peter Shadd is a bad person, so he must have killed Garrett Nickel—because we don't know who else might have. Well, Garrett Nickel had enemies, lots of them. He started his criminal career as a world-renowned graffiti artist—and I'll bet you didn't realize a graffiti artist could have such a reputation. I sure didn't until I started work on this case.

"From graffiti, Garrett Nickel graduated to burglary, then armed robbery, and then kidnapping and ransom. It got worse, I'm afraid. He was in jail for killing three people—three that we *know of.* But I think even Mr. Dillingham would agree that putting Garrett Nickel in jail for just three murders was like prosecuting Al Capone for tax evasion—it got him off the street but didn't approach justice for all his crimes. There are more than a hundred unsolved killings in this city, and we'll never know how many belonged to Garrett Nickel. How many people have sworn revenge on the Nickel-plated Outlaw? Who else would have wanted him dead? Well, lots of people."

Martin paused there. That was it. He was out of material.

Hmmm, probably should sum it up for them.

"It's my job to point out holes in the state's case," he continued, making it up as he went along. "It's my job to tell you what Mr. Dillingham won't—because he doesn't have to."

Martin let the point penetrate, and then he lightly tapped his hand on his hip, a covert signal to Peter, who looked up from his notes and for the first time met eyes with the jurors.

"The state cannot prove its case beyond a reasonable doubt," Martin told the jury, "because you're looking at an innocent man."

twelve

Near the end of Billy's exhausting shift of shoveling the historics of the dead into the computer, the fax machine spit out a paper soul who had died in a car crash. The paper had covered the crash in the news pages, before the funeral arrangements had been made. Billy had avoided the news coverage. He had no choice but to read the obituary.

He typed with clattering fury.

PROVIDENCE—Heidi M. Ward, 20, a senior at the University of Rhode Island, originally from Bar Harbor, Maine, died last Saturday in a two-car accident on Route 1 in Narragansett, on her way home from Scarborough Beach. Police have charged the driver of the other vehicle with operating under the influence of alcohol and motor vehicle homicide.

He closed his eyes and touched-typed.

Heidi was only twenty years old. Can you goddamn believe this? She was 20. This is not a typo, ladies and germs. 20 FUCK-

ING YEARS OLD!! She was a premed student ranked eighth in her class at a pretty damn good school, so we can assume she was a decent person, unlike the hateful son of a bitch who killed her on the highway and who probably will get away with it. Because that's the way things work in this corrupt little state!!! So Mr. and Mrs. Ward should GET THAT awful truth THROUGH THEIR SKULLS if they think they'll ever see justice for their little girl. Why do I keep typing, since I know I have to erase this and do it all over again??? Jesus Christ, I need help because I AM LOSING IT. I think I need to take a pill.

Billy rested his head in his hands, elbows on the desk.

He wiped tears on his palms, deleted the unusable paragraph he had just typed, and finished the obit the way the funeral home had written it. Then he filed it to the electronic queue for the editors to slap into the paper tomorrow with cold efficiency. To the layout editor who would arrive in the morning, Heidi Ward would be a seven-inch block of type, to be shoehorned around the advertising in a daily jigsaw puzzle, along with the box scores and the bus schedules.

Suddenly, the newsroom annex went nearly dark as the preprogrammed computer turned off all but one light. The clock on Billy's desk agreed that it was quitting time.

Billy looked around. While he had been working, a janitor had swabbed the tile floor, and had left his mop and an A-frame WET FLOOR sign for the day crew to put away. Billy couldn't even recall seeing the cleaning crew. He was exhausted from the trial all day, and then work all night. And when he slept, he had dreamed of murder.

The doomsday clock on the wall said six minutes to midnight.

Billy scribbled "DONE" on Heidi Ward's obituary fax, then filed it in a plastic tray.

He rubbed his eyes and watched the faint yellow fireworks on the inside of his eyelids. Then he stared at his computer screen for a minute.

Quitting time . . . I should go. . . .

Instead, he dialed an in-house number and punched a code to turn on the lights.

Then Billy cleared his computer screen, created a new file, and typed.

PROVIDENCE—Charles J. Maddox, a police officer retired on a disability after an auto crash last year, has died. He was brutally murdered.

Billy read over what he had typed. The letters on his screen seemed to grow brighter. He looked away and let a rush of light-headedness pass. What he had written wasn't quite right. He deleted the word *brutally*. All murders were brutal, weren't they?

The sentence read better with that little edit. Then Billy replaced *murdered* with *executed*.

He was executed.

No—wrong word. That was political spin. Journalistic standards called for the more general term: murdered.

Billy switched it back and read it over again. The paper's style required the age of the deceased in the first line. How old was Charlie Maddox?

Billy got up and went to the one semimodern computer in the annex, a PC three generations past its prime. The machine was tied into the paper's electronic archives. He did a keyword search with Maddox's name and the word *crash*, then waited while the computer sorted through thousands of news stories. The search was a tall job for the old machine.

Christ, Billy thought, *I could do math faster than this thing.*

Finally, the machine showed Billy what it found: three stories on the crash that had killed Angie.

Billy had never read them. He paused for a moment, then clicked on the earliest story, headlined PROVIDENCE WOMAN KILLED, OFF-DUTY COP HURT IN CRASH.

The text appeared on his screen. The reporter who had written the piece, a kid Billy had never met, had done a good job. All the relevant information was high in the text, including Maddox's age—forty-nine.

God, he looks a lot older than that.

Billy was about to exit the program, when he noticed a link to another section of the archives, entitled: "Unpublished Photos."

That was odd. . . .

Billy had never seen any pictures of the crash. Had there been a photographer at the scene?

He clicked. He felt his face flush.

The first picture had been taken from inside the car, looking out at a forest, through a windshield cracked with a giant *X*. The bull's-eye where the two cracks crossed was smeared red.

He clamped a hand over his mouth, against a surge of stomach acid. He swallowed hard to force it down. His other hand fumbled with the computer mouse and dispelled the picture. He coughed. His throat burned like he had been gargling with Tabasco.

Of course that picture had not been published—a family paper wouldn't run such a gruesome photo, especially when the skull that had cracked the windshield had belonged to the former wife of a former star reporter.

"Are you okay, man?"

Billy whirled. He shouted toward where the voice had come from. "No! I'm fine! There's nothing here."

The security guard recoiled a half step. "Whoa," he said, blinking. His eyes were slits.

Billy hurried to his terminal and spiked the first line of Maddox's obituary. "Just finishing up," he said. "It's all, uh, fine here."

Not knowing where to go, he wandered back to the PC and fiddled with the mouse. Part of him expected the guard to club him and cuff him, then march him straight to prison, the theme from *Dragnet* blasting through the halls. Ridiculous, of course—the paper's security man could never have caught a criminal; he was too stoned. He couldn't have caught gonorrhea in a whorehouse.

The guard's walkie-talkie barked. He spoke into it. "Yeah, I'm at the annex—it's cool, man. No break-in. Just the obit dude staying late." He nodded, saluted Billy with the radio, and then shuffled off.

Billy watched him leave, then collapsed into the chair. He felt a crying jag coming on and clenched his teeth against it.

No, not now.

He fished a pill bottle from his pocket. He popped two antianxiety tablets without water. The label said BuSpar, but who knew what they were? Billy had bought them off the Internet.

What would it be like in prison?

How much space does a man need to make a life?

Billy had never been out of North America. He had already proved that a man doesn't need the whole world to make a life. Could Billy get along inside a thousand square miles? That was about the size of Rhode Island. How about a hundred square miles? Or just one?

Could he make a life inside seventy-seven square feet?

That was the size of a cell in the state prison. Eleven feet long, seven feet wide. Could he survive in such a small space? Maybe he should lock himself in the bathroom for a few years to try it out.

He thought about Peter Shadd.

Peter was facing a sentence of natural life for premeditated murder. With any luck, Peter wouldn't live too long. One of the last stories Billy had written before he was demoted to the obituary desk was

about the prison ban on tobacco. For men doing the rest of their natural lives in prison, cigarettes had been one way to shorten a sentence.

He absentmindedly tapped Peter Shadd into the computer, then
commanded the machine to search.

The older stories were about the escape, and then Garrett Nickel's
murder, and the discovery of his body snagged at the mouth of the
Providence River. Of course the judge had ordered the jury not to
read about the trial, but these stories were old. What did it matter?

The stories said that Peter had been arrested in an old boathouse—
alleged crackhouse, in newspaper language—at 66 MacKay Avenue,
near the city waterfront. Billy knew the street from his days as a police reporter; he had spent many nights there watching the cops
stretch yellow tape around atrocities the detectives might solve but
could never explain.

The computer automatically searched the text of the story and offered cross-referenced links to other articles, listed by headlines. Several were about drug abuse, or the state prison budget. One caught
Billy's eye. The computer had matched the address of the boathouse
and the date of the story about Peter Shadd's capture and had offered
a link to a story headlined HOMELESS MAN DEAD IN VACANT HOUSE.

The story was dated three days after the cops had arrested Shadd.
The text of the story was short; the piece seemed like something a
harried police reporter had dashed off in five minutes.

PROVIDENCE—Police discovered the mutilated body of a
homeless man in a vacant boathouse at 66 MacKay Avenue late
last week during an investigation, police said yesterday in a written press statement.

The body had no identification, and detectives have been unable to determine the name of the person. A staff member from the
Manger, the Providence-based homeless shelter, made tentative
identification of the man as a frequent client of the shelter, who

never gave his full name and whom the shelter staff had been encouraging to participate in substance-abuse programs.

Police would not say how the man died, though they are treating the case as a homicide.

The cops had found a dead body in the same boathouse where they'd arrested Peter Shadd? Around the same time?

A *mutilated* body? Why the hell hadn't that come up at the trial?

Billy paused a moment and held his chin, thinking. Shadd's lawyer must have won a motion to exclude any mention of the body at the trial. Made sense—if the cops couldn't find a way to charge Shadd with killing a homeless man, then any mention of the body at trial could unfairly color the jury's thinking.

Just like it's coloring my thinking right now.

"Cripes!" Billy said aloud as he banged the keyboard and dispelled the story. No wonder Lady Justice wore a blindfold.

Billy glanced at his desk clock. He knew that if he stayed too long, the light of dawn would pull him up College Hill to the East Side, where he might find Maddox on his morning walk. He sighed and struggled to stand under the weight of his world pressing down on his shoulders. On his way out, Billy grabbed the janitor's mop and stood below the doomsday clock. With the mop handle, he nudged the big hand ahead to three minutes to midnight.

thirteen

Billy pulled the van to the curb on a dark and empty street and studied his map under the dome light. Aha. He was close. He headed toward the waterfront. The road cut through a field of house-size storage tanks for the petroleum industry, and then a dense cluster of duplexes and apartments houses. Billy made two quick lefts, turning onto MacKay Avenue. The street sank steeply toward the bay and then turned to soft dirt and angled gently into stinking black mud at the edge of the water—this was a boat ramp, though for nothing much bigger than a canoe.

To the right of the ramp, the shuttered and dilapidated boathouse had been built into the slope, so that the front of the building was on land and the back reached out over the water on log piles.

Billy made a clumsy six-point turn that would have gotten him flunked out of driving school. He studied the building in the driver's side mirror. The nearest streetlight was two houses away, but Billy could see that not much had changed from the picture of the boat-house in the newspaper's archive. A tattered ten-foot tail of police tape fluttered from a railing. The front door had been barricaded with plywood, but somebody had stolen the boards over a first-floor window, leaving a black hole like a rotting cavity. The building was missing dozens of cedar shingles from its sides, and its floating dock had been dragged ashore, piled in sections, and left to rot.

The boathouse was barely half a mile from Roger Williams Park, where Peter Shadd had supposedly robbed his former cell mate. Shadd could have walked here from the park, but why come all that way just to shoot up? How had he known to come here? Had he bought heroin on the street and then staggered around at random? Would those questions be answered in court?

Billy pictured Lady Justice peeking out from behind her blindfold. *I shouldn't be here.*

If caught, he'd be thrown off the jury. Billy was supposed to decide the case on the evidence he heard in court, nothing else. The problem was that justice *wasn't* blind in this case—Peter Shadd wasn't getting his fair shake. He was junkie, a convict—sentenced to jail in the first place because he *deserved* to be there for armed robberies. Billy had sensed that most of the jury already assumed Shadd was guilty of killing Garrett Nickel. They didn't care about the evidence or the circumstances. They wanted to cast their votes and go home.

His thoughts drifted. Angie had never gotten justice, either. Maybe Lady Justice needed Billy to pry open her eyes.

That's when a leg, clad in black jeans and a tall black leather boot, slid out the open window in the boathouse to the building's front porch.

Billy jammed the gearshift to drive and watched.

A woman climbed out the window. She was barely five feet tall, curvy, dressed in black. By her short spiked hair, Billy guessed she was young, mid-twenties, maybe, but he couldn't be sure. Shadows hid her face.

She watched Billy watching her for a few moments.

Then she clasped her hands above her head and gently rolled her hips in a subtle little dance on the porch, in the dead of night, for the stranger in the van.

Billy hit the gas. The van spurted up the hill.

He hit the brake.

Why am I running away?

"Why do you do this work?" Billy asked her.

"Because my father froze on the fucking street," she said.

"Isn't it dangerous? At night, in these places, especially for, um . . ." He caught himself about to put a sexist thought into the atmosphere.

She leaned back on the dirty sofa, tore off a bite of strawberry licorice, and crossed her big black boots.

"For a woman?" she said, finishing his thought. "Would I be safer as a man?" She laughed and lifted a thin brown eyebrow. "I realize men think their dicks have magic powers, but do they protect you from street crime?" She clicked her flashlight on and illuminated Billy's face.

Some strange emotion sizzled on Billy's cheeks. He wasn't sure what it was. Embarrassment? Not quite. She had zinged him, and he had enjoyed it.

She shut off the light and held out the open bag of licorice. Billy took another piece.

He had learned her name was Mia Elizabeth Kahn.

She was an outreach worker for the Manger, a homeless shelter in Providence. Her job was to persuade the drunk, the drugged, and the mentally ill to come in off the streets. The boathouse near the waterfront was on her regular rounds. Billy had wanted to ask her about the dead body found in the boathouse, and whether she had heard of Peter Shadd, but she wouldn't talk on the street, or in his van.

"In the house," she had suggested, leading Billy by the hand onto the porch.

Her hands were small and strong, the skin buttery with an un-scented moisturizer. What had looked like a braided bracelet around her left wrist was in fact a tattoo. Mia had slipped through the window with the grace of a cat burglar, and then had coaxed Billy through. Inside, the boathouse smelled like somebody had burned dried leaves in a gas station's rest room.

When Billy had clumsily entered through the window, invisible creatures had scurried away beneath strata of ankle-deep trash. He sat with her on a dirty sofa.

She was twenty-four, Billy guessed—younger, maybe, but no older. Her red hair was cropped short, dyed blue at the tips, and gelled straight up, like bristles of a toothbrush. Her left ear was pierced at least a dozen times, with silver hoops every quarter inch from the bottom of the lobe to the top of her ear. A tiny metal bar, like a silver tie clip, pierced her right eyebrow, and a blue gemstone twinkled from outside her left nostril.

"Why were you watching this place?" she asked. Her voice was scratchy, and a little lower than Billy might have expected. "Are you a cop?"

"No," he said, answering the second question, the one he didn't mind answering. "What happened to your father?"

She shrugged, then took another stick of licorice and sucked on it. "When he got moody and compulsive, blowing up anytime somebody spilled Kool-Aid, we thought he was just being an asshole," she said. "But my dad was a prepsychotic schizophrenic." She tore into the licorice and chewed a bite down.

"Mine's just an asshole," Billy said.

"I remember when he swung an ax at my mother and stuck the blade in the ceiling. That was the last day he lived with us. He was on the street when I was in high school. I remember him wearing a back-pack with everything he owned, and empty cans dangling from it. He grew a beard down to his crotch. I never knew he smoked until I saw him outside a movie theater picking butts off the ground and smoking what was left. Lots of people were afraid of him."

"Were you?"

"I was more afraid of becoming whacko, like him."

Billy leaned back and looked at the ceiling. Copper wires dangled from a hole.

She asked, "Are you afraid of being like your pop?"

"I'm already an asshole."

She laughed, saying, "I'm not nuts yet—I'd knock on some wood, but in here I'm afraid I'd knock a hole through it." She laughed again, loud and hearty. If her family story was difficult for her to tell, she didn't show it. "The last time I saw him was at a softball play-off my senior season. The restraining order said he wasn't allowed within a hundred and fifty feet of me and my brother, so he watched from beyond center field. Just him. Standing out there alone. He never waved. I don't think we ever made eye contact. I pitched pretty good. We won; he left." She shrugged again. "My brother was the last one in the family to see him—again, at a game. He played football at Cranston East."

"Is that Craig Kahn? Playing now at Brown?"

She nodded, impressed. "You certainly know local football."

"I know they're favored by eight against Cornell," Billy said, a roundabout way of confessing his gambling habits. "Your brother is the best offensive tackle Brown University ever had—their whole offense runs behind him." Bill looked her up and down, then chuckled. "How'd you end up with a brother who weighs three hundred pounds?"

"Three thirty-five," she said. "He used to steal my dinner."

Billy smiled, paused a moment. He was still curious about her father. "You said your pop froze to death?"

"Like a *Pop*sicle."

Billy groaned. *Is this chick serious?* "That's sick," he said. His disgust delighted her; he could see it in her eyes. Her delight infected him. Billy suddenly felt himself smiling. Her irreverence about death made her more alive than anybody he had met in a long time.

"I've tried crying into a towel," she explained; "it just made me feel like shit. The father I knew died years before that crazy bearded bum with a backpack. I mourned that loss long, long ago."

Long, long ago? What did that mean to someone so young? Five years? Billy had Tex-Mex leftovers in his refrigerator older than that.

"Why are you here, Billy?" she asked.

"A guy was found dead in this house about a year ago."

She turned toward Billy, brought her feet onto the sofa, and rested her chin on her knee. "In the attic," she said.

Billy leaned toward her. "You heard of him?"

"I found him."

He recalled the description in the paper . . . *a mutilated body.* "Oh Jesus—I'm sorry."

But he wasn't sorry. He could hardly have been more excited. Who knew what that body meant to the murder trial of Peter Shadd? Maybe nothing. Maybe there was a good reason that the jury had not been told about it. But why?

Billy didn't like the government to have secrets—even if they were intended for good. If the court thought the jury was too stupid to handle all the facts, how would anyone expect those dozen idiots to render a fair verdict? Billy had been an investigative reporter. Maybe his skills had eroded, and—more important—the fire in his chest had gone out, but the instincts were forever. As a reporter, he had never been very good at taking the information he was given without looking around for more.

Mia stuffed half a stick of licorice in her mouth and then peered into the bag. "Three pieces left," she said. "Two for you, one for me." She reached the bag to Billy. He took two pieces. "Are you a private eye, Billy?"

"I'm an obituary writer," he confessed. "Not that I *write* them too often. I mostly just type them."

She slapped her thigh and laughed. "And you're here in the middle of the night doing research, right? For a screenplay you're writing about a murdered street bum whose ghost crosses the River Styx in a shopping cart looted from a Benny's discount store."

"You're so close," Billy said.

Would she understand the truth? Or would she report Billy to the court clerk?

Naw, Billy decided. The boathouse was probably infested with rats, but Mia didn't seem like one of them.

"My name is Billy Povich," he said. "I'm a juror."

She smiled at him, squinted a little in surprise—hadn't thought of that one. "What's your case, Mr. Billy Povich? What's it got to do with this old shithole?"

He told her.

She listened without interrupting, then laughed and summed it up. "Are you trying to solve this case? To prove what?"

"I have some questions that the trial isn't answering."

She looked thoughtfully at him and then shook a finger. "I'm not sure if I'd want you on *my* jury, Billy Povich."

"Who was the dead guy you found here?"

She shrugged, saying, "There are people you get to know well at the shelter because they have their stories all bunched up inside and they don't need to be invited to spill them all over you. This guy was the other type."

"That would figure."

"He showed up at our place for the first time about, oh, maybe six months before he was killed. He'd be here a few weeks, then disappear for a while. That happened a few times. He looked about forty, but the street adds ten years, so I'd guess he was thirty. He didn't have any identification, and he never gave his full name.

"He said we could call him 'J.R.,' so that's what we called him. I have a police, uh, acquaintance who runs names through the department database for me. He tried running those initials and a personal description against missing-person reports nationwide, but he never found anything."

"That's a pretty close acquaintance, if he gives you access to internal computer records."

"As close as we both need," she said, being cryptic and smiling over it.

Billy wondered, *Is she sleeping with a cop?*

Mia spun on the sofa and clunked her boots on the floor.

Something scurried away under the trash.

"J.R. wasn't a junkie, not that I could tell," she continued. "But he drank himself crazy most nights, and slept here. Spent many days at our shelter. I tried to interview him for a client work sheet—sometimes we can get them benefits they don't know they qualify for. But he wouldn't cooperate. Oh, he was as polite and happy to chat with me, but he never gave up much of himself. His accent was wrong, not quite Rhode Island, though he had a familiar-sounding voice, the kind that made me wonder if I'd run into him long ago and never remembered."

"Why did he come here?"

She spread her hands. "He told me he came to see family," she said. "Goddamn—are we out of licorice?"

"Sadly so."

"You ate the last two pieces?"

"You told me to," Billy said. "J.R. said he was here for family?"

"That might have been bullshit, but maybe not," she said. "If he had come to start over and suddenly showed up with a suitcase on some second cousin's doorstep, it's easy to see how he could end up on the street. The week he got killed, he was in a good mood. First time I'd ever heard him talkative. He said he had come into good fortune and we might not be seeing him anymore—but that when the case of champagne arrived, we'd know it was from him."

"And then you found him here?"

"Upstairs," she said. "This place is one of my regular stops. There are about twenty places we know our clients regularly hang out. I try to persuade the reasonable ones they'd be better off in a bed. I'll tell the delusional ones anything they want to hear—'If radio waves are scrambling your brain, we got a shelter with a lead-coated roof.' "

"And that works?"

"Just listening to them usually works," she said. "I wouldn't normally have gone all the way into the attic, except that the trapdoor was open and the folding ladder had been pulled down. J.R. was up there." She bit her bottom lip.

"Are you sure it was murder?"

She looked away and lifted her eyebrows. "There aren't many accidental beheadings."

An intense sadness pinched Billy's windpipe. He swallowed hard. "I'm sorry," he managed to say.

"I had to recognize him from his clothes and the shape of him. He had a black thumbnail—that was what clinched the identification. There was so much blood. I called an ambulance from my cell phone, and that saved the life of the other dude—the one in the basement?"

"What other guy? You mean Peter Shadd?"

She nodded. "I searched the rest of the building while I was waiting for the ambulance and found that skinny guy in the basement— the room that leads out to the water—facedown at the bottom of the stairs. It looked like an overdose. His lips were blue. His nervous system was shutting down. The EMTs couldn't do anything for J.R., but they probably saved Peter Shadd."

Billy looked out the window. "Now twelve of his peers have to vote on whether he was worth saving," he said. "You're probably more qualified to sit on this jury than any of us would be."

"None of you is his peer," she said. "And neither am I. We could find a jury of his peers under an overpass I visited earlier tonight."

"At least those folks are smart enough to avoid jury duty," he said.

He still couldn't understand why Peter hadn't been charged with killing J.R.—unless there was no physical evidence. "You said there was a lot of blood upstairs. How much?"

"Do you want to see?"

The attic felt ten degrees warmer than the rest of the house.

The stain on the plywood floor looked like somebody had spread a quart of dark paint with a mop.

Billy had seen blood and bodies before as a journalist. But those bodies had been fresh, and the evidence of those crimes quickly swabbed away. This bloodstain was more than a year old. But then, in a decaying boathouse nobody seemed to care about, who would have cleaned it?

Billy borrowed Mia's flashlight and panned it around. The stain was roughly oval, about nine feet by fourteen. It went almost wall to wall across the width of the partially finished attic. The walls, formed by the pitched roof, angled up and met at the peak. Billy had to duck to walk around the splotch. The walls were unfinished and not insulated. Thousands of bent, rusted nails poked through the planks in straight rows, pounded there by roofers who had installed the tar paper and shingles.

Somebody long ago had begun converting the attic into usable space. The eaves had been blocked off with short vertical walls, maybe three feet high, which created crawl spaces that ran the length of the room. Billy pointed the light down a hole into one of the crawl spaces. A mound of soup cans, soiled clothes, newspapers, and other trash had been piled up in the gap.

Billy raised an eyebrow to Mia.

"Yeah," she confirmed, "people live in there."

She pointed to one end of the dark oval. "He was lying there. Faceup . . . well, I mean, he was on his back—put it that way." She rolled her eyes at her own slip of the tongue. "The blood was still wet when I found him, and it stank, a heavy metallic smell." Her nose wrinkled at the recollection. "There were a few footprints leading away . . . here." She pointed again. Billy aimed the light. The footprints were faded and nearly gone. "I guess they've been trampled and worn off. They were barefoot prints. Just the front of the foot, like somebody had walked away on his tiptoes."

"Did you see, uh, the head?"

"No."

"Someone stole his fucking head?"

She shrugged, saying, "Once you've committed murder, who cares about larceny?"

"And you said Peter was in the basement?"

"Facedown, in the dark, at the bottom of the stairs."

"Was he bleeding?"

She looked away a moment in thought. "He was bruised, as if he had fallen and whacked his forehead, but not bleeding," she said.

They started walking downstairs, with Billy holding the light. The stairs creaked like a rusty seesaw.

"Are you sure he wasn't bleeding? This must have happened fast for you."

"I spent an intense few minutes with him," Mia said. "I had to check if he needed CPR. I remember unbuttoning his orange jumpsuit and putting my ear to his chest. His heart was beating as fast as a hummingbird's. I would have noticed bleeding. There was no blood at all."

They returned to the front room, where they had entered through the broken window. A dry, scratchy drowsiness filled Billy's eyes.

"I can see why Peter Shadd wasn't charged in connection to J.R.'s body," Billy said. "No blood."

"Right—he didn't have a drop of blood on him," Mia said, her face brightening at the revelation. "So how could he have killed J.R., decapitated him, and chucked the head without staining his prison uniform?"

"Whoever did that thing upstairs had to have been drenched in blood," Billy agreed. He slouched on the sofa, sighed, and rubbed his eyes. "The cops have tests to pick up the slightest trace of blood on a person. Peter must have been clean." He shrugged. "I'm more confused that I was before."

"How's that?" she asked, vaulting over the arm of the sofa and landing with a whump. "You figured out why Peter Shadd wasn't charged with killing J.R.—he's not connected to it."

Billy had been a reporter too long to believe in coincidence. "If somebody finds you overdosing in the basement of a crack house, it's *possible* you might not be connected to a headless body upstairs," he said with a bitter little laugh. "Unless you just escaped from prison, and your cell mate is found shot to death in the river about ten minutes from here."

They sat in silence awhile. There seemed to be nothing more to say, either about J.R. or Peter Shadd's trial. Billy worried that Mia might leave. He studied her profile in the dim light from the street. Their conversation had been so intimate; he couldn't stand to let it end.

"Let's talk about something else," he said.

They whispered through the night.

Over the next few hours, he told Mia about how his career had begun to unravel at the dog track, and how divorce had crushed whatever journalist had been left inside him.

"I did not accept that she no longer loved me," he confessed.

"Who says you have to accept it?"

"She shacked up with another guy."

"So maybe she loved him, too."

"That, I *really* don't accept."

"Just because she couldn't stand to be around you doesn't mean she should join a convent," Mia argued. "Don't you think she could have loved more than one man?"

Billy said nothing.

"Tell me more," she insisted.

He told her about Maddox, about the crash that had killed Angie. He did not tell Mia about his dreams. She was, after all, still a stranger, and a crack house was not a confessional. But mostly he did not tell her because he did not want to scare her away.

She told him about watching her father drift into paranoia and madness, of learning to love a stepfather, and about her job poking through basements for people dying of self-neglect. Billy wondered what part of her story she might have kept from him.

She stretched on the sofa, rested her head on his lap, and closed her eyes. He could smell her hair, like lavender. Billy took her hand and lightly rubbed it, until he could not stay awake any longer and fell into a contented sleep.

Billy woke alone on the sofa.

Dawn had broken. He rose stiffly and shuffled through trash to the window. A breeze off the bay ruffled the sugar maples along the sidewalk. Sunlight slanted through their leaves and tousled with the shadows on the street.

"Oh shit," he muttered, checking his watch. If he didn't hurry, he'd be late for court.

Billy looked around for a note, a message—anything.

There was no sign Mia had even been there. His gut tightened with disappointment.

Poking his head out the window, he could hear the morning commute in the distance. He climbed from the boathouse and pounded
heavy-legged down the porch, heading toward his van.

A squadron of squawking geese soared overhead in a V formation.
Billy shielded his eyes and watched them turn with military precision
toward the bay.

He could find Mia at the shelter, he reminded himself. He knew
where she worked. He could walk to her office from his in ten minutes. Of course, she could reach Billy at the obituary desk nearly any
night of the week.

He climbed into the van, caught a glance of himself in the
rearview mirror, and shrieked.

"What the fuck!"

He looked more closely and laughed out loud.

Across Billy's forehead was a telephone number, inked on his skin
with a felt-tip pen.

How considerate of her, Billy thought, *to write the number backward
so that I can read it in the mirror.*

fourteen

Martin handed Carol his leather oxfords, then padded in stocking feet across his office to his desk and collapsed in his chair. It had been another long day at trial. His arches ached. He rubbed them.

"Is it smart for me to hide your leather shoes at my house?" Carol teased. "Somebody could get the wrong idea."

"You know how crazy my wife is about animal rights," Martin replied. "I'd rather she think *wrongly* that I was putting my pecker in my assistant than think *rightly* that I was putting my feet inside a dead cow." He gazed out the window, to the brick wall outside.

She snickered, then encouraged him: "You made the best of your opening statement the other day."

Martin waved off the compliment. "So unprofessional, to attack the opposing lawyer," he said. "Not something I could get away with again. Let's see the art while it's fresh. Please."

Carol opened a folder of eight-by-ten sketches of the jurors and began taping them to the wall. She arranged them in two rows of seven, in the order the jurors sat in the courtroom. With just a few strokes of charcoal and rough shading in colored pencil, the artist had accurately represented each juror, seven women and seven men.

"Frankie does good work," Martin said, looking over the drawings. "When he draws me for the newspaper, he always shaves off twenty pounds."

"Must save him a lot of ink." She winked at Martin.

Ignoring the dig, Martin nodded to the drawings and asked, "After two innings, what's our score?"

"Twelve to two, against us."

"Jesus!"

"With our rotten luck, we'll lose the two when they dismiss the alternates."

"I need six open minds to plant reasonable doubt," Martin said, scanning over the faces on the wall. "Gimme the bad news first."

"Dillingham has connected with most of the jury," Carol reported. "Take his opening statement, for example. I noted mimicry in the body language of several jurors—when Dillingham folded his hands or touched his chin, they did the same. It shows a subconscious connection."

"Meaning what?"

"Meaning Dillingham found their wavelength, and they accepted what they heard from him."

Consulting her notes, she pointed out pictures on the wall.

"Jurors one, four, six, and seven are especially affected by Dillingham," she said. "I note open hands, and heads tilted to the side, indicating interest." She sighed. "I'm afraid there has been very little negative body language toward Dillingham."

Martin flipped both middle fingers at the drawings and growled, "Read *my* body language."

"The jurors are, ah, less accepting of your case," Carol said.

"Don't sugarcoat it," he scolded. "If I gotta eat horse shit, let me savor the flavor. Makes me work harder." He fished his eyeglass case from his coat pocket, opened it, saw a spider inside, frowned, and closed the case.

"I'm noting a lot of fidgeting when you make your points—a sign of discomfort," Carol said. "Two jurors crossed their arms as you spoke today; another crossed her legs. It's defensive posture, an indicator of closed-mindedness."

"They don't like what they're hearing."

"Jurors two, three, and ten kept their heads down during your questioning this afternoon, which suggests they had reached negative conclusions. Worst of all, juror thirteen looked away and rubbed the back of her neck, which tells me she had mentally checked out of the process."

Martin looked at the sketch of juror thirteen, a heavyset fifty-year-old sales manager. "She's made up her mind to convict him already. Goddamn!" He sighed and wiped his hand over his face. "So who can I work with?"

Carol tapped a pen on the sketch of juror eleven, a pointy-chinned kid with a hard stare and a dark mustache as thin as a shoelace. "Alec Black," she said. "Age twenty-two, an art-school graduate who studied film noir."

"Now working retail at Pottery Barn," Martin guessed.

"The food-services industry," she corrected. "But he's all yours."

"The kid stares through me the whole time. I thought he hated me."

"He maintains eye contact and open posture for you, which is good. And he is the only juror who openly despises Ethan Dillingham. It couldn't be more obvious—he does everything but moon him."

"Skeptical of the law, eh?"

"That skepticism probably comes from trouble in his teens. He's got a juvie record, not serious—breaking and entering, vandalism, petty theft. He pleaded innocent but was convicted in a closed hearing in family court. Spent six months locked up at the training school. His counselor reported that he left more bitter than when he got there. But no arrests since he got out."

Martin raised an eyebrow at her. "Shouldn't that record be sealed? How'd you get that?"

She smiled and licked her lips. "When you put me on jury research, you told me to use all the tools at my disposal."

Martin covered his ears. "I don't wanna know—if I have to testify, I can say you never told me. Do you think Dillingham knows this kid is trouble for him?"

"I'm not the only one charting the jury. You wouldn't need an expert to see that this kid is solidly on our side."

"Which means Dillingham will try to get him kicked off. We can't depend on hanging the jury with one holdout. Tell me who else I got."

"This guy," she said, tapping juror twelve's picture. "William Povich. Worked for the paper as a reporter until a couple years ago—won all sorts of investigative awards, and was a Pulitzer finalist. Now writes obituaries on the night shift."

"Huh—a fallen star?"

"More like crashed and burned," she said. "He's not in your pocket yet, but he's got an open mind. Keeps his head up, very neutral posture. And he has held eyes with Peter several times. I'm reading curiosity and an honest desire to find the truth."

Martin stared at the picture in silence for a full minute. "I worry about the kid, Alec Black," he said finally. "He's young; he could be bullied. But not this guy, a former reporter—he could swing votes." He folded his hands into a little pyramid and spoke to the drawing, "How do I get inside your head, Mr. Povich?"

fifteen

Habits form fast: As the jurors filed onto the yellow school bus borrowed from the city of Providence, they did their best to re-create the seating assignments from the jury box. Billy plopped down beside juror eleven, Alec Black, the smoldering kid in the monochrome outfits, who was cultivating a bandito mustache.

"I love a field trip," Billy said in a low voice as the doors wheezed closed and the bus grumbled away from the courthouse with the jury, a court clerk, two sheriffs, both trial lawyers, a court stenographer, and a judge in a gray chalk-line suit but no robe.

"It's all an act," Alec said. "This is a Soviet-style show trial." He stared out the window, looking grim.

Billy recoiled from him, feeling singed. Then some long-buried reporter's instinct surfaced; he wanted to *know* this kid.

"How did somebody so young become so cynical?" Billy asked. It was an honest question, not a comment or a condemnation.

Alec looked at Billy. "How can somebody your age be so naïve?"

The bus inched along beside the river canal as they passed through the financial district, lurching from stoplight to stoplight in heavy morning traffic.

Billy smiled. The kid was sharp. The trial was only in its fourth day, and it was obvious most of the jurors were ready to vote their fears. They wanted Peter Shadd locked away, not because of the evidence—there wasn't much—but because he had already proven himself a criminal beyond any doubt; they believed he had an evil heart and that he might hurt them someday.

"My mind's open," Billy said.

Alec stared out the window again. Twenty pigeons pecked at french fries spilled over the sidewalk. "You and me are the only ones who wouldn't vote him guilty right now," he said. He put his thumbs together and made a U with his hands. He squinted through the U at the pigeons and then panned his hands to one side. "I'd film that scene in black and white, real low contrast, to let the birds blend into the sidewalk—it's symbolic of what they do: They're creatures of nature that blend into the cityscape and become almost invisible." He smoothed his thin mustache with a finger and then added with contempt, "Other than you and me, there's nothing but sheep on this bus."

Billy glanced around. They were not supposed to discuss the case, but he was confident nobody could hear them.

"What most people don't realize," Alec volunteered, "is that the justice system isn't as high-minded as on TV. The courthouse is a manufacturing plant, and the product isn't justice; it's convictions. Prosecutors are measured by how many convictions they ring up. Truth? Justice? No—can I *win* this case? If not, they don't prosecute. Instead, they pressure penniless kids with no lawyers to take deals, because the plea bargains help their case-disposal ratios. Just look at Dillingham. Why is he so anal-retentive? Why does he object over everything? He's trying to run for governor and he's protecting his conviction ratio."

Billy said, "You sound like you speak from experience."

"The best teacher."

The bus freed itself from city congestion and bumped over old trolley tracks, moving through the city's unofficial red-light district, past a topless bar painted pink and two kinds of porno shops—the kind that advertises with black stenciling on a nondescript door next to a loading dock, and the kind that advertises in flashing red neon, and in the sports pages.

"Take this field trip, for instance," Alec said. "There's no dispute that *somebody* shot Garrett Nickel, and no doubt he was shot by the waterfront, upriver from where they found his body. So why are we being taken to view where he went into the river?" He waited. The question seemed rhetorical, and Billy waited, too.

"This trip," Alec finally explained, "has been orchestrated by the prosecution to prime our imaginations for later in the trial. So that when Dillingham says Peter Shadd went to the waterfront and shot Nickel in the back, we'll already have the setting painted in our minds. We'll be ripe for his suggestion. Our imaginations will superimpose Peter Shadd onto our memories of the location. It's basic psychology."

Billy chuckled.

"You laugh because you think I'm wrong?"

"I laugh because I think you're right."

"Right from the opening statements, this trial has seemed like a railroad job," Alec said. "I'm not buying it."

"I can tell," Billy said. "You practically block your ears when Dillingham is questioning somebody. Everybody can see it."

"I don't care. He's a twit."

"He could be our next governor."

"Governor Twit," Alec said, raising his voice. A few heads turned.

Billy grinned. "I admire your passion," he said. "It will probably get you kicked off this jury before we deliberate, but I admire it."

"Would make a damn good movie script," Alec said. "The up-and-

coming filmmaker is kicked off the jury for refusing to be brain-
washed by a twit prosecutor in a bow tie."

The stream was about eight feet wide. It led into a drainage
pond that looked man-made—the edges of the nearly circular pond
sloped too evenly to have been made by nature—and then it flowed
slowly out toward the bay. A thick stand of phragmites had staked
territory on the far side of the pond; the reed plant loved to invade
wherever construction had disturbed coastline soil. A common yel-
lowthroat, brown and yellow, with a black mask, fluttered inside the
reeds. It sang for the jury: *Wichity, wichity, wichity, witch!*

The stream passed through an enclave of manufacturing buildings that would have had water views—*if* they'd had windows. An
unnamed access road ran alongside the stream. About a hundred
yards downriver, a homely concrete bridge carried the pavement over
the stream. The road then crossed a wasteland of pitted asphalt, heading toward a desolate cluster of corrugated steel buildings, which
looked untouched and forgotten, like a movie set for a film about the
end of the world.

Farther downstream, maybe a quarter of a mile, a tremendous
cargo ship, about as nautical-looking as a parking garage, had docked
for unloading. Four huge mechanical cranes, painted lemon yellow,
slowly turned in a million-ton ballet, moving steel cargo containers as
big as trailer homes. To the right of the ship—to the southeast—the
river widened into Narragansett Bay. To the north, giant storage
tanks squatted along the shore wherever the land jutted out into the
water. The tanks held oil and gas that had come by sea to one of the
oldest ports in America.

The bus hissed to a stop.

The stenographer dismounted first, carrying her clunky portable
note-taking equipment. The judge, his court clerk, and the lawyers

exited next, along with one sheriff; the other sheriff waited onboard with the jury.

Once the stenographer had set up on a tiny three-legged stool in front of her keyboard, the sheriff led the jury off the bus.

The air smelled swampy. A southern breeze blended the odors coming off the salty sea. The sun was hot on Billy's neck, and bright, too; he put a hand above his eyes as a visor. He could hear the distant hum of the cranes on the cargo ship. Otherwise, the place seemed deserted. A push to develop the area with new businesses had obviously failed. The building across the street was a half-finished tomb of steel and cinder block, festooned with graffiti. Maybe the contractor's paycheck had bounced, and he had packed up his crew and abandoned the job.

A short distance down the road, somebody had smashed the Plexiglas in a newspaper box chained to a utility pole beside the river. There was no traffic; a police car parked a quarter mile west ensured that the jury would not be disturbed. The jurors clustered in the street.

The clerk swore in a state police detective. The trooper was a monstrous man of six-five, in better physical shape than a Superman action figure. His hair had been buzzed to blond fuzz. He was in uniform: gray slacks with red piping down the side, and tall tan boots laced almost to his knees. He held his wide-brim hat under an arm.

Through gentle questioning by Dillingham, the trooper described for the jury what investigators had found. "The first blood spatter was over here," he said, walking toward the graffiti-covered building. He stopped a few steps from a wall decorated by spray-can Picassos. Balloonlike red letters crowded into one another on the wall. They said:

he that believeth shall not make haste

A philosophical vandal? Who had heard of such a thing?

"He was likely shot here by the building," the officer said. "And then he went this way, toward the stream." He walked toward the jury, which parted to let him pass. "We found a trail of blood on the street."

The trooper stopped at the rust brown pipe railing between the water and the road. "He would have entered the water somewhere around here," he said, "after going over the rail. He had been shot four times with a twenty-two-caliber firearm. Three of the four bullets entered through the back. He was also shot one time in front, in the rib cage—here." He lifted his right arm and gestured to a spot just below his pectoral muscle.

"The autopsy showed that Garrett Nickel drowned, though the gunshot wounds would have proven fatal," the officer continued.

He looked over the rail, to the stream.

"The water is approximately four feet deep. It's probable he was mortally wounded when he jumped or fell in and could not save himself, despite the shallowness. From this point, I believe that the flow of the stream carried the remains"—he slowly stretched a hand down the stream, toward the bay, mirroring the flow—"until the body reached open water and became snagged approximately three hundred yards south of here, where the remains were discovered by two teenaged brothers digging for quahogs. The body, dressed in tan cotton pants, a checkered flannel shirt, and running shoes, was positively identified through dental records as that of Garrett Nickel."

The trooper paused a moment to consult a flip-top notebook that looked toylike and silly in his huge hand.

He said, "The discovery of the body came three and a half days after Garrett Nickel escaped from custody. Due to the condition of the remains, which had been in the water for some time, the medical examiner was unable to fix a time of death with certainty." He folded his notebook and put it away. Then he nodded to Dillingham. He was finished.

Martin Smothers questioned the officer in a brief cross-examination.

"Did you find any blood at this site that belonged to Peter Shadd?"

"No."

"Did you find fingerprints here belonging to Mr. Shadd?"

"No."

"Did you find any clothing or objects belonging to Mr. Shadd?"

"No."

"Any physical evidence at this site—anything—that would prove Mr. Shadd was here?"

The trooper paused a moment. His big fists clenched and unclenched. "No," he said.

Martin smiled. "Then I guess we're done here."

sixteen

The first clue that Billy was in a dream: the five leg breakers chasing him in one white Caddy—five muscle men for five bookies and sharks, to whom Billy owed various amounts of cabbage. Since when did those guys work together?

Billy ran from them, around a corner, down an alley between two clapboard triple-deckers plastered with signs stenciled in a language he did not understand.

The leg breakers were in front of him. The five men had fused into one hulk, which was grinning like a madman, at the controls of a steamroller. Except that the *roller* part that flattens the asphalt was not smooth; it was spiked and made of chrome.

Billy stopped running and checked his watch.

The red second hand was turning the wrong way. He hid the watch under his hand for a second and then checked it again. Now his watch was digital. It said 42:42.

"This is a dream," Billy declared. He felt relief. The leg breakers were gone.

He heard the echo of a suggestion planted by his conscious mind: *Look at your hands.*

Immediately, Billy looked at his hands. They were blurry a moment, and then sharpened.

Experts in lucid dreaming recommend focusing on an object at the critical moment when the dreamer, still asleep, becomes aware he is in a dream. Your hands are always with you, so the experts say to look at your hands. For the past three months, Billy had performed lucid-dreaming exercises before bed—reminding himself to watch for dream "cues," the ridiculous events that happen only in dreams, and then to look at his hands. These were his last thoughts before he fell asleep.

When it worked, Billy could take conscious control of his dreams, usually for a short while before he woke up. He had begun these techniques to fight the random violence he had watched every night as his subconscious indulged in revenge against the crippled cop.

His hands in focus, Billy looked around the dreamscape.

He was in Roger Williams Park, the four-hundred-acre Victorian park of fields, lakes, and woods dedicated to the founder of Providence. It was winter and the ground was white. Lucid dreams are full of sensations, and Billy felt his face tighten against the cold. He could feel the weight of his body on the bottoms of his feet—a subtle detail that perfected the illusion.

Billy was on top of a hill, looking down a long road.

To his left, a broad slope of snow sank lazily away from the street. Hundreds of tracks left by sleds crisscrossed the snowfield. From his vantage point, Billy could see the Temple to Music, a monument of Vermont marble, hollow inside and fronted by stone pillars—looking like the Lincoln Memorial's little brother.

This was where Billy had seen Maddox several months after the crash. The mangled cop had been in a wheelchair that afternoon. Like Billy, he had come to hear jazz. That night, Billy's nightmares began.

In the dream, Billy saw Maddox again.

He saw him because he wanted to. This was Billy's dream. He was in control.

Maddox sat on a plastic lawn chair, alone, looking like he had come to a concert on the wrong day. Behind the stone temple, sunlight glared off the frozen duck pond.

Billy walked toward him. In his right hand, he felt his ice ax—twenty-five inches long, and yet less than eighteen ounces; it had a hardened steel head on an aluminum shaft, for mountaineering in the worst conditions. The hatchetlike head had a serrated blade that could have butchered a buffalo.

Billy had not used the ax in ten years, not since the first year he was with Angie. That winter, they had driven four hours to Mount Washington, in New Hampshire, where they had stayed in a majestic inn at the foot of the mountain. He felt his dream face smiling at the memory. He remembered the hot tub, the second bottle of merlot, and leaving the room at daybreak, while she still slept, to make for the mountain's summit alone.

He recalled little from the climb, just the scrape of his crampons against the ice and his white breath beneath his goggles. The summit that day had been encased in rime ice as sharp as a blade and as dainty as spider silk.

He had enjoyed the peak alone. The highpoint of his climb—the highpoint of his life.

Back then, Billy owed money to no one. He had started work in Rhode Island, covering crime for the paper of record. And in the red-roofed lodge far below, Angie waited. She would have been awake and at breakfast, probably, watching the mountain for Billy and drawing the faces around her—those of waiters and other diners—on her sketch pad.

Billy had killed Maddox many times in his lucid dreams. He had thought the dreams would satisfy his need to make Maddox pay for what he had done. Instead, the dream violence fed his fantasies. He had studied lucid dreaming to control the violence in his nightmares; now his nightmares had become rehearsals.

Billy felt his shoulders roll as he swung the ax. Hot blood splashed his face.

When he was done, he rested, feeling steamy sweat against his skin. The color began to drain from the park, like a Polaroid developing in reverse, and Billy realized he was waking up.

He saw Peter Shadd on the stage of the Temple to Music.

Peter looked at the mess at Billy's feet and frowned. He said, "That's some fucked-up shit."

Billy glanced down. His feet had churned up the snow and the blood and had spread it all around him. "Is this what you did, Peter?" he asked.

"Shit, man, you know I didn't do that."

"Everyone else thinks you did. I hear the other jurors talking. They're not supposed to talk about the case, but they do. They want to convict you."

"Do you believe in arithmetic?" Peter asked.

"I'm no good at it."

"Add something and then subtract the same. What happens?"

"The universe doesn't notice," Billy said.

"I didn't kill anyone."

"That's not you talking," Billy insisted. "It's not you; it's *me*."

"Save the innocent man, then kill the guilty one. The universe doesn't notice."

Billy woke into darkness with a little shudder. He was on his back, in bed. His T-shirt was dry. The hot sweat was just part of the dream. His heartbeat was calm, his breathing shallow and regular.

The radioactive clock glowed green. The time was 3:55 A.M.

Billy sat up, put his feet on the carpet, and passed his hands through his hair. His jaw was sore from grinding his teeth, and the foulness in his mouth smelled like sun-dried lizard. He took a BuSpar and swallowed it down.

Gathering his sheet into a ball, he wept silently into the cotton.

Billy cried because he had awakened into a world in which Angie was dead and Maddox alive. The dream had felt so real, as if Billy had really killed him. He wept because he would have to do it again. Billy bit on a mouthful of sheet. He thought of Angie, of the night she had told him she'd miscarried their first child. That night, Billy had locked himself in the bathroom and cried into the mildew on the underside of the bath mat, until Angie picked the lock with a knitting needle, took the bath mat away, and cradled Billy's head against her bare belly.

"Here I am," she had whispered to him.

With that memory, Billy's shoulders stopped shaking and the fit of tears passed.

He wiped his eyes on the sheet, blew his nose into it, and then tossed it to the corner. Switching on the lamp Angie had given him for his thirty-second birthday, he blinked the sleep away and let his eyes adjust to the twenty-five-watt bulb. Billy's dream journal was on the nightstand. The book was a hardcover binder with a shiny gold crescent moon on the cover. He flipped to the first blank page, wrote the date, the time, and the details of the dream.

The journal seemed radioactive, like the clock. It was a handwritten confession to a crime Billy had not yet committed.

If anything ever happens to Maddox, I must burn this book.

Unless, Billy thought, I want to be caught. Is that why I keep the journal?

Hmmm, no, that's ridiculous. Billy tossed the book back on the nightstand. Nobody *wanted* to be caught for anything—not speeding, not stealing cable TV, certainly not murder. But Billy had no doubt he would be caught. He wasn't a hit man. His revenge would not be done coolly for money; it would be a premeditated act of passion. And if it came to action, passion wouldn't care what clues it left behind.

From the hallway came a clunk. Then the old man mumbling, ". . . goddamn thing in the goddamn way . . ."

Billy went to the hall. The old man had steered his wheelchair into the doorjamb on his way to the bathroom and had gotten the footrest hung up on the trim around the door. A night-light low on the wall shone through the old man's wheels and cast a faint spoked shadow on the opposite wall.

"Pop?"

"This goddamn door jumped in my way."

"Mm-hm," Billy said, tugging the chair into the hall, and lining it up with the opening. "Why would a door do that?"

"Insurance scam, probably." The old man wheeled into the bathroom.

"Do you need help?"

"First thing I did out of the womb was piss on the doctor," the old man said. "If I did it then without help, I can do it now." He clicked on the light and flung the door shut in Billy's face.

Billy leaned against the wall and waited, listening to his father whimper, grunt, curse, and sigh. The toilet seat fell hard; the wheelchair rattled. Then silence for two minutes. And then the sounds of struggling began again.

The old man emerged from the bathroom more ornery than when he'd gone in. "All that work for ten fucking drops," he growled. "I tell you, boy, getting old ain't for sissies."

"Maybe you and I can switch bedrooms, so you'll have a straight drive across the hall."

The old man made a sour face. "Won't that be swell for you—trying to romance a woman in *my* room, the former cloak closet barely big enough for a twin bed and spare pair of underwear."

"I'm not doing any romancing."

The old man mocked him with fake surprise. "Really? You don't say?" He fingered the loose skin under his chin. "I haven't heard your headboard banging the wall recently, but I thought I was just going deaf."

"You should go back to bed, Pop."

"So should you—and get somebody in there with you."

"Can we drop this?"

"Pay her if you have to."

"I *don't* have to—" Billy caught himself as his voice rose. He glanced to Bo's bedroom door, then whispered calmly, "I don't have to pay to get laid."

"You're forty years old, son," the old man reminded him. "You wanna be alone forever? Listen to me—it sucks."

"You weren't alone often enough, if I recall my family history."

Anger stirred in the old man's blue eyes. "I played around too much, okay?" he said, a sudden rasp in his voice. "I got a lot of old memories of damp sheets." He frowned and held up his hands. The loose sleeves of his white T-shirt drooped beneath his wasted arms. "And now I have nobody. Who's gonna want me now? Your mistakes are opposite of mine, but just as bad—and they will turn you into me."

They stared at each other.

The old man looked close to tears. He had been nagging out of love, Billy realized, expressing his worries as best he could, in his own ham-fisted way. Something inside Billy melted. He said gently, "I hear you, Pop, but it's too soon—Angie's only been gone a year."

The old man looked away. He spoke down the dark hallway. "She's been dead thirteen months, but she was gone long before that."

Billy glanced to his bare feet. They were getting cold on the hardwood floor. "I had a plan to get her back," he said.

"Oh sure, your plan—to quit gambling, write your book, pay off your debts, and win her back. How much time did you think you had?

She shacked up with that asshole cop in the meanwhile. They was getting married."

"Never would have happened."

The old man sighed hard, a gasp in reverse. He said, "You and her—you divorced *five years ago*."

Billy's his head snapped up. "No. Five years?"

"Do the math—it's six years come January. That's how long you been alone."

The old man was right, though it didn't seem possible. Billy absentmindedly rubbed the spot on his rib cage where Walter had belted him. It didn't hurt anymore, but he had gotten used to rubbing it. "I didn't want anyone else," Billy confessed. "I was afraid it would feel like cheating."

The old man opened his mouth to speak, then stopped and did a double take down the hall.

Billy looked. A four-foot wraith in Batman pajamas and a Caped Crusader plastic Halloween mask crawled along the wall.

"Bo?"

The kid jumped to attention and whipped off the mask. "Yes, Billy."

"Look, it's Batman," the old man said. "Where's Robin? No—to hell with Boy Wonder—where's Catwoman? Remember her, Billy?"

"Uh-huh."

"Eartha Kitt!" the old man cried. "She can climb my scratching post!"

"Pop," Billy said, gently cutting him off. He asked Bo, "What are you doing out of your room?"

"Nothing."

"Um, have you been sneaking down to Mr. Metts's funeral parlor dressed as Batman in the middle of the night?"

A pause. "No."

It amazed Billy that a boy directly descended from a serial adulterer and a compulsive gambler could be such a rotten liar. Hadn't the kid gotten *any* DNA from Billy?

The boy yawned, big and phony. "I'm so tired! G'night, Billy! G'night, grandpa!" he said cheerily, and then vanished into his room.

"First time the kid hasn't tried to bum a dime off me," the old man said.

The mood had been broken; the father-son discussion was over. Fine with Billy—he had nothing more to say. "Can I push you back to your room?" he offered.

"Leave me here," the old man snapped. "Christ Almighty, I gotta piss again."

seventeen

The witness turned almost sideways, his left ear toward the jury. His peered, cyclopslike, through his left eye toward the prosecutor, who had called him to the stand.

"State you name," said the clerk.

"Lawrence Horne," said the cyclops. "But I like Larry." He spoke with a thick tongue, and if he hadn't come to court directly from jail, chained inside the sheriff's van, Billy would have assumed Horne was testifying through three vodka tonics.

He halfheartedly raised his right hand to be sworn in, like a recruit being forced to volunteer for some hated assignment.

The witness looked about thirty-five years old. He was unshaven and his stringy black hair was tangled. His face was sunburned and peeling, possibly from an outdoor detail, such as picking trash along Route 95. He was barely five-five and couldn't have weighed more than a buck twenty. Still, Billy doubted that many men in the cell block messed with Lawrence Horne. He was the sneaky-strong, wiry type, in good shape and hardened from a lifetime of street fights. As the prosecutor stood to begin his examination, Horne's lips puckered and his left eye narrowed. Though he was Dillingham's own witness, Horne seemed to be readying for a bitter argument. He looked like a man accustomed to throwing the first punch.

"Mr. Horne," Dillingham began, "are you currently a resident of the Rhode Island Adult Correctional Institutions?"

"The slammer?" he said. His demeanor brightened and he chuckled. "Yeah, I'm *residing* there for another eight to ten." He looked up to share the joke with Judge Palumbo, who stared through him as though he weren't there.

"Did you at one time share a cell with Garrett Nickel?"

"For three years, up at the Supermax, till we broke out."

"That would be the state's High Security Center, in Cranston, correct?"

"Call it what you want."

"At any time was a third inmate assigned to the cell with you and Mr. Nickel?"

Horne grimaced and stretched his jaw. He nodded toward the defense table. "Yeah, that little son of a bitch."

Martin Smothers bounced up. "Your Honor!" he objected.

Judge Palumbo calmed Martin with a nod and pushed him into his chair with the slightest gesture of his hand. "The record will show that the witness indicated that the defendant, Mr. Shadd, was his cell mate," the judge ordered. "Extraneous comments about his momma will be stricken from the record, and the jury will disregard. Move along, Mr. Dillingham."

"Mr. Horne," Dillingham continued, "can you tell the court about the first time you met the defendant?"

"Can I tell the court?" Horne repeated, looking around, seeming surprised by the question. He gave a little shrug. "Yeah—what the hell. I can tell it just like it happened."

Seated on the floor, Larry Horne gently dragged a string through the one-inch space under the cell door. The string had been painstakingly braided from threads pulled from a towel. The line was twenty-five feet long, long enough to reach two cells over. Nobody fished better than Larry. He would weight the end of the string with a paper wad and then flick it with a finger, casting it under the cell door, where it would extend as far as twenty feet. That was far enough to tangle it with somebody else's fishing line, and to make a person-to-person prison connection.

The odor of dinner arrived in F Block a few minutes before the meal.

Garrett Nickel reclined on the lower bunk and inhaled deeply. "It's the fuckin' meat loaf again," he predicted. "Hurry up and get the line in before it gets here."

"The meat loaf is made from ground kangaroo and rotten tomatoes," said Larry.

"Yeah, retarded kangaroo."

The skinny new guy said nothing. He sat on his footlocker, feet on the floor, his head leaning back against the concrete wall, eyes staring through the building.

The stencil on his jumpsuit read: "SHADD, Peter J."

The cell was about twelve feet square. It had been designed as a double room, but a prison-population boom had forced in a third bunk, crudely welded atop the other two. There was one metal toilet, a small vanity with cold running water, and three footlockers.

The cell door was steel, with a thick glass porthole. Below the porthole, the door had a horizontal trap just wide enough for a dinner tray. On the wall opposite the door, sunlight entered through a tall, narrow window, about seven inches wide, made of thick glass. Through it, the inmates could see a seven-inch slice of freedom be-

yond the prison yard and a twenty-foot chain fence. They could see
the former state insane asylum—now abandoned—a gloomy redbrick
fortress filled with nothing but old screams. And beyond that, civi-
lization: streets and stores and cars zooming along, drivers oblivious
to the eyes on them.

All three men wore bright orange jumpsuits. Orange meant trou-
blemaker; among Rhode Island prison inmates, the men in orange
were thought to be the most dangerous, or the hardest to tame. They
were held in lockdown in their cell, except for two showers a week.

Larry pulled a battered copy of *Newsweek* under the door. "Got
it," he said.

"What does it say on page thirty-three?" Garrett asked.

Larry flipped through the magazine and then read the handwritten scrawl. " 'We have our people on the outside looking for your
guy. . . . Will advise. . . . Stay tuned.' "

Garrett clapped twice. "Excellent!" He walked to the window and
peered out.

On the tiny window ledge, Garrett had left a shampoo bottle
nearly full of pink-tinted sour milk, topped with mold green curds
ripening in the evening sun.

With no ventilation, the cell was humid.

Garrett unbuttoned his jumpsuit to the waist and slipped his arms
out of it. He had been on a long, hard diet. His body had eaten whatever fat it had stored and then had begun consuming raw muscle; the
veins in his arms bulged just beneath the skin.

Garrett pulled out a six-inch shank from his sock and sharpened it
against the concrete wall, grinding lazily in little circles. He soon
tired of the work. "Where's my Bible?" he asked. Before anyone could
answer, he grabbed the book from his bunk and flipped through it until he found a tiny envelope of white powder. He dumped the powder
on the book cover, scraped the drug into a line with the envelope, and
snorted it.

He gasped hard, like a pearl diver breaking the surface after two minutes underwater. "Whew! Nothing better for losing weight," he said.

Larry Horne had been on a crash diet, too. But he was built smaller than Garrett and didn't need to lose as much. Still, Larry hated to deprive himself. He was envious of the new guy—he was already skinny enough.

A door buzzed down the hall, opened, and then slammed shut.

The chow was coming.

Garrett stashed the shank in his sock. "See if it's Flagg," he urged.

Horne grabbed his own King James Bible off his footlocker, a book identical to Garrett's, and yanked out a bookmark—a shard of plastic mirror half an inch wide and eight inches long. He slapped down the book, dived to the floor, and crawled to the bottom of the door. With his cheek on the concrete, he slid the mirror under the door and peeked into the hall.

"It's him," Larry confirmed in an excited whisper. "It's Frank Flagg."

Garrett rushed to the window and grabbed the bottle of rotten milk. With a hearty wet snort, he opened the bottle and drooled into the mixture.

A stench filled the cell. Peter grimaced.

Garrett pressed his palm over the bottle. "A good bacteria cocktail starts with whole milk," he informed Peter matter-of-factly. "That's the food—that's what bacteria eat. You add two teaspoons of blood as fertilizer and then seed it with the snot of a man with the flu."

"Rat shit works, too," Larry offered.

Peter tensed and looked around the cell, peering into the corners.

Larry laughed. "I think the new guy is afraid of rats," he said. "I guess we cancel our summer barbecue."

Garrett shook the mixture. He said to Peter, "Nice hot weather like this, mmmm, they grow good in five days."

Peter nodded.

"Spitting in here really had nothing to do with the recipe—that part's personal," Garrett confessed.

Larry climbed off the floor, saying to Peter, "It's your first meal with us—always ask for extra salt."

Peter sighed. He spoke his first words since being transferred from the medium-security prison half a mile away. "Is the food that bad in this building?"

"Who knows," Garrett said. "I only eat the crackers." He stepped beside the door and waited with his hand over the bottle.

The door trap creaked open.

"Chow time," said Flagg.

Franklin Flagg was about forty-five, heavy-browed and snaggle-toothed. He wore a sand-colored jumpsuit from the minimum-security building down the road, and served meals in High Security on work detail. He pushed a covered aluminum tray to Larry through the opening in the door.

"I want extra salt," Larry said.

"I know, I know. It's on there."

"The new guy wants extra salt, too."

"Fine." He pushed a second tray through. Larry set them on the bottom bunk and turned back to take the third.

Once the food was inside, Garrett leaned to the opening. He said, "The cops gave us a shakedown last week."

Flagg said nothing for a moment, and then: "Oh yeah?"

"Somebody told them I had a contraband: they ripped the cell apart."

"Huh."

"I barely had time to flush three grams of snizzle down the shitter. Do you know how hard it is to get that real Colombian shit into this building?"

"I don't need trouble," Flagg said. "I've done my time, every minute of it. I did six years in this building, and then worked my way down to minimum security by avoiding problems. In twenty-four days, I get paroled out of the system. I don't want to start nothing with you."

"I know somebody has been watching me," Garrett said. "You spying on me, Flagg? Is that how you won parole? Because I saw you in the rec yard. I saw you in the law library. I saw you looking at me at Bible study. And I'm seeing you right now."

"Look, Garrett, I got a lot of jobs around—"

Garrett jammed the bottle into the opening and squeezed.

Flagged shrieked, gagged, turned to run, skidded, slipped, crashed to the floor. "Help me!" he cried.

Garrett doused him with the putrid stream and then shoved the empty container into the hall. "Next time," he growled through the slot, "I stuff your heart in the bottle."

He yanked the trap shut, turned away from the door, looked to heaven, and shouted over Flagg's muffled cries, " 'And the captain of the guard took Jeremiah, and said unto him, the Lord thy God hath pronounced this evil upon this place!' "

"Amen!" said Larry.

Then Garrett asked cheerily, "So what's for chow?"

"Are you kidding?" Peter asked. He held his nose. "I can't eat after *that.*"

Larry uncovered the meals. "Uh, you can thank us later," he told Peter. The meat loaf was a steaming gray lump. The waxed beans might have actually been made from wax. Each tray also had one large wheat cracker, a battered apple, and a carton of milk. "You'll find that the meat loaf tastes like Jimmy Hoffa," Larry warned.

Garrett passed his nose over the food and sampled the aroma. "Mmmm," he said, mockingly. He bit into a wheat cracker and then collected three paper packs of salt from each tray.

"At least we got extra salt with the new guy here," Larry said.

Garrett opened the salt packs three at a time and dumped them into an empty milk carton.

"Don't you guys eat?" Peter asked.

"Not lately," Garrett said. He reached into his jumpsuit, briefly pulled out his cock, and squirted bright yellow piss into the carton.

"What the hell is that for?" Peter stammered.

Garrett adjusted his jumpsuit and then went to the window and stirred the mixture with an old toothbrush. "The salt is a corrosive," he explained. "And the piss is acidic."

He dipped the brush in the mixture and then carefully painted the metal frame around the window.

"How long you been doing this?" Peter asked.

"Two years."

The three men were silent as Garrett slathered the frame with piss brine. "How much longer?" Larry asked finally.

Garrett put the carton aside and retrieved the shank from his sock. He probed the frame with the sharp tip. "Hard to say," he concluded with a shrug. "There's some softening. I'd say a couple weeks, three at the most."

"Uhhhhh!" Larry moaned. "Three more weeks on this fuckin' diet."

eighteen

I'm glad you came back."

"I'm sorry about the way I left last time," Billy whispered.

"Think nothing of it," the priest said.

"I didn't wait for my penance."

"I'll sentence you to ten thousand Hail Marys if that would ease your conscience," said Father Capricchio. He chuckled.

Billy blew out a long breath. The silk screen bulged against it. "There's balance in the universe, isn't there?" Billy asked. "Hypothetically."

Father Capricchio's eyebrows climbed his head. Billy was here for business. He took a tug off his diet Moxie and considered the question. He began, "I guess that depends—"

"Because God puts things into balance," said Billy, interrupting. "There's the right amount of mass and energy in space, the right mixture of air and land on earth. When there is *crime*—let's call it sin—"

"Let's."

"—isn't there an equal amount of justice somewhere to counteract it?"

"God plays fair, if that's what you mean." Father Capricchio said. Billy had lost him.

"No, what I mean is—what if an innocent person is about to be harmed, while a guilty person goes free? Wouldn't God approve if somebody, um, righted the scales?"

Father Capricchio felt a chill, like a cool, damp wind. He squirmed in his chair, then said gravely, "You speak in terms of man's law, not God's. Our laws are fallible—for example, sometimes we let the guilty go free because we're not sure they're guilty."

"Reasonable doubt."

"There is no doubt in God's law—whatever errors we make with human justice, God will correct on His timetable."

"I'm sitting on a jury," Billy said.

Father Capricchio tried to lighten the mood. "You mean a sharp guy like you can't get out of jury duty?"

"It's a murder trial."

The cold wind blew again down the priest's back. He said, "We are not speaking in hypotheticals, are we?"

"Most people think it's an open-and-shut case—that the defendant is guilty. But I don't think so."

"You must follow the evidence, and your own conscience, of course."

Father Capricchio thought back to the morning newspaper. He had seen *something* about a murder trial. In Rhode Island, maybe?"

"I looked into his eyes, Father," Billy said. "And I didn't see it—whatever it takes to be a killer wasn't there. This kid has been in trouble, shot lots of dope into his own veins. He's a tough guy on the outside, but inside he's scared."

Father Capricchio had no intention of talking Billy out of his hunch. He believed God planted hunches to tell people what they could not know by mortal means. Father Capricchio had a hunch that Billy's trial had pushed him closer to committing murder.

"He's innocent," Billy said.

Father Capricchio sipped Moxie, thinking of what to say. Finally, he raised the courage to ask, "Do you believe that if you free this defendant, it will be okay to kill the man you hate?"

"We've already agreed that there's a balance in the universe."

Father Capricchio rubbed the back of his neck. The skin was damp with sweat. He probed: "You said last time that this man killed your wife. How can this be? Why isn't he in jail?"

Billy was quiet a moment. "It's complicated."

"Oh, bullshit it is," the priest scolded harshly. "If you're unwilling to trust the sanctity of the confessional, and the vows I took to perform this sacrament, and my love of Christ, which brought me to the Church in the first place ... uh, uh ..." Father Capricchio wasn't sure where he was going with his outburst. Was he threatening to throw Billy out?

"The guy used to be a cop," Billy explained calmly. "He took up with my wife after she threw me out."

"Oh," Father Capricchio said. His tirade had worked—no one could have been more surprised than he. He heard pills shaking in a bottle. "Is that medicine you're taking?"

"They ain't Tic Tacs."

"Why did she throw you out?"

"After I gambled away my stuff, I started losing her stuff, too. She told me I was sick and tried to get me some help. I convinced her that therapy was working. We even had a little boy. Then I lost the house and the game was up. She took my boy and the cat I gave her, and started over without me. The divorce was easy—we had no assets left to split."

"I hear a lot of regret in your voice."

"It was all temporary—I had figured—until I could win a few bets, get out from under the mountain."

"By gambling *more*?"

"Father, once you owe these people, winning is the only way out," he said. "But in the meantime, Angie—that's my wife—shacked up with this cop up on the East Side, in Providence. I didn't even know she'd been seeing anyone." He sighed. "I was still working as a reporter, though by then I was just mailing it in, mining the same old sources every day for a new fact to be mounted atop fifteen inches of background, to make a story. It's hard to get away with that for long. Somebody I worked with posted a sign in the bathroom near my desk: 'Reporters must wash hands after pulling articles from ass.' "

"How cruel," Father Capricchio said.

"I was juggling three bookies and a thin-skinned loan shark who thinks I miss payments to humiliate him—I don't pretend to understand *that*. On top of those debts, I was bouncing a dozen credit-card companies, using one card to pay off another."

"Ugh," Father Capricchio said, slugging soda. "I'd rather owe the loan shark."

"And then my old man got sick—can barely butter his own bagel—and moved in with me."

Father Capricchio chuckled gently, not making fun, just sympathizing. "We all have our crosses to carry," he said, "but it sounds like you had enough to tow."

"Mmmmm," Billy said, sounding detached. "And then Angie was dead."

He fell silent.

Father Capricchio held his breath and waited, waited. Pressure built in his chest. He passed thirty seconds without air, forty, forty-five.

"They had been at dinner," Billy continued. "Angie and the cop."

The priest closed his eyes and silently eased out the breath he had been holding. He inhaled deeply and smelled his sweat.

"Some Mexican restaurant, a bring-your-own-bottle place—I won't eat there," Billy said. He sounded annoyed. "This cop was known to like the sauce. Three years ago, he nearly got fired after the Massachusetts staties bagged him for DUI on the turnpike."

"Dee you eye?"

"Stands for driving under the influence," Billy said. "Don't you ever leave that little booth?"

"In body only."

"I don't know what kind of wine they had, but a waitress remembered a bottle of Captain Morgan, and their register receipt said they bought ten Cokes. How well does rum and cola go with taco salad?"

"They had an accident, didn't they?"

"Not an accident," Billy said sharply. "A *crash*. There's a difference."

Father Capricchio tugged off his white collar. It was getting warm in his confessional. He wet his lips with diet Moxie and then echoed, "They crashed."

"The car swerved off a back road, traveled sixty-six feet into the woods, and rammed a white oak that had stood on that spot for ninety-four years," Billy said. "After I cut the goddamn thing down, I counted the rings."

Tears filled the priest's eyes.

"Angie was dead at the scene," Billy said.

"God bless her," Father Capricchio whispered under his breath.

"And the cop—that drunken son of a bitch—he lived. He got mangled, but he *lived*. His cop buddies who arrived at the scene to *assist* the local PD whitewashed the crime. They sat on the accident report for a week, protecting him. When they finally released it to the public, it said he had fallen asleep at the wheel. They never drew blood at the hospital to test his blood-alcohol level, so there was no way to convict him for motor vehicle homicide—there's no fuckin' proof."

No proof? "Then how do you know," Father Capricchio asked, "that this *wasn't* an accident?"

Billy cleared his throat. He leaned closer to the screen. "I got bumped from my reporting job pretty soon after," he whispered. "I couldn't look at a police report anymore without seeing conspiracies and lies—poorly written ones, too."

Father Capricchio heard the pill bottle shaking again. More pills? He wanted to speak up, but he slapped himself lightly over the back of the hand.

Don't be his mother.

"I was a shitty reporter at the end, but I had been good in my day," Billy said. "I still had sources, people who owed me. I learned off the record that the original accident report—the one filed the night of the crash—had been intercepted *and rewritten.* They sanitized the paperwork. All copies of the original were obliterated—on paper and in the department computer. When I heard this, I tipped off a reporter buddy of mine. He investigated—the way I *used* to do it. He got the department to admit that the report had been rewritten, though they claimed it was only because the original had been misfiled and lost."

"You don't believe them?"

"Christ! Would you?"

Father Capricchio frowned heavily. He was not supposed to lie—period. But certainly he must not in the confessional. He tipped back the soda can and drained it. He said, "I suppose I wouldn't believe them."

"So instead of jail for killing my wife," Billy said, "he got a disability pension."

nineteen

The moment Alec Black left the smoke-free mall for the parking garage, he satisfied a craving with an organic American Spirit cigarette. The smoke smelled like dry leaves in a campfire. He tried to think about the movie he had just seen—how he would have shot it better—but the plot was so dumb, the acting so flat, the happy ending so horribly Hollywood. His thoughts drifted back to the trial. He was a juror, the target audience of the production. What if the trial were a movie? What director would have cast a bug-eyed freakazoid like Peter Shadd in the role of defendant?

Only a genius, of course.

A Kubrik or a Kazan. Or Fritz Lang—Alec planned to be the next Fritz Lang.

He let the butt dangle between his lips, put his thumbs together, and made a window with his hands. If the trial were a movie, how would Lang have filmed the testimony from Larry Horne? He panned his hands across empty parking spaces. Fritz would have shot it in black and white, naturally, starting with a close-up of the cell door—

shot in silence for thirty seconds—before slowing pulling back to reveal the three convicts.

Alec puffed his butt and looked around. At midnight, the garage was empty. He had exited the mall on the wrong floor. His car was one level higher.

He took a long drag and headed for the stairs.

"Lose your car, too?" someone asked.

Alec jerked his head around. A man fell into step with him toward the stairwell. He was dressed in black jeans, a black turtleneck, black sports coat, and tight black leather driving gloves—just as Alec was dressed, except for the gloves.

"You scared the shit outta me," Alec said. He chuckled and patted his hand over his heart. "Didn't hear you behind me."

"Daydreaming?" the man asked. He smiled.

"Thinking about a movie."

"I saw you in the theater. I saw the same film. Not much to think about, was it?"

Alec dragged on his cigarette. He didn't remember the man from the theater. "It was a dumbed-down adaptation of a pretty good book," he said. "The relationship between the senator's wife and the mandolin player wasn't sexual in the book. It was emotional. His free sprit was supposed to teach her about the limitations of being a political wife, despite the money and the fame. The movie squeezed out the subtlety from their kiss on the roof, and then the director had to paper over the lack of character development by introducing the bodyguard as a heavy. There was no heavy in the book. It's too bad. But that picture will probably make a hundred million dollars."

"Wouldn't the studios make as much with a good *story*?"

"You'd think."

Their footsteps echoed through the garage. A pigeon flapped overhead. They watched it nestle in a nook between steel beams.

"Spare a smoke?" the man asked.

Alec fished the soft pack from his jacket. He shook a butt from the pack and offered it to him. "Organic," he warned.

"I'm easy," the man replied. They stopped walking long enough for Alec to flick his lighter and put flame to the cigarette.

I'm easy? What the hell does that mean?

Was this guy trying to pick him up? In a parking garage outside the mall and the megaplex? Alec was straight, though he realized his style of dress and his finicky tastes in the arts could jam a person's gaydar and thus give the wrong impression.

The stepped together up the stairs.

"You know a lot about film," the man said.

"Studied it in school," Alec said, adding a white lie to put his sexuality in context: "My girlfriend says I'm the next Fritz Lang."

The man blew smoke and laughed. "What's a film student doing at the megaplex? You should be at the indie theater."

He hadn't flinched at Alec's mention of a girlfriend. Maybe the guy just enjoyed free tobacco and enlightened conversation. "I'm just killing time," Alec confessed. "I'm on jury duty and I can't stop thinking about the case."

At the garage's top level, Alec's twenty-year-old Volvo faced the railing across a wide swathe of white concrete unevenly lighted by flickering fluorescent tubes. To the left, the open-air garage overlooked a highway interchange. Even at midnight, cars streamed off Route 95 in a sweeping cloverleaf that flowed into downtown Providence. Beyond the highway, Federal Hill clubs and restaurants brightened the hillside with colored lights. Parallel rows of glowing yellow dots marked the residential streets of Mount Pleasant.

Alec flicked ash on the floor. "I'm parked down this way," he said.

"So what about your case?" the man asked, keeping pace with Alec. "Is he guilty?"

"I'm not supposed to talk about it."

The man sucked hard on the butt and drew his cheeks in. Exhaling, he said, "There's nobody here. I'm just interested. You can tell me now and kill me later, if you're afraid I'll squeal." He raised an eyebrow at Alec and smiled. The man's green eyes were narrow and sleepy.

"I think the prosecutor is full of shit," Alec offered. "I can say that much." He drew on his cigarette. There were just four cars on the entire level. "Which car is yours?"

"The Taurus," the man answered instantly. Raising his voice above the grumble of a trailer truck on the street below, he asked, "Why is the prosecutor full of shit?"

"They all are, aren't they?" Alec replied. "They care about convictions—their won-loss records—not the truth."

Which of those cars was a Taurus? Didn't look like any of them were. Alec quickened his pace. The man jogged a step to catch up, then matched steps with Alec, as if he expected a ride home. A prickling sense of danger combed down Alec's back. Who was this guy? Alec put his head down and marched double time for his car, fishing his keys from his pocket. "Well, take care," he said, bidding the man good-bye without a glance, and lunged for his car.

That's when Alec heard the blade click.

He whirled. The man's face was calm, his body language casual. Only the switchblade in his hand indicated evil.

"Your wallet," the man demanded.

The knife paralyzed Alec. He blurted, "I'm fucking broke."

The man never raised his voice. "Your wallet." He gave a little nod. "Take out your wallet. I'm not going to hurt you."

Alec caught himself blinking furiously at the man, and at the five-inch blade, which reflected the maroon ugliness of Alec's battered sedan. He drew his brown leather wallet from a back pocket. "I got, like, fifteen dollars here," he said, holding the wallet in the space between them.

The man took a last puff of his free cigarette, dropped the stub on the floor, and twisted a toe over it. Then he took the wallet.

"My Visa is maxed out," Alec said. Not even a lie.

From his own pocket, the man took a folded wad of white paper. He slid the paper into Alec's wallet and then handed it back to him.

Alec couldn't move. "What is this?"

"Take it."

"Take it for what?"

"Take back your wallet," the man ordered, "and put it away."

What the fuck's with this guy?

Alec complied. He kept his eyes on the blade and slid the wallet back into his pocket.

If he had been a split second faster, he might have figured it out.

The man's forearm flashed up at Alec. The blow caught him square in the Adam's apple. Alec gagged, clutched his throat, and spun away, hitting the side of his car. His eyes watered from the pain. He tried to scream but heard only a dry whisper. By instinct, he staggered two steps away from the attacker, saw the railing, empty space beyond, and braked in terror.

Not that way.

A forearm into his spine drove Alec against the rail. He bent over it, looked straight down six stories to a bridge over the flaccid Woonasquatucket River flowing shallow and brown beneath the mall in a man-made trench of granite blocks.

He bounced off the rail. The man punched him in the lower back.

Alec tried to scream but managed only a wet gurgle from his bruised windpipe. The man rammed his shoulder into Alec and drove him back against the rail. Alec slapped an open hand feebly on the attacker's head. The man jammed a hand between Alec's legs, grabbed him under the groin, and lifted him.

He growled as he rolled Alec over the railing.

Alec slapped a hand on the rail and clung to life, dangling sixty feet above the concrete. Glancing over his shoulder, he could see through a glass wall into the mall's food court. The lights were off and the place looked closed. Some janitor had leaned a mop against the glass.

Alec imagined the movie: The camera would start tight against the hand, close enough to see the tendons stretching and the little black hairs standing on end. Then the camera would pull back, revealing the arm, the body, the wall. Faster, the camera would retreat, the wall growing ever higher, until the ground appeared at the bottom of the frame. No good director would show the fall, of course. Instead, the camera would switch to the attacker showing him battering Alec's fingers on the rail with the butt of his knife, until one final blow dislodged the hand, and then—for only an instant—the camera would film a shadow on the wall, plummeting.

twenty

The jurors gathered as they did each morning in the jury lounge, sitting in the order of their numbers, around a long, crooked conference table shaped like California.

The seat next to Billy was empty.

At quarter past ten, a sheriff with a clipboard entered to take attendance. He reminded Billy of a buzzard—long neck tucked between hunched shoulders. His skin was gray and he smelled like cigar smoke.

"The lawyers have been arguing for an hour," the sheriff told the jury. "We're, um, down one juror, and the judge had to consider whether we should go forward with just one alternate. He just ruled against declaring a mistrial, so we'll go ahead and resume the testimony this morning."

He beckoned with a wave of his arm. The jurors got up and filed past him to the courtroom.

We're down one juror?

Where was Alec?

Billy was the last one out. He leaned toward the sheriff and asked, "What happened to Alec?"

"I'm not supposed to say. We should get moving."

"Did he get kicked off the jury? What did he do?"

"Mr. Povich—" the sheriff began.

"I like the kid," Billy said, interrupting. "I want to know what he did to get kicked off."

The sheriff sighed. He peered down the hall, saw that it was clear. In a low voice, he said, "Alec Black killed himself last night."

Billy chuckled. "All right, come on!" he begged. "Just tell me what he did to get kicked off, so I won't do the same thing."

The sheriff stared at Billy.

"Oh Jesus," Billy said.

The sheriff made the sign of the cross. *In the name of the Father . . . the Son . . . and the Holy Ghost . . .*

"How?" Billy demanded. "How could this happen?"

The sheriff shrugged. "He told his roommate he was going to the movies, and then he jumped from the top of a parking garage, late last night. He died instantly." The sheriff turned away. Billy grabbed his arm and rooted him there.

"But why would he do that?" Billy stammered. "We're in the middle of this trial. . . . This kid had strong opinions." Billy suddenly gasped. "Somebody killed him!"

The sheriff clapped Billy on the shoulder, a comforting gesture. "I guess Mr. Black had a lot of personal problems," the sheriff said. "It was a suicide—they found a suicide note in his wallet."

The sheriff paused a few moments and then urged him along. "We really need to get to the courtroom."

Billy relented, nodding. He walked slowly toward to court. Alec Black . . . a suicide victim? Billy couldn't picture it. The kid was so cynical, such a pain in the ass. He had a sarcastic comment for everybody; he loved sticking his thumb into the eye of the powerful. Why would he have killed himself and wasted fifty or sixty years of perfectly good scorn?

In the courtroom, the actors were at their marks.

Peter Shadd stared into outer space and absentmindedly cleaned his glasses with his necktie.

On the stand, his former cell mate Lawrence Horne was ready to continue his testimony. Horne shot nervous glances around the courtroom, like a rabbit that had wandered onto a greyhound track.

The night was moonless. Garrett had insisted they wait for the new moon.

The dim glow from the yard lights put Garrett's face in silhouette in the window. He worked the shank around the metal frame, driving it in with the heel of his hand and then wiggling it out. "Like butter, baby," he whispered.

"I can't *wait* for butter," Larry moaned. "First meal I'm gonna get is a half-pound burger, real rare, so that the juice runs down your hand from the first bite. Cheese all over it. Cheddar. Real sharp. Mm-hm. Couple slices of Canadian bacon melted so deep into the cheese, they almost disappear. Sliced tomato. Some crunchy iceberg lettuce. Spanish onion. And butter, baby—both buns grilled crispy in butter." He laughed and pumped his emaciated arms in the air. "The diet ends tonight."

"My mouth is fuckin' watering," Garrett said. "Thanks, asshole."

"Say, Shadd? You coming?" Larry asked.

Peter sat up in the second bunk, swung his legs off the side, and rubbed his eyes. "I ain't been dieting," he said.

"Skinny shit like you don't need to."

"I can't handle any more years on my bid."

"They can't jail what they can't catch," Garrett said.

Larry asked, "How many years you got?"

Peter exhaled hard and then counted the years silently on his left hand—from pinkie to thumb, back down to pinkie, and back up again. "About fifteen," he said.

Larry slapped a hand over his chest and staggered in a make-believe heart attack. "By the time a young guy like you does fifteen fuckin' years, there's no guarantee his dick would still work when he got out. Maybe you should come with us," he advised.

A shard of metal from the window frame went *plink* on the concrete floor. Garrett snickered.

"Destroying state property is a crime," Larry joked.

"A misdemeanor," Garrett answered, never taking his eye off his work. He hummed a few bars of some hymn and then said, "Freedom lies in being bold."

"Amen," Larry said. "Book of Leviticus?"

"Gospel according to Robert Frost," said Garrett.

Another shard went *plink*.

"Where will you go?" Peter asked. He sounded flabbergasted, like he was trying to talk them out of something so *obviously* stupid, like cliff jumping without parachutes. "So maybe you get through the window and into the yard? So what? Say you get over the fence. *So what?* The guards never start the nighttime count later than one-thirty. You won't get two miles before they're after you. Every cop in the state will be working overtime. Your faces will be on TV, in the papers. How far can two guys dressed in orange get on foot? All this effort . . . seems like a lot for one night of exercise, and then three extra years on your bid. Three more years to listen to Larry mumbling about food in his sleep."

Garrett stopped work for a moment. He looked at Larry. "In the month he's been here, that's the most I ever heard him say." He went back to work on the window.

"How far can you run?" Peter asked.

"Not *running* anywhere," said Garrett.

"You think you can moon-walk to Mexico?"

"I can crawl as far as Pontiac Avenue, and that'll be far enough."

"And then we'll get my stash," Larry said.

"You hush about your stash," Garrett ordered.

Nobody said anything for a while. Peter and Larry watched Garrett work the pick around the window. Every half minute or so, Garrett stopped for a few seconds and all three men strained to hear danger in the silence—the boom of a distant door, the clink of a key, a guard's footsteps.

They heard nothing.

Garrett attacked the window with persistence. He was like a battlefield surgeon—not fancy, but quite skilled with a knife, like Jack the Ripper.

Peter broke the silence, "What do you mean? Crawl to Pontiac Avenue? That's right outside—what happens when you get to the street?"

Garrett chuckled. He said to Larry, "Notice how he says *when* we make it to the street, not *if*. Interesting, huh?"

"He's getting religion," Larry agreed.

After another minute, Peter demanded, "Are you getting help from the outside? A car? Somebody picking you up?"

Garrett snorted. " 'And some believed the things which were spoken—' " he said, glancing at Larry.

" '—and some believed not,' " his longtime cell mate replied, completing the verse from the Acts of the Apostles.

Garrett wrenched the tool with sudden violence.

A chunk of metal went *clank* on the floor.

"Yahtzee!" he said.

He put the shank aside and wormed his fingertips into a crack between the window frame and the wall. With a foot braced against the wall, he steadily pulled. His body quivered. He pulled without success for nearly a minute, and then the metal frame squeaked faintly in surrender and abruptly tore off in Garrett's hands. He held it to his face and grimaced at Peter, showing off his canine teeth like two fangs.

He looked like the devil in a picture frame.

Larry clapped lightly, excited. "I'm gonna dig up my stash, buy a bottle of Crown Royal and a crystal glass," he promised.

Garrett flipped the frame on the bottom bunk, grabbed the shank, and went to work on loosening the window glass. "The seal is all dried out," he said. "This won't take long."

He worked in silence for ten minutes.

Larry watched over his shoulder.

Peter lay on his bunk and stared at the ceiling. Eventually, he asked, "Who on the outside would ever help you get out of here?"

"I don't care if you come or not," said Garrett. "But if you stay, you better keep your fucking mouth shut."

"I'm wondering why anyone would help you."

Garrett paused a moment and wiped the back of his hand over his brow. He was breathing heavily from his struggle with the window. "I'm not without certain talents," he said to Peter. Then he laughed and got back to work.

He jammed the tool in the crack above the window and pried. The glass suddenly fell inward, like a tree toppling without sound. He caught the glass, whisked it across the cell, and propped it against the door.

"Holy Jesus," Larry said.

Peter roused from his bunk and climbed to the floor. "I never thought . . ." he said, trailing off as a breeze carried the scent of freedom into the cell, which chased away the stink of body odor and despair.

The three cell mates inhaled deeply, standing spellbound and silent, smelling grass that had been cut that day, and a blend of summer pollens. They found joy in a whiff of ragweed. They heard distant cars on the highway, a trailer truck burping between gears. Crickets cheered for them to escape.

Garrett finally broke the spell of the outside world. He slid Larry's mirror from his Bible, eased it through the opening, and peered around.

"Well?" Larry asked.

"Paradise lost," replied Garrett. He stripped off his jumpsuit and pushed it out the window, then his shoes, socks, and underwear. Naked, he grabbed a can of petroleum jelly and smeared it over his ears and his torso.

Larry, too, began to strip.

"Grease my back," Garrett ordered.

Larry shuffled to him, pants at his ankles, and quickly slathered the gel over Garrett's back and shoulders. He slapped Garrett's flesh. "You're good to go," he said. Then he kicked off his pants and shoved his clothes out the narrow window.

Garrett said to Larry, "You're first."

"Me?" asked Larry. He was about to protest, but Garrett smacked petroleum jelly on his back and spread it in two hard swipes. Larry greased his chest, thighs, and ears.

"Lay flat, tight against the building, until I'm out."

Larry nodded and went to the window.

He paused a second, sizing it up, and then climbed onto a footlocker and reached his right arm out into freedom. The window was a tight squeeze. But the diet had shrunk his body to its minimum. His greased-up shoulder slipped through the opening. He turned his head and pressed it into the frame.

There's no way. . . . this hole is too small.

"Push, push," Garrett urged.

Larry closed his eyes, relaxed his jaw, and wormed his head deeper into the opening. He winced at the pain. Tears streamed along his nose. Just when it seemed impossible to push any more, his head slipped through, and Larry looked up into the star-filled sky. He blinked away his tears, steadied himself in the opening, exhaled deeply, and pulled his sunken chest through. Reaching a hand below the window, he steadied himself again, and then let his legs slide through. He dropped five feet to soft earth. The ground was moist and cool. Long-dormant memories revived the moment he touched freedom. Panting, he put his nose into the grass and inhaled deeply. For a moment, he was five years old again, sneaking through the weeds to scare his sister.

He struggled into his jumpsuit, socks, and sneakers. The perimeter fence was thirty yards across a flat lawn of tightly cropped grass. The fence was of little concern. Larry had learned to conquer chain link and barbed wire early in his career as a delinquent.

But after the fence?

Larry needed Garrett.

He looked up to the window. He had been outside alone for several minutes. Where the hell was Garrett?

Larry felt a brief burst of dread. Had the guards come for an early head count?

He rose to his knees, slowly pushed to his feet, and peered into the cell.

Garrett flipped the shank in the air. It spun once before he caught it by the handle. "Last chance," Garrett whispered to Peter. "Those are the terms."

Peter closed his eyes a moment and inhaled fresh air. He pulled open his jumpsuit and said, "Gimme the grease."

twenty-one

The Batman mask had a special place under the bed, next to a baby food jar that had once held strained peas but now held Bo's coin collection. These were coins he must never spend: one bicentennial half-dollar, six Rhode Island state quarters, and a silver dime from 1959, which was older than Billy, but not older than Grandpa, who was older than any coin Bo had ever seen. Billy had said the dime was worth more than a regular dime because it was so old. How much more? Bo didn't know. Maybe it was worth a quarter. Maybe a hundred dollars.

He grabbed the box with the mask and pushed himself from under the bed.

The Incredible Hulk clock on the nightstand had green numbers. The numbers were thick and blocky and Bo thought they looked mad sometimes. Maybe the numbers were mad because Bo was out of bed at four o'clock in the morning.

He put on the Batman mask. His breath through the little holes in the nose whistled like Darth Vader. He squeezed the penlight Billy had given him. It went on when he pinched it and off when he didn't. He aimed the light through the pickle jar on his bureau. The coins in the jar were the ones he could spend. The jar's shadow on the white wall was tall and crooked. The jar held thirty-seven dollars and twenty-two cents. A fortune. Yet still not enough.

Time for Bo to go on his mission.

He grabbed his toy pistol. It was metal and heavy and looked just a like a real gun. The gun made Bo feel less alone in the dark. He opened his bedroom door, peered into the dark hallway, and listened.

Silence.

He tiptoed to Grandpa's room, put his ear to the door, and heard nothing. He turned the knob, pushed the door open, and stepped inside. Grandpa was under the sheet. His wheelchair was beside the bed. Bo felt a chill. The chair never bothered Bo when Grandpa was in it, but it scared him when it was empty.

Bo would not face the empty chair without his mask. The chair called to him. It wanted him to sit. Bo was afraid the chair would never let him up. Or that he would like having wheels so much, he would never want to walk.

With one eye closed, he couldn't see the chair. He could see Grandpa on his back. His pillow was under his shoulders and his head was bent backward at the neck. That looked like it would hurt. Grandpa's jaw was open. Bo pinched the light and shot the beam into his grandfather's mouth. His teeth were tan and the cavities greenish black, the color of a deep swamp, deep enough to drown it. Bo got scared and cut the light.

He stepped closer and listened. Grandpa made a soft wheeze. His breath smelled spoiled. Bo pinched the light and saw Grandpa's chest rise and fall through the beam.

He was not dead.

Satisfied, Bo retreated to the hall and silently snicked the door closed.

He went next to Billy's room. The door was already open two inches. Bo put his ear in the space.

The sheets rustled.

Bo listened a little longer; he wanted to hear breath—that was how he knew people were not dead. Talking was good, too. One time, Bo heard Billy cry in his sleep. Bo had been happy to hear his father cry; it meant that Billy was not dead.

Bo had missions every night to make sure Grandpa and Billy were not dead, and that he was not alone.

There! He heard it—Billy's breath—a snort like a pig.

Bo clamped a hand over his mouth. He didn't want to laugh. He zoomed down the hall in stocking feet, to the top of the wide carpeted stairs that led down to Mr. Metts's funeral parlor.

His mission had made him feel safe. He probably could have fallen asleep. He thought about going to bed.

Then he lighted the stairs with the flashlight. This was the scariest mission of them all. Maybe he would just go partway. He stepped down, down, down, to the first floor. The door there had a gold knob shaped like a lion's head. But it was a friendly lion. Bo turned the knob and pushed into the funeral parlor. It smelled like flowers.

He turned left, into a big room with rows of soft chairs that faced the table where Mr. Metts would put the coffin with the person who was dead. The carpet was spongy and it felt good under his feet. Three big windows looked out to the street. The streetlamp outside was yellow. Bo could make out the black outline of the Armory castle at the far end of the park.

Mr. Metts's silver telescope stood on three legs near the window. The undertaker had showed Bo how to read license plates across the park with the telescope. Someday they were going to take it out at night and look for Mars, and for spaceships.

Bo passed into another room and froze. Fear tickled inside his stomach.

There was a coffin there. It was white. Giant baskets of purple flowers, as tall as Bo, had been placed at each end of the coffin. The coffin was closed. The flowers smelled so thick and sweet, Bo became light-headed. He knew there was a dead person inside.

"I'm sorry," he whispered.

He put his head down and marched past the casket, went into the hallway. He stopped at a white door with a little gold sign that said PRIVATE.

He tested the door. Locked. It was always locked.

Bo dropped to his knees and aimed the light at the floor. He lifted the edge of the carpet—as he had seen old Mr. Metts do. There, Bo found a gold key. Feeling brave behind the Batman mask, he unlocked the door and pulled it open.

Inside, a brown coffin stood straight up on one end.

Bo looked up to a window set in the coffin. In the window was a face.

Feeling less brave, Bo blessed himself with the sign of the cross. He cleared his throat and greeted the corpse formally. "Good evening, Sal."

The dead man's skin was gray and tight. His eyes and mouth were closed. Bo didn't look too carefully at the mouth—he didn't like to see the stitches through the lips. Clumps of Sal's hair had fallen out. He had bald patches. The hair he still had was straight and black, like a witch's hair.

A newspaper story glued to the coffin told the story of Salvatore Genovese.

Bo had learned the story by heart, from Mr. Metts.

Sal had worked in a traveling carnival that had come through Providence in 1929. While he was here, he had died—murdered, some people said. A man who said he was Sal's father made a deposit with Mr. Metts's grandfather for a funeral. The father never came back. Mr. Metts's grandfather refused to do the burial until he was paid the rest of the money. He put Sal in a special coffin with a window and displayed him in the funeral home. People came from all over to see it.

It was still in the lobby when Mr. Metts was a little boy.

But then some people didn't like it. And Mr. Metts's father, who was dead now, put the coffin in the closet and showed it only to his friends. Bo's friend, Mr. Metts, showed the coffin only to Bo.

Panning the light over the newspaper story, Bo scanned for the number. . . . There it was . . . the balance Sal's father owed for the burial—$125.

Bo could hardly imagine such a sum.

"I made thirty cents bringing newspapers down for recycling," he stammered to the corpse. "We're up to thirty-seven dollars and twenty-two cents. That's not counting my special money collection under my bed, but I'm not supposed to spend those coins."

He aimed the beam at the dead man's face in the window.

Tears of pity stung Bo's eyes. He was afraid of the corpse, but he loved it, too, because Sal needed Bo to help him get buried. Dead people cannot take care of you anymore—you have to take care of them.

Gingerly, he reached a hand to the coffin. He tapped it for a split second, as if afraid it might burn him.

"G'night, Sal. I'll come back as soon as I can." He closed the door, spun the key in the lock, and tucked they key under the carpet.

He marched back the way he had come, into the room with the coffin. He faced away from it.

What was that?

A white flash, from the park outside.

Maybe it's a robot!

Bo killed his flashlight and dropped to all fours. Since he and Grandpa had watched *The Day the Earth Stood Still* on television, Bo had been waiting for a robot to appear in the park.

He crawled to the big window that faced the street and peeked his Batman face over the sill.

There was a man in the park.

The man was watching Bo's house.

The stranger was dressed in an overcoat and a brimmed hat, like a gangster. He was a big man. The man's hands were in his face. There was another white flash. Bo gasped.

He's taking pictures of our house.

Bo dropped to the rug. He looked straight up at the window and began to shiver. Why would a man in an overcoat be taking pictures at night? Did he know that Bo had sneaked downstairs to the funeral home? Maybe he was Sal's father. . . .

Suddenly, a face appeared in the window above Bo. The man looked in through cupped hands.

Bo tried to scream for Billy, to dash upstairs and yell for the police, all at once, but he found himself frozen on the floor, looking up through the plastic mask at the stranger. The man's face was wrinkled. His gray eyebrows were bushy and grew in crazy swirls. Bo was glad for Sal in the closet. At least Bo was not alone.

What did the man want? Did he want to put Bo in a coffin in the closet, where Bo would not be buried? He imagined Mr. Metts sharing the secret in the closet with another boy. Bo hoped the other boy would visit him.

In a moment, the man vanished.

Had he seen Bo?

No, he'd never looked right at him.

Bo regained control of his body and didn't waste an instant—he crawled, trembling, to the stairs and then up to the apartment. He knew he never should have gone downstairs that night, and now he had to live with a frightening secret. He promised himself never to tell Billy about the stranger who was watching the house.

twenty-two

The three escaped cons found the mango-colored Oldsmobile in the parking lot of a box company, in an industrial park across the street from the state prison complex. Garrett reached behind a tire, tore off a piece of duct tape, pulled a silver key off the tape, and unlocked the car.

"Shotgun!" Larry called.

"Nobody's riding shotgun," Garrett said. "Both you assholes, in the back." He slid in behind the wheel.

"Massachusetts plates," Peter noted as he tumbled in. "Who left this for us?"

Larry piled into the back after Peter. His undershirt was wrapped around a cut on his wrist, from scaling the barbed-wire fence. "It's got a Rhode Island inspection sticker," he said.

Garrett gave a sour look over his shoulder. "You two working at the DMV? It's a fuckin' stolen car with hot plates. It has an expiration date of about two days, so let's shut up and get moving."

The Oldsmobile stuttered in surprise when Garrett turned the key. He pumped the gas and hammered his fist on the dash, telling the car, "You work for the Nickel-Plated Outlaw, you son of a bitch."

The engine huffed to life. Garrett laughed like a madman, jammed the transmission into drive, and stomped the gas. The car lunged forward.

"My stash," Larry said. "I need my stash!"

"Five minutes," Garrett snapped. "If I could go *five minutes* without hearing about your fuckin' stash, I could die a fulfilled human being. Jesus, Larry!" He thought for a moment. "I'll dump you in the park; then me and Peter will take care of some business. We'll pick you up later, and then drive through the night. We'll be in Bangor by morning. There's a ferry to Nova Scotia. We'll dump this shitbox and steal new wheels on the other side."

"I can't get my stash myself," Larry cried. "I can't swim."

"What? Then how did you hide it there in the first place?"

"It was January—I walked on the ice."

Garrett muttered to himself. He turned right onto Pontiac Avenue, heading north, away from the prison. They passed a twenty-four-hour gas station lighted up brighter than an operating room. "That wasn't here when I went in," Larry said. He pointed to an on-ramp. "Ooo—take the highway."

Garrett shot him a hard look in the mirror and then jerked the car onto the ramp. Larry tumbled into Peter, who tumbled into the door. "It's been awhile," Garrett explained in what seemed like an apology for his driving. He raced onto the highway, steadying the wheel with his knee as he slipped his arms out of the orange jumpsuit.

Larry rolled down his window, leaned against the door, and felt the wind strafe his face. What a rush, to be free. "Now I know why dogs do this," he said.

"Take Peter," Garrett ordered. "Get the stash. Meet me the same place I drop you off."

At an interchange, he swerved onto Route 95, toward Providence, hiding the Olds among a handful of long-distance truckers plowing north at eighty miles per hour.

Larry blanched. To leave Garrett Nickel alone with the wheels? "Won't take long to get the stash," he pleaded. "Come with us."

"I got an errand," Garrett said. He glanced at Larry in the rearview mirror. Something monstrous stirred in Garrett's eyes, and Larry felt a stab of fear in his chest.

Garrett wrenched the car off the highway, cutting off a tractor-trailer in a squeal of tires and a howl of horn on the way to the exit. Larry tumbled again into Peter, who clutched both hands on the door handle. Larry whispered to him, "Sneak past a rifle tower, climb a razor fence, get killed on the fuckin' highway."

Righting himself, Larry imagined that the windshield was a movie screen and what he saw there just a scary flick.

Garrett rode the bumper of black Nissan up the ramp. "Learn to drive, asshole," he cursed.

He swerved around the car, plowed through a stop sign, and bounced the Oldsmobile down a narrow and pitted city street. He yanked the car left and right, curb to curb, around the potholes. Outside Larry's window, dangerous objects flew past the car—poles, mailboxes, hydrants, a bungalow. He clung to the door and licked salty sweat off his upper lip.

The Oldsmobile zoomed down another ramp, heading west on a darkened suburban highway divided down the middle by a concrete barrier. Up ahead, the road bordered a dark, forested edge of Roger Williams Park, which looked more like wilderness than picnic grounds.

"When I slow down," Garrett shouted, "you two jump out and get the stash."

"Where do we meet you?" Larry cried.

"What do you mean, jump when you *slow down*?" asked Peter.

Garrett checked his left wrist, though he hadn't owned a watch in nine years. "I need a couple hours," he said. "Get the stash, and then come back and lay in the weeds, right where I leave you. On my way back, I'll tap the horn so you know it's me."

"What do you mean by 'slow down'?" Peter repeated.

Larry scrambled up the grassy slope after Peter. At the top, he examined the painful dark spot on his forearm. He licked it. Blood. A scrape the size of a silver dollar.

The Oldsmobile roared down the road, then vanished.

"I think he was going twenty when you pushed me out," Peter bitched.

"Be thankful—he was about to hit the gas again." Larry took a moment to look around and get oriented. The woods were silent. "This way—Jesus!"

He grabbed Peter by the arm and dragged him to the ground.

Headlights approached.

"Not a sound," Larry warned.

Laying flat in the underbrush, the two cons watched a Providence police cruiser slowly motor along a park road. The police took their time—they could have jogged faster. The cops probed the woods on the other side of the street with a white searchlight. Darkness gobbled up the light as they passed.

"Are they looking for us already?" Peter whispered after the cops had gone.

"Doubt it," Larry said. "The slammer won't miss us for another hour. The park closes at nightfall. They're looking for dope sales and sex orgies. They have them here sometimes."

"Hmm—how much time do we have?"

"Whoa—" Larry said. "Did you just make a joke? Congratulations— your first joke. How does it feel?" He didn't wait for an answer.

"There's no time for shooting smack and getting laid. We gotta get to the boathouse, but we can't use the road. And not a fuckin' peep once we get moving. There's no highway noise in the park, so any sound will carry a long way."

They skittered across the road like two bugs, heading into the woods the cops had just searched, then up a steep slope. Larry winced at every snapping twig. "Do you have clubbed feet or something?" he complained. "Why are you so loud? You might as well be playing the accordion."

Dropping to their bellies, they wormed their way to the crest of the hill. Below them, the slope eased down through hardwood trees to another park road and then to a lakeshore. The lake at that hour was a dark plain dotted with one clump of trees on one tiny island. The gabled boathouse on the shore looked like a mansion at the edge of outer space. Far in the distance, downtown Providence twinkled white and yellow.

Larry pointed to a light moving along the far lakeshore. "The cops are down by the zoo," he said. "Let's get to the water."

They hustled between giant ash, down the hill, across the road, and to the boathouse. Larry led the way around the building, heading to an L-shaped aluminum dock that reached into the lake. Eight plastic paddleboats floated motionless in the water.

"You left your stash here?" Peter whispered.

"Six years ago, before I went inside."

"A thousand people come here every day."

Larry clucked his tongue. "Best place to hide shit is right in everybody's face. Wait here a second." He knelt on the dock, crawled to the end of it, and then scampered back. "The paddleboats are tied down with wire, padlocked to eye hooks in the dock."

"And?"

"And you need to swim under the dock and loosen one of the hooks so we can take a boat."

"Think about what you're saying," Peter said. "We don't have time to shoot smack and get laid, but we have time for paddleboating?"

"Two jokes in one day," Larry said dryly. "You're on fire." He pointed to the water. "Get under there."

"Why can't you?"

"I told you I can't swim. Can't even dog-paddle," he said, exasperated. "I'll drown, and then you'll have to face Garrett alone—without the stash. Think about *that.*"

"Aw, cripes," Peter said. He shook his fist at nobody in particular and then began to strip.

"Slower, shithead," Larry whispered. "You're making too much splash."

"I just want to get there."

The convicts pedaled the two-person boat away from the boathouse, toward the black stalks of trees on a tiny island.

From across the lake, the angry snarl of a caged tiger slashed the silence. Goose bumps erupted on Larry's arms.

"Jesus, you hear that?" Peter whispered. "Is that from the zoo?"

"Mm-hm."

"I hope that thing ain't escaping, too."

"All that time locked up together and *tonight* I find out you're a comedian," Larry said.

The cat snarled again—a high-pitched ripping noise.

Larry clutched the side of the boat. He was already surrounded by death in the little craft. They had found no life preservers at the boathouse, and Larry swam like a hunk of marble. "I might drown out here," he said, "but I refuse to be eaten."

In a few minutes, they approached the teeny island, not much bigger than a whale's back. They aimed into it. The boat's plastic hull ground against sand and roots and became beached. They climbed out into a grove of skinny pine and silver birch, thick underbrush, and a soft, damp rug of moss. Larry could smell the wet earth under his feet. He reached down, tore up a handful of moss, and stuck his nose in it. "Never smelled anything so good, even when I was free the last time."

"Where's the stash?" Peter asked. He sounded impatient.

"Other end."

They fought through underbrush, heading toward the other side of the island. They sank into the wet moss and made suction noises when they lifted their feet. *Plup! Plup!*

"In that stump," Larry said.

The stump was two feet high, half as wide, and was decaying to mush. A determined person could have pulled it apart with his bare hands. The center of the stump had rotted out and had been filled with coarse sand.

Larry began to dig out the filling. He paused to watch the police car and its cone of light as the cops crested a hill across the lake and then dipped out of sight.

Peter stood aside. "Where did you get this stash?" he asked.

"It's a week's worth of productive work. An Exxon station, a nightclub after closing, the lottery drawer of a Seven-Eleven." He reached deep into the sand and found something. "Heeeeeello! Tell our two contestants what they have won on *Digging for Dollars*."

He pulled out a package wrapped in plastic, slightly bigger than a softball.

"My pistol," he said casually, rolling it aside. "We may need that."

He dug some more and pulled out another pack in plastic. He rolled it toward to Peter. "Rip it open and count it," he said. "I had three packs of two grand and one of three. . . . Here's another one . . . and another." He fished deeper into the stump, growing excited about their chances of actually escaping all the way to Canada, because nothing smoothed problems like cash.

"And Garrett laughed at me for hiding my shit in here," Larry said, a smack of "I told you so" in his voice. "Hmmmmm . . . ah, got it."

He pulled out the last pack of cash, looked at Peter, frowned, and then said flatly, "You fuckin' double-crosser."

Peter leveled the pistol at Larry's face. "Put the dough down and get behind the stump," he ordered.

"Garrett should have punctured your lung before we left the room."

"The money."

"I should have insisted," Larry said, "or done it myself."

Peter motioned with the pistol for Larry to drop the money.

Would he really waste me out here?

Larry didn't know Peter Shadd well enough to be sure. But no altar boy ever got assigned a cell with the Nickel-plated Outlaw, so it had to be *possible* that Peter could pull the trigger.

Larry dropped the money, spat at it, and then moved behind the stump.

Keeping his eyes—and the gun—directed at Larry, Peter gathered up the cash and stuffed the packs in his jumpsuit. Then he backed away, retreating all the way across the island.

"What can you do?" Larry asked, keeping his voice low. "Kill me here? The cops will hear the shot."

With his foot, Peter pushed the boat free.

Larry stumbled toward him. "I can scream for the cops," he threatened. "If I scream, they'll be here in two minutes. I'll do it."

Peter sat on the left side of the boat and pedaled backward from the island. He put the gun away.

Larry stepped into the water. The paddleboat's tiny wake lapped at his knees. The water paralyzed him; it grew so deep so quickly and seemed pleased to suffocate him if he lost his balance. He could go no deeper.

He couldn't yell for the cops, either. Peter had called his bluff—

after smelling the land, Larry could not betray himself by screaming for the police to take them both back to prison.

Peter turned the boat in an arc and headed for shore. With just one man aboard, the craft listed to the port side.

"I'll kill you," Larry promised, his voice barely above a whisper.

Peter probably couldn't hear him. But he'd know.

twenty-three

The café's patio overlooked the cobblestone Riverwalk, which bustled with people moving at two speeds: Half were in a hurry; half had no place to go. Below them, the river followed its man-made canal of granite into a round basin, where Martin's wife had often dragged him to see Shakespeare performed in a Rhode Island accent. Beyond the basin, the river vanished beneath the mall, where Martin's favorite juror had been found dead, his skull broken.

The sky was bright. Sunlight skipped off the river and blinded him. Martin stared down the canal, listening to two voices: one from across the table, the other in his earpiece.

His tenderloin had arrived on a gold plate, presliced and arranged in a fan around a spiral tower of red Bliss mashed potatoes. Martin rarely ate so fancy a meal. A covert hamburger at the Haven Brothers diner, down by City Hall, usually satisfied the inner carnivore he kept secret from his vegan wife.

He liked the view from the patio. He could see the best of the "new" Providence—the river park, the graceful arched bridges, the new office buildings, which combined brick and glass to look modern and classic at the same time—all built upon the ruins of what the *Los Angeles Times* had once described as "a dreary little mob town." The view of the new Providence gave Martin hope that he could still puncture Ethan Dillingham's case against Peter Shadd, though he was running out of time.

"Martin?" Carol said. "Are you listening?"

"Mm-hm." He jiggled the earpiece deeper.

"Want to run away together?"

"Absolutely."

"Let's invite your wife to a bullfight."

"Mm-hm."

She threw an olive at him.

"What?" he cried, indignant, wiping the wet spot on his shirt.

"I knew you weren't listening."

Martin held up his tiny radio. He said, "It's this asshole from the talk show—Pastor Guy. I don't know why I ever subpoenaed him."

"You wanted him to testify because he's a minister, he's semifamous—at least by voice—and he's the only person outside of prison who knows Peter personally."

Martin held up his hand. "Commercial is over," he said. "I should hear this."

Pastor Abraham Guy continued his radio rant:

"So how do we LOVE an enemy who takes advantage of us?" he raged into Martin's ear. "An enemy who steals what we have earned through HARD WORK, who cheats our elderly out of their pennies, who hurts our children, mugs our sisters, and robs our brothers at the point of a gun?"

Carol turned her palms up, asking, "What? What?"

Martin put a finger to the earpiece, like an FBI agent on a stakeout. His other hand grabbed a fork and stabbed a slice of steak.

The voice in his ear continued:

"In my career doing GOD'S WORK, I have tried to bring the ministry to the enemies of hardworking folk—that's right, I have carried the Scripture WITHIN THE WALLS of the state prison, and more than once . . ."

Martin grumbled, "More than once? More like every week for five years. I hate this guy—he's so afraid of getting tarred as too liberal."

Carol folded her arms and scowled. "I can't hear what he's saying," she reminded him.

Pastor Guy ranted along:

". . . What can one poor minister do where the government of the state of Rhode Island has failed so miserably? Our judicial system is an ABOMINATION. The jails are so near full. How long before the ACTIVIST JUDGES say we must release the short-timers to make more room? Does this make you feel safer for your children?"

Martin groaned. Carol reached for another olive. He explained, "He's setting up a tough-on-crime position for his run for governor."

"On his show?" Carol asked. "Aren't there campaign rules about that?"

"Politicians make the rules for themselves, so there're loopholes," Martin explained. "Until he declares himself a candidate, he can say what he wants, and the radio station doesn't have to give any opponent equal time."

Pastor Guy fumed:

"We will be releasing people back into society who ARE NOT READY to go back. Where is the rehabilitation in our prisons? We ought to be transferring these potentially dangerous criminals to facilities in other states if we don't have room to hold them here. Sure it costs money, but how much are we willing to pay for peace of mind? I've been in our prisons, folks. I've looked into eyes BRIMMING with evil. Eyes that could belong to THE DEVIL HIMSELF—that's what I've seen in there."

Martin slapped the table in anger. "Asshole!" he shouted.

Carol nodded and smiled to diners nearby, then glowered at Martin.

"Half of what he says is wrong, and it's killing my strategy in Peter's case," Martin said, disgusted. "He says the prison is full of evildoers."

"Isn't it?"

"Mostly—but how can I call him as a witness now? I'm trying to portray Peter as the class dunce who got in over his head."

"You have deposition transcripts," Carol reminded. "Pastor Guy told you—under oath—that Peter was mild-mannered, respectful, interested in the Bible."

Martin said bitterly, "I didn't think to ask the son of a bitch if he had seen evil in Peter eyes."

She shook a finger at him in jest. "That's no name to call a pastor."

"He's a politician," Martin said, staring off to a yellow-brick cupola on top of the mall. "At his core, he's a self-promoting asshole— any accidental noble qualities are secondary." He yanked out the earpiece. "It's risky now to call him to testify. I could use his deposition transcript to keep him on the reservation during my direct exam, but I don't know *what* he could say on cross."

He chewed cow. "But I don't have much else," he admitted. "Larry Horne has been more credible that I had expected—it's damning for Peter to be seen in cahoots with his cell mates."

"He escaped with them," she said. "I'd call that cahoots."

"If I can't separate Peter from those other two thugs, we're screwed."

Martin grabbed his steak knife. The blade reflected the sun. He stared at the knife, at the tiny serrated teeth that moved so easily through the beef. He saw his reflection in the silver.

He had an idea.

"Pen!" he called out.

Carol dug a red felt-tip from her alligator purse. Martin snatched it and furiously scribbled his thoughts on a starched linen napkin.

"Are you separating Peter from the other escapees?" Carol asked.

"Don't have to—any one of our jurors would have escaped that night, too. Just like Peter Shadd. I only have to show them why."

He wrote. She waited a full minute.

"Why?" she begged.

Martin stabbed the knife into the table and stuck it there. "Because if Peter didn't go, Garrett Nickel would have cut out his guts."

"Is that a fact?"

"It's a possibility," he said. "With a maniac like Nickel, wouldn't that be enough?"

twenty-four

Ethan Dillingham stood at the far end of the jury box. As any good lawyer knew, if he could hear the witness clearly from there, so could the jury. His voice rang a little thinner than usual that morning, after three long days leading the direct examination of Lawrence Horne.

"When we left off yesterday, Mr. Horne," Dillingham began, "you had testified that the defendant, Mr. Shadd, *menacingly* pulled a gun on you. . . ."

Martin bounced up. "Objection!"

The judge glanced at the clock. "Two minutes past nine and we have our first objection," he said. "Could be a new record." He read Martin's mind, and told Dillingham, "Let's do this thing with less *colorful* adverbs, okay?"

The prosecutor lifted his chin an inch to acknowledge the objection as minimally as possible, then continued. "And so after Mr. Shadd pointed the gun at you, and left you stranded on the island in the lake, what did you do?"

Three days on the witness stand had started to wear on Larry

Horne. His hair had grown greasy. The flesh under his eyes had softened and puffed up. He had been a competent witness all three days,
describing the escape and Peter's betrayal. But he suddenly seemed
agitated. Martin had watched Horne as the sheriffs escorted him to
the stand. He counted three dirty looks toward Peter. Horne had
ended his testimony the day before by describing the double cross.
Maybe he had been stewing over it all night.

Let's hope so.

"I waited awhile, thinking maybe he'd turn back," Horne said.

Martin made a note. That seemed like a lie. He took his eyeglasses
from their case and slipped them on. The spider clung to the lens over
Martin's right eye. It looked as big as a bearskin rug. Martin eased the
glasses off and closed them back in their case.

"The sun started coming up," Horne said. "I had to do something,
so I tore my shirt into strips and lashed a bunch of sticks together."

"To make a raft?" Dillingham asked.

Horne frowned at him as if he were an idiot. "To make a little float
I could hang on to and kick my way to shore."

"And you made it?"

"Actually, I got halfway back and drowned," he deadpanned. He
raised an eyebrow and looked away, as if to say, *What's with this guy?*

Jurors giggled and smiled at one another.

Martin bit his lip. The jury knew that Horne was a punk, but they
liked him anyway. They had come to see him as an amusing rouge,
which was dangerous for Peter. The only juror who seemed unmoved
by Horne was William Povich, but who knew what Povich was thinking? He was inscrutable behind a wrinkled brow and lively eyes that
scanned, never stared.

"Mr. Horne," Judge Palumbo scolded.

Horne looked up at Palumbo, shrugged, and complained, "It's a
stupid question, Your Honor. If I'm here, I must have made it."

Even Palumbo broke into a tiny smile. He glanced to Dillingham and said playfully, "This court does not discriminate against stupidity, but perhaps Mr. Dillingham would like to rephrase?"

"I would, sir," Dillingham said. He chuckled at himself and then said to the judge, "We lawyers have long appreciated this court's tolerance for our less insightful moments."

Martin was shocked. Self-deprecating humor from Ethan Dillingham? The jurors adored it. That little joke was Dillingham's finest moment in three days, and the first time he had connected with the jurors as a human being.

The bastard.

Dillingham flattened his smile, turned to Horne, and corrected himself. "What I mean to ask is, how did you make your escape without being apprehended?"

Horne shrugged. "Little bit of luck—I made it to shore and then laid there to rest. The sun was up. By then I knew the prison was looking for us, so I had to get out of the orange pj's, right?"

"Mm-hm. Go on."

"So I crawled across a road into somebody's backyard, okay? And they hadn't brought their laundry in from the clothesline, so I helped myself to some painter's pants and a couple shirts. The fit was real good. Maybe a tailor lived there, I dunno. I stuffed my jumpsuit in their trash and then tested out my new clothes in the neighborhood. It's important to look casual, see? Take it slow. If you gotta run, you better be in gym shorts, or you're gonna look suspicious. That's what Garrett used to tell me. I thought maybe he had read that in the Bible."

Dillingham seemed perplexed for a moment. How did they get from fleeing the island to gym shorts and the Bible? He checked his legal pad and found his place. "Three days later, you were arrested in Maine," he said.

That was a statement, not a question. Martin could have objected to the form, just to be an ass, but he let it pass. No use getting on the jury's nerves so early in the morning.

Horne said, "I hitched some of the way, hid in the back of a pickup, too. It ain't hard—you don't need a passport to get to Maine. I didn't know that the little bastard had already shot Garrett."

"Objection!"

Judge Palumbo agreed with Martin. "The jury will disregard that last comment, and the witness with keep his opinions to himself. Anything more, Mr. Dillingham?"

Dillingham checked his legal pad. He flipped the page, and then another, as if he didn't want to let Horne go after three days of direct examination. "No, Your Honor," he said finally, "I'm done with this witness."

To prepare for his cross-examination, Martin had studied Horne's criminal record and then looked up old newspaper stories about the crimes he had committed. He had read the quotes from Horne's victims and had allowed a dark spot of contempt to grow on his heart. In court, he tapped into that dark spot and exaggerated the hell out it.

"Do you remember Daryl Archer?" Martin asked.

Larry Horne leaned forward and squinted his cyclops eye at him. "Who?"

"Daryl. Tall guy. Was a neighbor of yours. You bloodied his skull with a shovel."

"Objection!"

"Remember him now?"

Judge Palumbo signaled for a time-out and then beckoned both lawyers to the bench for a sidebar conference, a huddle the jurors could see but not overhear.

The judge leaned over the bench. The two lawyers leaned in tight. Martin could see the curly gray hair up Palumbo's nostrils. The judge nodded to Dillingham. "Talk to me," he said. "It's your objection."

"Mr. Horne is a witness, not the defendant," Dillingham whispered. "Mr. Smothers should not be allowed to rehash every time Horne spit on the sidewalk."

"I'll leave out the spitting and stick to his violent assaults," Martin replied. He could feel Dillingham's hot peppermint breath on his hair. "Your Honor, this courthouse should put in a revolving door for this guy Horne. He's played nice with Mr. Dillingham for three days, but I should be allowed to use his own record to dirty him up a bit."

Palumbo turned to Dillingham for an answer. The prosecutor ummed and aahed, huffed, and then began to speak. "I reiterate, Your Honor—"

"Then you don't need to talk anymore," the judge said, cutting him off.

To Martin, the judge said, "You can use his history to probe his credibility, but stick to the court record, and spare us the blood. Got it?" He shooed the lawyers away with a little backhand wave.

Martin spent the next two hours in a tense and bitter exchange with Horne over his record of bar fights, traffic altercations, and the time he stomped a guy who had beaten him at darts.

"Your appearance here is not due to your love of truth and justice, is it?" Martin asked, giving Horne a sarcastic wink.

"Objection!" Dillingham yelled, popping up.

"Rephrase," the judge said.

"What kind of leniency," Martin asked, "has Mr. Dillingham offered you in exchange for your testimony?"

Horne looked at Dillingham. "Uhhh . . ."

"He can't help you," Martin barked. "What kind of deal did you get?"

Horne licked his lips. "Immunity on the escape."

Martin summed up the exchange so that the thicker jurors would not overlook it. "So in exchange for testifying against your former cell mate, Mr. Dillingham agreed not to prosecute you on the charge of escaping from Rhode Island's most secure prison, is that right?"

"Yeah."

"A free ride on your escape?"

"Ain't that what I said?"

"And you could not have gotten that kind of largesse from Mr. Dillingham unless your testimony was useful to him in his case, isn't that right?" Martin asked.

"Objection!"

"Sit down, please, Mr. Dillingham," the judge said. "The witness may answer."

Horne looked at Dillingham, who stared back, unblinking. Horne said, "He wanted me to talk about the escape."

"If you had nothing bad to say about Peter Shadd, you wouldn't be here, would you?" Martin shouted, jabbing his finger at Horne. "You couldn't get your cushy immunity deal without offering some dirt, could you?"

"Objection!"

"And you'd say anything to get that deal, wouldn't you?"

"One question at a time, Mr. Smothers," the judge ordered. "Anything to say on this objection?"

Martin was confident he had made the point. "I'll move on, Your Honor."

The judge leaned back in his chair.

Martin paused to allow the jurors to process the testimony, and then he looked over his handwritten scribbles. Discrediting Horne had been easy—Horne was a natural-born asshole. The next part of his cross would be harder, and more important for Peter's defense. Martin would try to carve a refuge for Peter within Garrett Nickel's notorious reputation.

"Let's go back to the night you escaped," Martin said.

"Weren't just me who escaped," Horne said, nodding at Peter. "He did, too."

Horne was pissed and trying to be difficult. Martin ignored him and plowed ahead. "You were first out the window, is that correct?"

"Yeah."

"When you went out, did you expect Peter Shadd to join you that night?"

Horne shifted in his seat. "I didn't know." He looked at Dillingham, who pretended to be fascinated with his note taking and didn't look up.

Martin feigned surprise. "You didn't know?" he echoed. "Well, it seemed that the details of this planned escape were exquisite. A cell mate who had been expressing doubt for weeks seems like a significant loose end, wouldn't you say?"

"I don't know what you mean."

"Mr. Horne," Martin said, trying to sound like he was beginning to lose his patience, "are you saying that after months of preparation, you and Garrett Nickel never thought about what to do about your cell mate? Were you just going to leave him in the cell, to call the guards the moment the two of you went out the window?"

Horne tugged at a one shirt cuff and then the other, seemingly oblivious that every person in the room was staring at him, waiting for an answer. He looked up suddenly and said, "Garrett was going to take care of Peter."

"Take care how?"

"Like you said, Garrett didn't want to leave Peter in the cell—he never trusted the little bastard, and with good reason." He glared at Peter.

Martin let the curse slide. Why not let the jury hear what was in Horne's heart?

"He was going to give the little bastard a choice that night," Horne said. "Either he tagged along or Garrett would cut his throat."

Jurors gasped. Dillingham fumbled his pen out of his hand. The revelation stunned even Martin, who had intended to *suggest* Nickel had intimidated Peter, but had never imagined . . .

"Right there in the goddamn cell," Horne added without a prompt. "Let the cops clean him up in the morning."

The words hung in the courtroom a few moments.

"Nickel told you this?"

"When Peter was in the shower."

"He threatened to kill him?" Martin said, restating the answer to buy a few moments to collect himself.

"He planned to slit his throat—usually fatal, wouldn't you say?"

The point *had* to be clear to the jury—Peter had no choice but to escape or die. Under those terms, who among them wouldn't have slipped out that window?

Martin moved to his final point. "You testified that after Mr. Shadd marooned you in the lake, you waited hours, is that right?"

Horne gave Martin a hard cyclops squint, as if he suspected a trap. "Yeah."

"Hours, you said."

"A few hours."

"Did anybody see you out there?"

"Doubt it."

"It's fair to say, isn't it," Martin said, "that if anyone had seen you on that island, they would have called the cops?"

"Maybe."

"They would have called *somebody*, don't you think?"

"Probably."

"I mean, a man in an orange jumpsuit, stuck in a lake, is something a citizen reports."

"Yeah, fine," said Horne. "They probably would."

"But nobody did."

"Nobody saw me." Horne wiggled in his seat and grinned, as if he had won the argument.

"So there's no proof you spent *hours* on the lake?"

"Huh?"

"No proof at all, is there?"

"It was hours."

"You could have spent twenty minutes out there before you paddled to shore and then hunted down Garrett Nickel yourself, isn't that true?"

"Objection!" Dillingham yelled.

"Mr. Smothers," warned Judge Palumbo.

"That ain't what happened," Horne said bitterly. "I wouldn't."

"Objection!"

"Wouldn't you?" Martin shouted over the cross talk. "You'd let Nickel knife Peter Shadd in cold blood—because you're just as much a monster as Garrett Nickel!"

"Fuck you!" screamed Horne.

"We can't trust a thing you're saying!"

"Objection! Your Honor!"

Palumbo rapped the gavel four times, hard enough to drive nails into concrete. "Enough!" he roared. When all was quiet, he rapped three more times. His face glowed crimson. "Do you have any more questions for this witness?" he demanded.

"No, Your Honor," Martin said merrily. "We all have better things to do."

twenty-five

The coffee shop called itself a "shoppe" and seemed the kind of place that used hand-pumped milk from free-range holsteins raised on kosher diets grown from seed blessed by the College of Cardinals. Franklin D. Flagg didn't care if the farmers read Milton to the cows before tucking them into bed; he just wanted a cup of coffee.

The shoppe's staff dressed in nothing but black. Always scowling, they looked like constipated ninjas.

Signs all over the shoppe promised that a percentage of the profits would go to this or that good cause. Maybe that was why the employees were cranky. If you donated something like 162 percent of your profit to feeding the tree slug and educating the octopus, there wouldn't be much left to pay your staff.

Flagg used pocket change he had panhandled to pay the anorexic android with the skin tone of skim milk. He took his coffee outside. Traffic moved like an advancing glacier. Pedestrians—laughing, chatting, flirting in person and on their cell phones—outpaced the cars down the neighborhood's main artery. Flagg had walked half an hour from downtown to this enclave of hip bars and mid-scale ethnic restaurants, where you could browse for modern art made from car mufflers, get acupuncture from a senior citizen fluent in Mandarin, pick up some bisexual company for the evening, and get sloshed on thirteen-dollar martinis—all within sight of your parking space.

Flagg had come for none of those things.

He had come to use the phone.

He could not risk being spotted by anyone from the shelter, nor anyone from his former life, before prison, when Flagg had made book, fenced on the side, and directed the thrashing of deadbeat gamblers, all from the back room of a newspaper and magazine store on Federal Hill. That was a long time ago—so long ago that Flagg's memories of that era were sepia-toned.

The pay phone at the corner gas station was outdoors, at a utility pole in a small parking lot, at the edge of a handsome redbrick sidewalk. Flagg jammed a Rhode Island state quarter into the machine, the coin with the sailboat on the reverse, and dialed a number he had already looked up and memorized.

The phone rang five times.

Flagg didn't want to reach an answering machine. This was not the kind of message he could leave on tape, and if he had to hang up, the phone would keep his quarter.

"Well, hello," Flagg said as somebody finally answered. "You know who this is, eh?"

Flagg listened a few moments and then interrupted. "No, you listen to me. I'm scheduled to testify this week in the murder trial of Peter Shadd. The son of a bitch lawyer who subpoenaed me thinks I'd make a good defense witness because of an assault claim I filed against Garrett Nickel for serving me a bacteria cocktail. . . ."

He listened.

"What?" Flagg said. "No, it's bacteria in a bottle—oh, shut the fuck up and pay attention. We both know what I saw when I was in the joint."

Flagg waited, heard nothing, and finally meandered to the point. "I can make this easy on you, or I can make it tough."

He listened some more, and then he got annoyed. "I'm telling you how goddamn much," he said. "Don't interrupt me, or this conversation will end and the next time anybody hears from me, it'll be from the witness stand. I'll sing like an opera star."

He listened again.

"Fifty thousand," Flagg offered. "I'm hungry, not greedy." He listened and then said, "Of course in fucking cash. Do you think I got a MasterCard machine in my backpack?"

Flagg sensed he was about to close the deal. "You'd hardly miss the money," he said, "and you'll never, ever hear from me again."

twenty-six

The headlights on the car behind Billy looked like cat's eyes.

Christ, it's three in the morning. . . . Who's following me?

The car was a sedan, black or dark blue. It had been on Billy's ass since he had left the newsroom annex, hanging back several hundred feet and matching Billy's speed. He had tested the tail with a few turns through downtown Providence, into the financial district, rumbling over cobblestone intersections, and zipping down dark alleys that during the day would be blocked with delivery trucks. Several times he had thought he had lost the sedan, or that he had just imagined it had been following him, only to see again the cat's eyes in the mirror.

Was a collector following him? Did another broken nose await when he finally stopped at home, or ran out of gas? That didn't make sense. Why would a collector follow him to his house just to bust a tomato stake across his knees? Leg breakers were not known for brains, but if one was smart enough to find Billy at work, why not jump him in the annex parking lot? Who would have been there to save him? Not the unarmed security guard with the munchies.

He considered briefly that Maddox was coming to get him, before he could get Maddox. But that was silly—unless Maddox had discovered mind reading.

Billy pushed the accelerator and bounced the van over potholes, past former jewelry factories made from red brick, now crammed with nightclubs trimmed in pink neon, and twenty-four-hour tattoo parlors. The licensed bars had let out hours ago. The drunks had finished their fistfights, and everyone had staggered home, except for small bands of twenty-something kids from out of town, who couldn't find the all-night raves but who were too high to be discouraged.

He aimed the van onto the highway and floored the gas. The engine moaned in surprise. The steering wheel pulled hard left and Billy battled to keep the old van under control. His sudden burst of speed had gained some space on the sedan. He zoomed south, watching the mirror as much as the road ahead.

The little sedan must have been a turbo, because the cat's eye headlights appeared at the top of the ramp, less than a quarter mile back.

Goddamn that little thing.

There could be no doubt: The car was following him.

Billy felt a hot flash as adrenaline juiced him for survival. The steering wheel stuttered in his hands like a living thing. He briefly let go with one hand and wiped sweat from his eyes. A motorcycle screamed around him, startling Billy. The wheel slipped. The van screeched into the middle lane.

"Cripes!"

Billy wrestled the car under control and watched the little sedan gaining in the mirror.

Got to get off this highway.

Light filled his mirrors. The sedan closed on his bumper; a tractor-trailer pressed close to the sedan.

Billy was passing an exit. It seemed too late to take it.

On impulse, Billy wrenched the wheel to the right.

The tires screamed. The van swerved across an empty lane of highway, strafed a road sign with a thundering clang and a metallic screech. Billy hugged the steering wheel. He listened to his own hoarse howl and then straightened the van down the ramp.

With a trailer truck on its tail, the little black sedan could only drive on. The next exit was a mile south. No way the driver could double back and find Billy.

At the bottom of the ramp, Billy drove into a village thick with two- and three-family apartments, markets that advertised in Spanish and Portuguese, and small clumps of kids on the streets—even at three o'clock in the morning—smoking, talking, kicking beanbags back and forth. Billy turned down streets at random and lost himself deep in the neighborhood.

He panted and felt his heart drumming double time in his chest. Sweat from his palms had matted the shag-covered steering wheel. The van's shaky wheel alignment had grown worse; even at twenty miles per hour, the machine fought over who was in charge.

Billy pulled over, shifted the transmission to park, and wiped his shirttail over his face. He thought about the people he owed money, and who among them would have bothered to scare him on the highway.

That's when a darker notion slipped inside his skull and slithered between the folds of his brain. What if somebody had killed Alec Black, and now they were after him?

Did they think they could kill the whole jury?

Or just those jurors who still had some reasonable doubt?

The kitchen light was on when Billy got home.

Bo and the old man were at the table. The old man smeared apple jam on toasted Wonder bread. Bo plopped chunks of margarine into a steaming bowl of Cream of Wheat.

The old man had pulled the hanging lamp low over the table, illuminating the late-night breakfast like an illegal poker game.

"What the hell are you two doing?" Billy demanded. "It's three-
thirty in the morning."

Neither Bo nor the old man looked up.

"I told you he'd be mad," Bo said. He used a teaspoon to carefully
excavate the Cream of Wheat around three globs of melting margarine.

"Bo is having trouble sleeping," the old man explained.

"Just when it's dark," Bo said.

"And since I'm up and down all night, we figured we'd start the
day early and then take naps," the old man said. "Winston Churchill
slept that way." He glanced up at Billy and frowned. "You look rotten."

"Tough commute," Billy said. "Pop—"

"There's coffee in the carafe," the old man said, interrupting. "It's
decaf."

Billy bit his lip and turned his attention to Bo. He asked, "Why
can't you sleep?"

Bo shoveled Cream of Wheat in his mouth.

"He won't say," the old man said. "Something spooked him."

Fatigue had Billy by the back of the neck. He dropped hard in a
chair, poured himself a cup of decaf, and ate a slice of bread. He
watched his son scoop and eat around the three glops of margarine in
his Cream of Wheat, leaving little volcanoes topped with pools of yellow oil. Billy used to eat his Cream of Wheat the same way. Had the
old man showed that to the kid? Naw, he decided. When Billy was
growing up, the old man had never been home at breakfast.

"I'm full," Bo suddenly announced.

"I'll finish it," Billy said.

"Brush those teeth," the old man urged.

Bo sprinted to the bathroom.

"Why does he *run* everywhere?" Billy asked.

"You should know."

"I didn't run like that when I was his age."

"Not what I mean," the old man said in his scolding, superior tone, which usually preceded a zinger. "The kid has lived here a year, and you don't know why he runs like that. You're his father and you don't goddamn know."

"I'm not a child psychologist," Billy said, too tired to mount much defense. He spooned tepid Cream of Wheat into his mouth. "Why do kids run?"

"*Your* kid runs because he's on a *mission* to brush his teeth," the old man said, still scolding. "He's a task-oriented little feller—the boy likes missions. He wants to be a superhero's helper, or, if he can't get that kind of job, he wants to be a secret agent with a code name and a radio, and an endless supply of missions. Policemen and soldiers do missions, too, so those are options."

"My kid, a cop?"

"Until you graduate from gamblers anonymous, I'd steer him away from the Police Academy—so he don't lock up your bookies. The kid has even mentioned being a reporter, because they do missions and write about them for the paper. He doesn't know that you don't do those missions anymore."

Billy stared at him. "He told you all this?"

"I asked him."

Billy looked down into the bowl.

"At your age, I was a fuckup," the old man said, no longer scolding. "But you've seen how that went, so you got no excuse. Why do you keep that kid at arm's length?"

Billy took the cordless phone to his room and dialed the number he had memorized before scrubbing it off his head.

The clock read 4:35 A.M. He hoped Mia was awake, but he doubted that it mattered much—she didn't seem the type to get upset about sleep.

"Hello?" She sounded awake. An intercom blared in the background on her end.

"Did I wake you?"

She laughed. "You found my cell number, I see."

"I had to scrub my head with gasoline and Lava soap," Billy said. "You know, there's this invention known as paper. . . ."

"You can lose paper."

"I suppose."

"Though," she said, "if you had lost your head in the boathouse, you wouldn't have been the first."

"Oh Christ!" Billy blurted. "You're evil."

She laughed. "He's dead, Billy. Dead people don't care what we say about them, and they can't be brought back by reverent, somber bullshit. The best way to live is by flipping your middle finger at death. Try it. It's liberating."

The intercom blared again on her end.

"Where are you?" Billy asked. "The airport?"

"The emergency room. I drove my brother here. He was lifting weights barefoot at our mom's house and dropped a forty-five-pound plate on his foot."

"Your brother lifts weights barefoot?"

"In the nude, actually," she said, deadpan. Billy couldn't tell if she was joking. She added, "You should see the gash. He won't be walking for a while. They're stitching him up as we speak."

Billy told her, "Somebody followed me from work tonight. I nearly killed myself trying to lose him on the highway."

"Somebody you owe money?"

"The guys who collect the money are pros," Billy said. "If they had been following me, I wouldn't have known until my nose got broke."

"Hmmm. Maybe something to do with court?"

"I dunno. There's no court tomorrow—the judge has a conflict, so I was hoping to spend a day not thinking about the trial." He was exhausted, babbling.

"Did you call the police?"

"To tell them what? A car I can't identify followed me around downtown, and then I ran over a road sign to get away from it? I saw the headlights, that's all. Are they supposed to look for a car with headlights?"

"You don't trust the cops," she said, cutting to the truth.

Billy had already moved on. He said, "I've been wondering if my old man'd be capable of raising my kid, if anything were to happen to me."

After a moment of silence, Mia asked, "What's going to happen to you, Billy?"

He switched the phone to his other ear, leaned back on the bed, and rubbed his sore eyes. "I've been worrying about it," he said. "The old man uses a wheelchair most of the time. His fuckin' legs are sturdy like two pieces of wet rope. It's a mystery how he even gets on the toilet—and not a mystery I care to solve. I always thought the kid liked the old man. . . ." The thought drifted from him.

"It takes more than affection to a raise a kid," she offered.

"I feel stupid—I've wondered if my father could raise my son, but I realized tonight that the old man has been doing the job for thirteen months."

"Since your ex-wife died."

"Yeah."

She sighed. The intercom blared. She asked again, "What's going to happen to you, Billy?"

Tell her.

To hell with the secrecy of the confessional, he thought. Confessing to Father Capricchio hadn't exorcised his feelings about Maddox; confessing his dark urges aloud had only brought them into the real world, where they had grown stronger. Mia was not sworn to secrecy. Telling her would guarantee he would be caught, should anything happen to Maddox.

Burn the boat. Smash the bridge. Obliterate all hope of escape.

If Maddox died, then so would Billy, if much more painfully, in jail. It seemed like his best chance to save himself.

Tell her.

He took a deep breath. "Mia—"

"Hey!" She called out. "Hey, Bigfoot! Over here." She laughed.

"Wha—"

"It's my brother, Craig," she told Billy. "He's stitched up like Frankenstein, and walking like him, too." She let Billy eavesdrop on a conversation on her end.

"How's it feel?"

"Shitty."

"Did they numb it?"

"Told him not to."

"Ooo, tough man. How long are you on those crutches?"

"Ten days."

Mia gave a sad moan. "Awwww."

"When you're off the phone," a man's voice said, "I gotta call coach. He's gonna chew my ass off for getting hurt like this. I gotta sit down."

"I'll come get you." To Billy, she said, "He's fuckin' bummed!"

"Ten days ain't so long."

"At least he's not bleeding over the floor anymore," she said. "Our poor mother is probably still scrubbing her shag." She giggled.

Bleeding over the floor . . .

Billy bolted up with a revelation. "Oh Jesus," he said.

"You were telling me about your son," Mia reminded him. "Billy? Billy? Shit . . . did we drop the call?"

He said, "I think I know who butchered your friend J.R. at the boathouse."

twenty-seven

At eight o'clock on the morning he had planned to pick up his money and disappear, Franklin D. Flagg scraped together forty-nine dollars—a fortune assembled from bottle deposits, a day of hard panhandling, two pints of B-negative sold to the blood bank, and a fiver lifted from a snoozing wino. He walked to the brass and brick Biltmore Hotel downtown and asked the doorman in the hard round cap to whistle him a cab.

Taxicabs were key to Flagg's plan to get the money and get out of town.

He sent the driver south on Route 95, to Cranston, around Roger Williams Park, and then onto Broad Street, heading north toward South Providence. Flagg's head twisted back and forth. He scanned for tails. Didn't seem to be any. They passed a great stone church in a village square, within screaming distance of a family-planning clinic, where America's official national argument played out daily between clients and demonstrators.

As the cab pushed deeper into Providence, the neighborhood changed to a mix of street-level storefronts and two-family homes with double-deck porches. It seemed that anyone in the neighbor-hood with expertise in *anything*—karate, fixing radios, dying hair, dancing the tango, or making pan gravy—had opened a shop on the street, amid Spanish and Asian markets, beeper stores, fast-food chains, dance clubs, and check-cashing outlets. The buildings were white and blue and red and Day-Glo green. Somebody with talent had painted a mural on the side of the U.S. Post Office of a dark-skinned Eve, serpents gathering at her feet, against a deep blue sky and a full moon.

The sky was clear blue, the air dry. The cab drove past churches and cemeteries, schools and a synagogue. Businesses that didn't open until nine or ten o'clock were still shuttered with roll-down grates. People walked the sidewalks. The cab stopped every few hundred yards for red lights, or to let packs of high school girls cross the street.

Flagg ordered the driver to let him off at a soul-food restaurant. There was a pay phone outside. The meter read seventeen dollars. Flagg stuffed three fives and two ones through a hole in the plastic shield that separated the crazy riders from the fearful driver and then got out. Flagg must have seemed like a crazy rider, paying double for a roundabout trip to a restaurant just a few miles from where they had started.

Flagg watched the cab disappear, then shoved a quarter into the pay phone and called a cellular telephone.

The phone rang just once.

"So you're ready," Flagg said. "You have the money? . . . Good. In a paper sack? . . . Very good. Do you have a cab waiting like I told you? . . . Excellent." Flagg felt flush with authority. He was giving orders, which someone else was following. *This is like being an execu-tive in the bank building downtown,* Flagg thought. He liked the feeling. No wonder those bank people worked long days.

"Have the cab drive you around awhile," Flagg said. "Don't leave the city limits. I'll call you back within thirty minutes and tell you how and where we'll meet."

Flagg hung up before there could be any argument.

He went into the restaurant, ordered smothered pork chops with two fried eggs, grits, and coffee perked on the stovetop, with heavy cream and three sugars. He savored the meal for the full thirty minutes and then paid his tab and made another call.

"I'm ready to meet," Flagg said. Breakfast rode low in his gut. "Head down Broad Street." He gave the address of the restaurant. "I'll be out front. Have the cab pull over. Leave the dough on the seat. Pay your fare, get out, and go inside the restaurant. Try the pork chops—the meat falls right off the bone. I'll get in the cab, and when it drives off, you'll never see or hear from me again. No tricks. No eye contact. Don't say anything to me. Don't do anything to attract attention."

He hung up.

The cab's backseat was red vinyl, worn and slippery.

Flagg slammed the door and grabbed the paper sack.

"Drive," he ordered.

"Where to?" asked the driver.

"Just go. I'll tell you in a minute."

The driver shrugged, slipped the transmission into drive, and pulled into traffic, heading north, toward downtown Providence.

Flagg peeked in the bag, saw the money bundled with rubber bands, and felt a delicious cold tickle, as if a naked woman was dragging her fingers across his belly. Flagg could afford as many naked women as he could handle; he figured on handling lots of them. He giggled out loud; he couldn't help himself.

The cab passed a hospital and then a high school as it approached the southern end of the downtown district.

"I can drive all day, mister," the cabbie said through the perforated plastic barrier, "so long as you know the meter is on."

Flagg needed a long-distance bus or train, but not from the downtown station, where so many other bums knew him. "Other than Providence," Flagg asked, "where's the nearest bus or train?"

The driver was silent a moment, and then offered, "I could take you to Kingston station, but that would be a half-hour ride, and sixty bucks."

Flagg chuckled. "I think I can spare that much."

"Mm-hm. You're the boss."

Flagg liked that. . . . He had the money. . . . He *was* the boss.

The driver zigzagged through traffic, blared his horn at a pedestrian waddling in his path, and then merged the cab onto the highway. Flagg clutched the paper sack in his fists and sat back. Where would he go? Out of state, of course . . . far away, for sure . . . but where? Before he got the money, Flagg had been afraid he'd jinx his plan if he thought too far ahead. He remembered an old cell mate who had grown up in northern New Hampshire. Flagg couldn't remember the guy's name, but he remembered his stories.

He asked the driver, "Ever been to northern New Hampshire?"

The cabbie stole a glance at Flagg in the mirror. He wore sunglasses with mirrored lenses and a Boston Celtics cap. He needed a shave. Flagg wondered if the scruffy look was in. Did women like it? He would need to know these things if he was going to make a new life, with money, in northern New Hampshire.

"Been as far as Manchester a couple times," the cabbie said.

"Ever been up north, way up north?"

"Nah."

"I'm thinking of going there," Flagg said.

"Mm-hm."

"Yeah—" Flagg caught himself. Could this cabbie identify him to the police? Did cabbies have privilege, like a lawyer and a client? Flagg decided to lie. "But I think I'll probably end up someplace else. Like New York City, you know?"

"I been there."

"Lately?"

"Nah."

"I may go out west, you know? Someplace with mountains. You ever been out west?"

"What for?"

Flagg peeked into the bag again, felt the same cold tickle, and grinned. "I like to see new places."

"Mm-hm."

Flagg wet his lips with his tongue. "You're a real talkaholic, eh?"

"I drive the cab."

They drove twenty minutes before the taxi abandoned the highway for a rural route that pitched and rolled like a river. They passed fields of cornstalks and gigantic turf farms, nothing but green grass for a mile. Flagg caught a whiff of the sea. The cab turned hard and bounced down an old country road that was patched all over, looking like an extreme close-up of a gum-spotted city sidewalk. They left the farmland behind. Trees closed in on either side of the road. They drove five minutes without seeing a house or another car.

"We lost?" Flagg asked, breaking a long silence.

"Nah."

Flagg looked around. "This don't look like Kingston."

"It ain't yet," the cabbie said. From his tone, Flagg imagined the driver's eyes rolling behind his sunglasses.

"I never been this way," Flagg said, readying for an argument. He had the money; he was the boss.

"Mm-hm." The cabbie sounded dismissive.

Through the trees, Flagg glimpsed a high-speed passenger train running roughly parallel to the road. It shot past the taxi in seconds.

"Oh," Flagg said. He leaned back. Flagg had read about the high-speed service from Boston to Washington, D.C.; the train hit its top speed in Rhode Island—130 miles per hour.

At a fork, the cab turned left, away from the railroad tracks, down what seemed like a paved oxen path. The woods grew thicker. The meter was already at sixty-six dollars. This guy was running up the tab, taking Flagg for a ride.

Where the hell are we?

Flagg started to ask, then paused to check the driver's name on his taxi license, posted on the seatback: Galeno M. Gomez.

Odd . . . this driver ain't Hispanic. . . . Was he adopted?

The bushy brown hair on Flagg's forearms lifted straight up.

He was in a stolen taxicab. They were driving in the woods, heading down a cart path that probably was a dead end, at least for Frank Flagg.

Double-crossed.

They're going to kill me.

The cab was rounding a curve at twenty-two miles per hour when Franklin D. Flagg threw himself from it. He hit the ground with a grunt and let his momentum carry him into a roll. The pavement scraped his elbows, knees, and shoulder blade. Flagg rolled into a wet gully, lay there, and groaned. He was still holding the paper sack. The money was soaked.

Brakes squealed.

Flagg clambered to his feet. The driver calmly stepped from the cab. He had a nickel-plated pistol in his right hand. He jabbed the gun in Flagg's direction and fired.

The bullet whistled over Flagg's head.

"Jesus Christ!" Flagg screamed. He hugged the money and ran up the road.

Bang.

Bang.

A slug hit near Flagg's feet and ricocheted. Flagg yelped and dashed into the woods, staggering over a fieldstone wall, knocking stones to the ground.

I promised I'd disappear. . . .

Flagg stomped through the forest, plowing through underbrush with the grace of a rolling boulder. He panted and whimpered as he ran, lost and without direction, crashing, bashing through the thick forest, cradling the money against his heart. Branches raked his skin. Sticks and roots grabbed for his feet and tried to twist his ankles. His eyes watered from pain and from fear.

It was only fifty thou. . . .

Bang.

A white-hot drill bore into his left calf.

He shrieked from deep in his belly.

Flagg stumbled, fought to stay on his feet, knocked his head on a downed tree, saw wisps of white cloud twisting in a circle against a perfect blue sky, and then tumbled down a steep hill, still clinging to the money. He landed with a thunk on a path of packed stone dust. The ground beneath him trembled. Lifting his face from the dust and shaking his head clear, Flagg recognized the railroad ties, laid side by side like piano keys, and the steel rails upon them, shining like mirrors in the sun.

Around a bend, an oncoming train grew louder. Flagg crawled. He rose, wobbly, to his feet. His chest ached. His thighs had turned to pudding. The pain in his gunshot calf spread down his leg, like he had one foot in a bucket of lightning. He staggered ten paces.

Bang.

The slug slapped Flagg's neck and he could no longer breathe. He watched his own feet stumble onto the tracks, between the rails. He felt drunk, or like he was watching somebody else's feet.

The high-speed train was on him in an instant. He pushed the money at it. Hit it square on the nose.

twenty-eight

To sneak into the boathouse during daylight, Billy and Mia approached by sea. They slipped their kayaks into the bay about half a mile to the south. Billy's used thirteen-foot fiberglass boat was banana yellow, scuffed like a tiger's scratching post, tight on his hips and fast in the water. Mia paddled a rented twelve-foot plastic boat, lollipop red, fat, as stable as a beached rowboat, and slow. Not that speed mattered; no matter how anxious they were to search the boathouse, they wanted to look like recreational paddlers braving the dark and ugly water of the upper bay.

"Let's stick together," he told Mia. "We look like a happy couple enjoying the sun on a day off from jury duty."

He watched the ying-yang symbol tattooed on Mia's upper left arm. The symbol flexed as she worked the paddle. Billy felt a squirt of embarrassment.

A happy couple? We could almost be father and daughter.

They stayed a hundred feet off a shoreline that cut in and out like the ridges of a key. They passed beach houses on their left, mostly small bungalows, more than fifty years old, with back porches and tiny lawns that dropped off at concrete retaining walls, cracked and pitted by the tides. Many of the homes had small wooden docks. Others had just stairs leading down to the water, or, at low tide, to beaches of foul black muck. The water smelled vaguely of sewage. Billy tried not to think about the untreated waste that oozed into the upper bay each year, carried there when heavy rain overwhelmed the treatment plants. *When was the last big rain?* he wondered. He was glad he couldn't remember.

They paddled around a stone breakwater, like a finger laid in the bay to protect a small cove from storms. Stray cats watched them from between the rocks, or tore at baitfish left by anglers. Seagulls gathered on the rocks, flapping up nosily when a cat came too close.

Billy pulled the paddle as much with his abdomen as his arms. Ahead on the left, the boathouse appeared suddenly as they rounded a small, jutting peninsula. The front half of the boathouse was built into the slope; the back half stood on twenty wooden piles. The gentle dark cove water rode up and down the posts. On the back of the building, three sheets of plywood covered what had been a panoramic window overlooking the water. A dozen steep wooden stairs led from a short dock to a door. Glass in the door had been smashed and crudely repaired with silver duct tape and cellophane plastic.

Billy threaded between the piles and beached his kayak in mud under the boathouse.

Mia's boat slid up close to his. She said, "Are you going to tell me what we're looking for before I help you search the place?"

Sitting in the kayak, Billy slipped off his life jacket and stuffed it between his legs. "You saw barefoot prints in blood leading away from J.R.'s body," he said.

"Somebody walked away on tippy-toes."

"We assumed that Peter Shadd didn't slaughter J.R. because he had no blood on his prison jumpsuit, and none on his sneakers."

"And his hands—his hands were clean." She whipped off her life jacket.

"I try to pay attention to the testimony in court," Billy said. "Though sometimes I feel like the only one who gives a shit. Early in the trial, we learned that Garrett Nickel's body was found south of here, having floated down a small stream."

"He was shot at some industrial building, you said."

"I've been wondering what Garrett Nickel was doing at that shitty industrial building; he should have been driving to Maine. But I had overlooked the three items of clothing he was wearing when he went into the stream." He ticked off the items on his fingers. "One pair of cotton pants. Checkered flannel shirt. Running shoes."

She nodded each time, waited for more.

"Where the bloody hell," Billy asked, "was his orange prison jumpsuit?"

In the boathouse attic, Billy toed the edge of the bloodstain but did not step on it. He avoided treading on the stain as he would stepping on a grave. Billy was not squeamish over blood—he had seen plenty flow from his own nose throughout a decade of phoning bookies with his bad hunches. So why couldn't he step on the stain? Why did his feet refuse to do it?

Mia stood hands on her hips and tapped her foot in the center of the goddamn thing.

"Garrett must have had extra clothes with him," Billy said.

"How would he get the clothes?" she asked.

"If what his cell mate said in court was true, then somebody on the outside helped Garrett get a stolen car," Billy said. "Throwing some old clothes in the trunk would have been easy. Do you know how often J.R. hung out here?"

"Only to drink," she said.

"Was that often?"

"He could have gotten his mail here."

Billy rubbed his chin in thought. He realized he hadn't shaved in three days. "If there was no blood on the stairs, let's assume he killed J.R. here," he said. Billy looked around the room. Old newspaper, forty-ounce beer cans, shopping bags, and a hundred other distinct pieces of trash littered the corners. "And if Garrett killed him here, then his jumpsuit could still be around."

"He could have run off and changed someplace else," Mia said, not with doubt, just offering the possibility.

"Don't think so. We know he walled away barefoot—I'd guess he was naked. He stripped off the prison outfit, wiped his hands on it, and shoved it somewhere. Then he put on clean clothes someplace else. Downstairs, maybe."

Trash was piled in front of the crawl space over the eves. Billy dug through it. He took Bo's tiny flashlight from his pocket—the kid had been honored to lend it for his father's mission. The beam made long shadows behind lumps of trash. He grimaced at the sour stench of rotting waste. "Like the outhouse at a leper colony," he said.

She clapped him on the shoulder. "This will be good training if you ever want my job," she said.

"This tunnel," he grumbled, "smells like the shortcut to hell."

Clenching the flashlight in his teeth, Billy crawled on hands and knees through the trash and into the hole. The stench brought tears to his eyes. He blinked past them and breathed through his mouth. Floorboards creaked under his hands. He swiveled his head to shine the light around. A cluster of stubby white candles, burned nearly to their bottoms, sat in a puddle of congealed wax. There were dozens of empty cigarette boxes, crumpled fast-food wrappers, balled-up blankets, an old army-issue sleeping bag, foam coffee cups, piss-stained sheets, batteries bleeding their corrosive guts.

Mia called to him in the singsongy rhythm of a limerick. "There

once was a guy name Billy, whose ass was looking quite silly—
crawling through a smell, down the shortcut to hell—where a hundred degrees would be chilly."

She giggled.

Billy laughed, too. "You're a h'ain in de h'ass," he told her, the
flashlight still clenched in his teeth.

He pawed through debris as he crawled, trying to keep his hands
out of the smears of human waste. The tunnel ended at a wall of
planks and two-by-fours. There was no room to turn around.

"Anything?" Mia called down to him.

He grunted no.

Where did you hide it, Garrett?

Billy backed slowly the way he had come, shining the light
around. Black ants scurried from the light like it was the end of the
world.

Wait a sec—would Nickel have had a flashlight?

Billy closed his eyes. If he had no light, how would he hide something here?

His hands groped.

He found a crack to his left, where the plank floor met the sloped
roof. The space was just wide enough to sink his fingers in. He pulled.
It was stuck fast—at least at this spot. Billy backed up three feet and
tried again. The board creaked but would not yield.

He backed up three more feet, wormed his fingers inside the
crack, and yanked. A narrow two-foot board popped up and whacked
Billy in the forehead.

"H'uck!" he cried. He spit out the flashlight and repeated, "Fuck!"

"What?" Mia yelled. "Are you all right?"

He rubbed his head. "This boathouse attacked me," he yelled.
Billy grabbed the light, aimed it where the board had been, and
gasped.

A thousand black ants bustled in happy chaos over two bloody sneakers crushed down the hole. He could see the orange jumpsuit below the sneakers; it was stained deep brown.

"Hey fellas," Billy whispered grimly to the ants. "I think I saw a Snickers bar a few feet down that way."

"Are you talking to yourself?" Mia asked.

"I'm trying to con some ants, but they're not falling for it."

"They've seen your type before."

Billy grabbed the sneakers and the fabric, wrestled them from the hole, and shook them. Ants dropped, their hard little bodies sounding like soft rain. They went berserk—this really was the end of their world. Probing beneath the clothing, Billy found a thick book, crusted with dried blood, a knife tucked in it like a bookmark. He gathered all the items from the hole and backed all the way down the crawl space. He tumbled out with an "*Ahhhh*."

The jumpsuit had dried in the rectangular shape of the hole. Mia snatched it from Billy and pulled it back into shape. Nearly the whole thing had been stained with blood.

"Jesus, what a mess," Billy said.

Above the chest pocket a stencil read:

Rhode Island Department of Corrections
NICKEL, Garrett

Black ants crawled over the jumpsuit.

"The son of a bitch killed J.R.," Mia said softly, as if awed.

Billy stood behind her. He imagined his finger lightly tracing the bump of her spine on the back of her neck. She turned around.

"No skull," Billy blurted.

"Huh?"

"No place to hide a human skull in there that I could see."

"The bastard stole his head?"

Billy brushed ants off his chest and then examined the book. It was four inches by six, two inches thick, and bound in faux leather. He turned it over.

Gold lettering said simply Holy Bible.

Billy opened the front cover. "It's the King James Version," he said. "Stamped by a prison Bible-studies group."

"Not the kind of reading you'd want after stealing somebody's head," Mia said.

The eight-inch hunting knife with a green rubber handle had been stuck in the Second Book of Kings. The blade was jagged and sharp, frightening even at rest in a Bible. Without touching the knife, Billy read one verse aloud.

" 'And he did that which was evil in the sight of the Lord.' "

"For sure," Mia said.

Billy closed the book. "The clothes and the Bible came from the prison," he said. "Whoever helped Garrett Nickel with the getaway car must have left him this knife."

"How does this affect the trial?"

Billy thought about it. "It proves that Nickel and Peter Shadd were both in this place on the same night," he said. "They must have come together. That's bad for Shadd. It means he was probably here when Nickel killed J.R."

Maybe the rest of the jury is right. . . . Maybe Shadd is another Garrett Nickel, just in more sympathetic packaging

"Couldn't Shadd have shot Nickel by the river and then wandered here by chance?" she asked.

"Possible, but I don't like the coincidence."

"We should call the cops," Mia urged.

Billy grimaced. After ten years betting with bookies, he had gotten used to avoiding the cops. "I can't," Billy said. "I'm a juror and I'm defying a court order to stay ignorant about the case except for what happens in court. If I get thrown off the jury, then Peter Shadd gets convicted in five minutes. I can't let that happen while I still have doubt." He drummed his fingers on Garrett Nickel's Bible. "*You* call the cops . . . tell them you were here, doing your job, and you stumbled onto this stuff. They'll have no choice but to accept the story if you stick with it."

She looked down to her black canvas sneakers. "I can't," she said.

"You can be totally believable," he encouraged.

"I won't lie to the police. I can't, Billy—my stepdad . . . he was chief of detectives. Retired now, but still in touch with his guys."

"Ah," Billy said as he fought the crazy urge to run. So that was how she got access to police computers. He thought about the secrets he had shared with her. He drummed his fingers on the Bible again. He regretted he hadn't yet told Mia about his dreams. He wanted to share himself with her, but he could not tell her now.

A cop's daughter?

"We can't just hide this stuff again," she said. "We solved an open murder case. The killer is dead—but so what? Somebody out there might care about J.R. They'll want to know who murdered him. Somebody besides me."

Billy thought for a minute. "There's one person I trust—though he's not going to like it."

twenty-nine

The box from FedEx on Martin's desk was wrapped tighter than King Tut.

Martin sawed at the box with a metal ruler. His attention was on the radio. Pastor Abraham Guy was getting close to announcing his candidacy for governor on Galaxy AM:

". . . The lack of morals among those who have run our state the last few generations has left Rhode Island in a precarious position. State services are being cut because of declining revenue. Why is revenue declining? Because business doesn't want to be here. They don't want to move their operations, and their high-paying jobs, to a medieval BACKWATER where the local politicians expect to be GREASED for every building permit they issue, or every sewer tie-in they allow. . . ."

"He's in top form today," Carol said. She jotted down the pastor's quotes in shorthand, in case he mentioned anything inflammatory about criminal justice.

Martin twirled the box, looking for a weakness to exploit with the edge of the ruler. The package, a littler bigger than a shoe box, was light and made no noise when he shook it. As a defense lawyer for the poor, the deranged, and the despised, Martin got a lot of weird mail, mostly incomprehensible letters scrawled in near madness with a leaky ballpoint. But this package, which had been express-shipped from across the city, intrigued him. The return address was simply "J.R."

That was what the headless bum in the old boathouse had called himself.

Martin was an expert in that unsolved murder. He had battled ferociously in pretrial motions to forbid any mention of the mutilated body at Peter Shadd's trial. If Dillingham wasn't going to charge Peter with killing J.R.—and he couldn't because of a lack of evidence— then Martin had to be sure the state couldn't use the body to poison the jury against Peter. Winning that motion had been a great victory, though Martin had begun to think it might have been the high-water mark of the defense.

On paper, it might have seemed that the trial was going well—the prosecution had rested, with no direct evidence having been presented that would link Peter to the shooting of Garrett Nickel, and Martin had undercut Larry Home, the star witness of the state's circumstantial case. But jury trials are more than logic on paper. Martin sensed the jury slipping from his reach. He had lost his best juror to a leap from a parking garage. Those who remained would never agree to acquit Peter Shadd. The best Martin could do was persuade one or two to hold out against the majority and force a mistrial. A do-over.

". . . What this state needs is a return to the principles of morality on which it was founded," the voice on the radio raged. "It needs leadership that is not afraid to shine the light of truth into the dark corners of political sleaze, which for generations has dragged our state down and slowed our progress. Our state symbol, the anchor on our state flag, should not stand for the terrible weight of corruption. . . ."

"It's getting riskier every day to put him on the stand," Martin said. "Then don't."

"I have no choice, especially now that Franklin Flagg has disappeared."

"You still have the assault report Flagg filed against Garrett Nickel."

"There's not much emotion in a piece of paper. I wanted Flagg on the stand so the jury could feel the fear Nickel inspired."

"So what about the pastor?"

"He's the only character witness I've got," Martin said. "He's a big name—something to get those brain-dead jurors to perk up and listen." Martin stabbed the corner of the box and chewed his bottom lip. "I'm down by three runs in the bottom of the ninth—I've got to swing for the fences."

"But you'd still be down by two."

"It's a metaphor."

"Shouldn't you work the count? Get a few men on base and extend the inning? Make Dillingham go deep into his bull pen?"

"My perfectly fine metaphor assumes the bases are loaded."

"With two outs, a double to the gap would score three," Carol said. "It's better to play for the tie at home and then win in extra innings."

Martin sighed. "There's only one out."

"All the more reason to work the count."

"Do you enjoy torturing me?" he asked. "When do I ever torture you?"

"Every week in my paycheck." She laughed.

"Got a goddamn answer for everything," Martin mumbled, shooting her a smile and a sly glance.

He wormed the ruler through the tape and slit open one side of the box.

"My hope," he said, abandoning his metaphor, "is that Pastor Guy doesn't care what I ask him—that he just wants to get the better of Dillingham. I'll get him to say that Peter was the most respectful, courteous, nonthreatening student of the Bible you'd ever wanna see. Then for the pastor, the cross-examination with Dillingham can be the first debate of the campaign."

". . . The entrenched politicians of this state are part of a dysfunctional political family of hacks, retreads, and wanna-bes, each of whom got where he is today because he happened to be related to some other hack, retread, or wanna-be. Political hacks breed like germs, and it's time this state elected somebody with the guts to disinfect the culture. . . ."

"I suppose he'll be running as the outsider," Martin deadpanned. He slit more tape, pulled open the box, and recoiled as if it had been electrified.

"Jesus, Mary, and the junk man!" he yelled.

Carol bolted up.

"Ants!" Martin said.

"Oh, you wuss."

"What the hell—

Martin pulled out an orange prison jumpsuit stained with blood. He read the name printed above the pocket and then set the item on his desk. He took blood-encrusted sneakers from the box, one Holy Bible, and one hunting knife with a vicious serrated blade.

"What's all this?" Carol asked in a whisper.

"No note, no nothing," Martin said.

He checked the return address on the box again.

"Oh shit," he said, suddenly understanding. He thought for a moment, then said, "Get Dillingham on the phone. He'll need to test DNA on this stuff and compare it to what they have on J.R., the bum in the boathouse."

Carol dialed. "What should I tell him?"

Martin blew twenty black ants off his desk blotter.

"Tell him that Garrett Nickel cut J.R.'s fucking head off." He sighed and added ruefully, "All that work to keep the body out of the trial, and now *this*. It puts Peter and Garrett in the boathouse that same night. We need to change strategy—Peter has to explain this to the jury. But first he's got to explain it to me."

thirty

Peter lay faceup on the concrete floor, his bent legs on the lower bunk, as if to do sit-ups. Martin nodded to the guard. He grimaced when the door boomed shut.

Peter barely glanced at him. The young convict locked his fingers behind his head and stared at a ceiling so brown with nicotine, you could have scraped off a pinch to put between your cheek and gum.

"We're losing," Martin said.

"You did good with Horne."

"You're going to have to testify."

Peter shot him a hard glance but said nothing.

Martin folded himself on the floor, grunting all the way down, lay on his back, and put his feet up, as Peter had done. The floor smelled like mildew. "This would be more comfortable if I get you transferred to a padded room."

"The floor is good for my back," Peter said.

"You're too young for back problems." Hmmm, Peter was right: It *did* feel good on the back.

Peter rubbed his palm on his face, as if wiping tears Martin could not see. "Sleep on a one-inch mattress every night and then tell me about back problems."

"Nobody can find Flagg."

"You check the shelters?"

"Without Flagg, we've got nobody else to help paint Garrett Nickel as a monster who intimidated you into joining the escape," Martin said. "That was our strategy, Peter. You were the patsy; he was the ringleader. You didn't want to break out, but what choice did you have once threatened by the Nickel-Plated Outlaw?"

After a few moments of silence, Peter said, "Are we really losing?"

"Our best juror killed himself. One of our witnesses has vanished. Ninety percent of the jury hates you, me, or the both of us. Your Bible-study teacher is running for governor against the prosecutor, which means calling him as a character witness is playing Russian roulette with a machine gun. My pretrial strategy is in tatters, and I'm yanking out what little hair I've got. So—fuck, yes!—I'd say we're losing."

Martin paused, let the bitterness drain from his tone. He needed Peter's cooperation to save him, and he needed some truth. "I busted my ass to exclude any mention of the headless bum in the boathouse from your trial," he said calmly.

"I was so fucked-up that night—I didn't even know that guy was up there."

"I've gotten some anonymous information that suggests Garrett Nickel killed that guy, the night you were there."

Peter gave a tiny shrug.

"You told me that after you left Horne on the island, you bought a needle and some smack on some street corner you can't remember and then shot up in an alley you couldn't recognize."

"That's what I said."

"And that you wandered in a haze and then stumbled into the boathouse at random."

He shrugged again. He would not meet Martin's eyes.

"You and Garrett were at the boathouse together that night."

Peter rubbed away another invisible tear. "Like I said, man, I was so wasted. . . ."

"I need to know, or we will lose."

Peter's brow wrinkled. Without looking at Martin, he said, "You told me before that there was some stuff you couldn't hear as a lawyer and still represent somebody." Real tears gathered in Peter's giant bug eyes.

Martin swore, "I won't abandon you."

A tear raced down Peter's cheek to the floor. *Funny thing,* Martin thought—*the kid didn't wipe the real ones.*

"When Horne was in the shower, Garrett would talk to me," Peter confessed. "He said Horne was an idiot who couldn't be trusted and would just get us caught if we didn't do something about him. He told me to pretend I didn't want to break out, to keep pissing on the plan. To act weak. To let Horne bully me, so that he'd let his guard down."

"So that bullshit from Horne about Garrett forcing you to escape at knifepoint?"

"All bullshit," Peter confirmed. "Playacting." A second tear raced down the wet track left by the first. "On the night we broke, Garrett fixed it so me and Horne would go for Horne's stash—he knew Horne couldn't get the stuff alone."

"You had no use for Horne, but you needed his stash."

The wet bug eyes flicked to Martin for a moment and then back to the ceiling. "Garrett told me to take a shank," he said. "To give it to Horne in the ribs once I got the money."

Martin's throat tightened. "Did you take the knife?"

A third tear tracked to the floor.

"I didn't want to use it—I never done anything like that," Peter said. He closed his eyes and pushed another tear out. "I had Horne totally snowed, man. He gave me his fuckin' gun? How stupid do you gotta be?" He opened his eyes. "Once I saw how scared he was of the water, it was easy just to leave him on the island."

"You met Garrett after that?"

"Right where he left us off," Peter said. "He had all this coke, smack—all sorts of shit in the car. Garrett told me to help myself." His eyes widened and rolled in their sockets. "It never hit me like that before."

"You had detoxed in prison," Martin said. "Your tolerance was back to zero. That's why you overdosed and nearly died."

"Garrett said we had to stop at a boathouse—to make some quick money before we split for Maine. He had this big fuckin' knife, and a picture of some guy, I didn't recognize."

"Did he say who was in the picture?"

"Some buddy of his," Peter replied. "Garrett said we were going to look the guy up." He finally wiped his face, and then looked at Martin. "I just assumed it was the person who left us the car."

Martin nodded gently.

"And I was telling the truth about the dead guy upstairs," Peter said. "I don't remember much about what happened once we got inside, but I know I had nothing to do with his death." He looked away. "Though later, when I found out that somebody was killed there with a knife, I assumed Garrett had done it."

They both lay there in silence for several minutes.

"I didn't shoot Garrett," Peter blurted, as if suddenly remembering he had forgotten something important.

"Mmm," Martin said. He was thinking. His pretrial strategy to make Peter the patsy had been naïve. He had hoped to get Peter off without any extra time on his sentence, but that was no longer possible. Truth was against them. Even if they could hang the jury on the murder charge, Peter would have to do three years for the escape—every second of it in punitive segregation as an escape risk. Peter had a tough dozen years ahead of him, at a minimum.

But Peter didn't kill Garrett Nickel—Martin believed him. He said, "You have to testify. You have to admit your role in the escape and the plan to rob Horne. Dillingham will kick our ass over the body in the boathouse unless we steal his thunder and lay it out in direct examination. We'll shake things around and put you as the first defense witness—as if you *can't wait* to get up there and deny you killed Garrett Nickel."

Peter smacked his lips. "Okay," he said in a tiny voice.

"Can you tell it to the jury just as you told it to me here?"

Some tears would be nice, too.

"I can do it."

Peter yanked the tourniquet with his teeth and then tapped the vein. Plump and firm after so long without the needle, almost a virgin again.

Garrett raced the Oldsmobile along the highway.

"Hold it still while I do this," Peter said. He gasped softly when the needle went in. He pushed the plunger and cooed. *Whoa.* The rush was almost instant, a pins and needles feeling, as if he had traded his blood for carbonated soda. A sense of heavy weight formed in his stomach. By the time he pulled out the needle, he was euphoric. *He has stunned the world to win Olympic gold. A billion fans are screaming his name across the oceans.* Peter soon grew drowsy and settled into the world's warmest and safest embrace, as if nuzzled into the bosom of God. They were on the run from prison? A thousand cops on their tail?

Who gives a fuck?

Garrett was yelling at him, "Hey, you fucking scag addict, I'm talking to you!" He jerked the wheel back and forth and jostled Peter to attention.

"Huh?"

"Did you waste Larry?"

Peter chuckled, thinking of his cell mate marooned on the little island. "I took care of him," he said.

"Is he dead?"

"He won't bother us."

Garrett growled, "That's not what I asked. Is he fuckin' dead?"

"Sure," said Peter, lying, "he's bled out by now."

"No chance he crawls for help, or somebody finds him?"

"He's dead, man." He leaned back and sighed.

Garrett chuckled. " 'He's dead, man,' " he repeated cheerily. "You're a mean little double-crosser, ain't you?"

"Mmmm."

"You like the feel of that Mexican shit? I thought you'd like that. That's why I arranged to get a few grams. Old habits die hard, don't they, little double-crosser?" His tone sharpened. "Hey—is that Larry's gun in your belt?"

"Mm."

"Don't shoot your dick off."

Peter said nothing. He was dancing cheek-to-cheek with a ghost made of nothing but love and the wind.

"Or mine," Garrett said.

Peter listened to the engine's raunchy purr. The car jostled him as it left the highway and zipped through neighborhoods that seemed familiar but which he could not place. They drove for what seemed a long time, though Peter did not mind. When they stopped, time suddenly seemed to compress, and Peter realized they had been in the car only a few minutes.

He watched Garrett stuff clothing into a garbage bag. He put a knife in there, too. Then Garrett studied a photograph of a man Peter did not recognize.

Garrett whispered to no one in particular, " 'And when they had found him, they said unto him, All men seek for thee.' " He grinned and tucked the photo into his shirt. He turned his Bible upside down and shook it. Nothing came out but dust. He put the book in the bag.

"Get out and shut your door, but be quiet," Garrett ordered. "Holy Jesus—look at them eyes. Can you fuckin' walk?"

Walk? Sure, why not?

"Mm-hm."

Outside, the moonless black sky was brilliant.

Garrett walked with the bag. Peter followed one step behind. He watched Garrett's feet and kept in step. Left, right, left. They walked for what seemed a long time, down dark streets, cutting across light to safety in the shadows.

They reached a boathouse that looked like wreckage washed ashore by a murderous storm.

"What a dump," Garrett said.

Peter laughed into his hands. The entire world lifted itself up, spun once clockwise, and slammed down without a sound. Peter gasped and grabbed for the railing at the front steps of the boathouse. He stumbled up the stairs behind Garrett.

Garrett whirled, clenched Peter around the throat, and warned him in a spit blast, *"Watch the fucking noise."*

Inside, the room was dark and cluttered with trash.

Peter relieved himself in a corner. His listened to his piss patter on an old newspaper. When he had finished, he grabbed for a dirty sofa. He was nauseous, dizzy, starting to sweat.

Garrett appeared beside Peter, spun him roughly, and pushed him onto the sofa. "Stay here until I'm done," he said. "And no noise."

"Mmmm."

Peter listened to footsteps tap up some stairs. The floor above creaked. He leaned his head back and watched copper wires dangle from a hole in the ceiling. They just dangled there. . . . He waited for them to do something. It seemed he had been waiting a long time. He felt the slightest vibration from the sofa, as if a spirit had sat down beside him. He turned toward it.

A rat.

Peter gasped. Never had he seen such a tremendous greasy gray rat—a mop head from a sewer plant, slicked back with Vaseline. Its slithering pink tail was like Satan's limp cock. The rat's fleshy nose pinched the air in Peter's direction.

"Leave me be," Peter whispered to it.

Voices upstairs drew the rat's attention. It rose to its hind legs, nose twitching.

"Dear Jesus, it's as big as a cat," Peter said.

The world spun again, taking the blurred rat with it. Peter grabbed for the gun in his belt. When the world stopped spinning, the rat had advanced on Peter. It reached its dirty snout toward him.

Peter aimed the gun. The weapon weaved unsteadily. It seemed to float. Peter had trouble keeping his hands on it. "I'll shoot," he warned the rat.

The rat climbed slowly up the sofa and stood on the backrest. It was the same height as Peter.

Peter closed one eye and stared down the barrel.

The world spun, slowed, stopped, spun again. He blinked hard. Sweat poured down his face. He worked hard to breathe, as if the old boathouse had spun itself to the top of a high mountain. The rat taunted him with its twitching nose.

"One move and I'll shoot," Peter said.

A scream of terror ripped through the house.

Peter pulled the trigger.

Blam!

The gun kicked in his hand. The rat vanished. Peter inhaled the weapon's hot smoke. The world spun in a blur.

He heard Garrett shouting in anger, *"What the fuck—"*

Peter pushed himself to his feet and stepped onto the spinning planet. He staggered through trash. He had lost the gun.

He panted, sobbing, confused, his insides convulsing with dry heaves. He heard Garrett's voice again: "Are you crazy? I'll kill you for that."

Peter staggered toward a black rectangle on the wall.

He fell through it and tumbled down stairs to blackness.

"Pretty much the next thing I remember was hearing a woman's voice," Peter told the court from the witness stand.

"What did she say?" Martin asked.

"She was like, 'Can you hear me? Are you hurt?' Stuff like that." Peter leaned back and rubbed the stubble on his neck. "I remember a bright light and I thought I had died." He paused. "But I think she was just shining a flashlight in my eye."

"What happened next?"

"Then I remember I was outside on a stretcher. Red lights were flashing. I overheard an argument. I didn't understand at the time, but I think a cop was arguing with an EMT over whether I should go the hospital in handcuffs."

"Did you?"

Peter shrugged. "I don't know."

Martin paused a moment. Peter had done well on the stand—calm, believable, personable. He had explained the gunpowder residue on his hands. He had held the jury's attention.

This was the moment to ask the jury to believe him.

"Did you kill Garrett Nickel?" Martin asked.

"No, sir," Peter said. He sat at attention.

"Do you know who did?"

"No, I don't."

"Did you ever see Garrett Nickel again after he went upstairs in the boathouse?"

"No, sir. I heard him yelling at me, like I said, but I never saw him."

"Did you know at the time," Martin said, "that Garrett Nickel had gone upstairs to commit murder?"

Jurors snapped to attention.

"No way, no sir, I did not."

Dillingham stood up, frowned, and then slowly sat back down.

Martin grabbed papers from the table. "Your Honor," he said, "I move at this time to put into evidence the results of DNA tests, which show a highly probable match between a body discovered upstairs in the boathouse by the social worker who also found Mr. Shadd and bloodstains found on Garret Nickel's prison clothing, which was sent anonymously to my office."

Whispers stirred in the gallery. Jurors shot one another glances.

The judge took off his reading glasses. "Any problem with this, Mr. Dillingham?" he asked.

The prosecutor stood. "No problem, Your Honor. I was going to file my own motion to bring this new information into the case."

The judge looked away a moment, slipped his glasses back on, and peered over them. "Approach," he ordered.

The two lawyers went up to the bench for a sidebar conference.

Quietly, the judge asked, "What the hell is going on, Martin?"

Martin told him about the anonymous package.

Dillingham added, "The preliminary DNA analysis is compelling— the jumpsuit, the sneakers, and the knife were all covered in the blood of that John Doe victim, identified by a social worker as the homeless individual who called himself J.R."

The judge took his glasses off again, bit on the end of one bow for a moment, and then decided. "We'll recess. You two lovers will talk, eh? You will come back to this court with a list of facts to which both sides can stipulate. Facts in dispute will be settled by a duel between the two of you. No pistols—chain saws with rusty chains. So it would be better if you can agree on what the jury will be told about this. *Capiche?*"

thirty-one

The man following Billy wore a tan raincoat and an olive green Stetson, pulled low to the top of his sunglasses. From the quick glance Billy managed to sneak as he walked around a corner, the man looked like the average big-shouldered brute. He limped slightly, maybe from an old football injury, or maybe he'd been wounded in a war, or had been punished by the mob. From a hundred yards away, the man looked anywhere from 35 to 135.

Who could be following me?

Maybe the same guy who followed me on the highway.

Who is this guy?

A collector, maybe? But then why does he follow at a distance?

Billy detoured on his walk to the courthouse. He headed through a neighborhood of single-family cottages, and three-deckers packed side to side, so close to the street that the front steps were part of the sidewalk. The houses were old and simple but in good shape. With no front yards, people with green thumbs settled for whiskey barrels packed with geraniums. The neighborhood felt old-fashioned—the kind of place that closed streets for block parties and where adult neighbors had authority over one another's kids.

Billy got lost in the maze of side streets. He zigzagged by instinct, until he heard the bustle of Atwells Avenue, the main artery of Federal Hill. The street was like an old village square, stretched out for a mile; a place to visit, not a place to drive through on your way to someplace else. The awnings on the restaurants and markets were the Italian colors—red, green, and white. The place always seemed thick with people. Locals lived in apartments stacked two or three high on top of the restaurants; tourists walked with noses in guidebooks that revealed where gangsters had been whacked into their linguini, back when Federal Hill had been HQ for the New England mob.

Billy glanced over his shoulder, saw the guy in the raincoat.

He walked into a wall in the shape of a man. "Ow!"

The wall said, "Billy Povich, I'm glad I found you. I was about to visit."

Billy looked up.

"Hey, Walter," Billy said glumly. How was Billy supposed to lose the guy tailing him while getting pounded in some back alley? *Wait a second* . . . Who would dare come after him with Walter the collector at his side? Billy repeated brightly. "Hey, Walter!" He grabbed the big man's right hand and pumped it three times. *What the hell* . . . He pumped three more times.

The main in the raincoat detoured, casting one glance toward Billy and Walter. He slipped down a side street and disappeared.

Walter frowned, looking puzzled. He took his hand back. "Mr. C. wants his money," he said. "He was *unpleased* I came back last time without the full wad."

"I'll write you an affidavit," Billy said, only half joking, "swearing that you whooped me as hard as anybody."

"You know I like you, Billy, but Mr. C.—"

"By Sunday, Walt—I'll have it by Sunday."

Walter put his hands on his hips and cocked his head at Billy. A pack of teenaged boys parted on the sidewalk and flowed around Walter like a stream around a boulder.

"Pounding my face today won't make Sunday come any quicker," Billy added.

"You'll have the interest, too?"

"All of it," Billy confirmed.

Walter's face softened. The bear smiled. Maybe there would be no beating that morning.

"I'm heading downtown," Billy said, sneaking a glance to where the man in the raincoat had disappeared. "Can we head that way?"

They walked toward downtown; Billy felt like his big brother had arrived to scare off a bully. He wondered why the man had been following him at such a distance. Why didn't the guy try to catch him in the neighborhood, before they reached the crowded avenue? Or was the man just waiting for the perfect shot? Had Walter saved his life without knowing it? Billy indulged in the mystery in silence.

Walter said, "So what's with Sunday? You getting paid that day?"

"It's payday," Billy agreed.

"What did you hit?"

"College football game," Billy said. "It's local, so you know how those point spreads are."

"Shaky, mostly," Walt said. "Especially early in the season, when the local books haven't figured out the teams yet. When was the game?"

"Uh, that's the thing," Billy said, violently scratching a sudden scalp itch. "The game's not until this Saturday—but it's a lock, a fucking lock. I laid everything I have on this bet, so I'll have Mr. C.'s money after I win."

Actually, Billy had laid more than everything he had—he had maxed out the cash advances on seven credit cards for the capital to put down this five-figured wager, which he hoped would be the last bet of his life.

If he lost, it certainly would be the last.

Billy had expected Walt to bonk his head or maybe restrict his oxygen for ninety seconds or so, to make the point that a live bet was not equal to cash in hand. But the big man just rubbed a fist into his palm. The gesture seemed almost subconscious on Walter's part, though Billy understood.

He had to win that bet.

Anxious to change the subject, Billy asked, "So how'd it go with your girl after that horoscope ran in the paper?"

Walter beamed. "I had to beg off the fourth time," he said. "Which gets me thinking. She has this friend—"

"Uh-huh."

"—who lives by the horoscope, same as my girl. Both Scorpios."

"That's probably why they're friends."

"This friend is *hot*."

"You wanna switch?"

"That would be no net gain on my part," Walter said. "I'd like to add her to the mix."

"Ah."

"Maybe I can owe you a favor?"

Billy grabbed his chin a moment in thought. He said, "They say three's a crowd, Scorpio—but there's nothing more fun than a happy crowd. Share and share alike!"

thirty-two

Dillingham's leg bounced under the table as Peter Shadd returned to the witness stand. The prosecutor reminded Martin of a racehorse in the gate.

The judge informed Peter that he was still under oath, then told Dillingham, "You may begin cross-examination."

The prosecutor exploded from his chair. "What happened to your gun?" he demanded.

Peter's eyes widened. He seemed stunned by Dillingham's aggressiveness. "Wasn't my gun."

Dillingham rolled his eyes dramatically. "Excuse me," he said, exaggerating the sarcasm, laying his hand over his heart and looking upon Peter as he would a bug. "What did you do with the gun you had stolen from your cell mate?"

"I dunno."

"You don't know." He pretended to be disappointed.

"I lost it."

Dillingham suddenly marched across the courtroom and stood at the back of the jury box. "Isn't it true," he called out, nearly shouting, "that after you robbed your cell mate Mr. Horne and stole his money in the park, you decided to kill Garrett Nickel?"

"No."

"You killed him so you wouldn't have to share any money with him."

"No!"

"You shot him, isn't that true?"

"Objection!" Martin yelled. "He's answered the question twice already."

"You shot him, didn't you!"

"I didn't shoot him," Peter cried.

The judge made a sign, as if signaling a base runner was safe. "That's enough," he growled, growing red-faced again. He shook a finger at the two lawyers and warned, "We're going to keep our heads during this cross-examination. We're going to speak one at a time. We're going to shut up if there's an objection, until I sort it out. We will do everything I say today, or we will spend the night downstairs in lockup. And by 'we,' I mean the two of you."

He looked for anybody who might disagree. Nobody dared. Returning to the testimony, the judge made his ruling. "The question has been asked and answered—the witness denies shooting Garrett Nickel. Let's move on, Mr. Dillingham."

Dillingham nodded in deference to the judge. When he resumed his cross-examination, the racehorse was gone and staid, plodding Ethan Dillingham was back—a Clydesdale again. "You mentioned in direct examination that when Garrett Nickel picked you up, you injected yourself with heroin, is this correct?"

"Yes."

"You had been years without the drug, correct?"

"In jail—yeah."

"The drug's destructive hold upon you is well documented, is that not true?"

Peter looked hard at him and then shrugged. "It screws me up."

"Mmmmm," Dillingham said thoughtfully. "Can you tell the court, then, why you immediately injected yourself with a substance for which you had no *physical* addiction at that time and which you knew contributes to self-destructive behavior?"

Peter looked away in heavy thought for a few seconds, searching himself for the answer.

"I shot up because I had been thinking about doing it from the day I got locked up," he said. "Getting high is all I dream about in prison— whether I'm reading, doing push-ups, working on my appeal, or, well, anything. I'm sorta dreaming about it right now, if you want to know the truth. I don't expect anybody who ain't in my shoes to understand, but there it is."

Dillingham flipped the page of his legal pad and read. He had no follow-up question for *that*. Martin suppressed a smile. Peter had done well.

Give the son of a bitch more truth than he can handle.

"So is it possible," Dillingham said, though it seemed his heart wasn't in it, "that you could have shot Garrett Nickel while in this drug-induced stupor?"

"I didn't shoot him."

Dillingham let it drop and flipped the page. He asked, "You have testified that the gunpowder residue on your hands came from firing at a rat, is this true?"

"I'm afraid of rats."

"I don't believe the police found a dead rat in the boathouse—at least not one mortally wounded by a bullet," Dillingham said. "The only gunshot body found anywhere near the boathouse was that of your former cell mate Garrett Nickel."

"Objection," Martin said, "Mr. Dillingham isn't asking questions; he's dictating a novel."

The judge nodded. He told Dillingham, "This is a Q and A format,

Mr. Prosecutor, so let's hear more Q out of you and more A from the witness, and perhaps we'll conclude this trial before I hit mandatory retirement."

Jurors chuckled.

Dillingham ignored the humor and plowed on. "What happened to the rat?"

"Maybe it ran away."

"With a bullet in it?"

"Maybe I missed."

"From two feet away?"

Peter tugged on his ear and fidgeted. He suddenly looked nervous. "I must have missed," he said. "Or I hurt it and it ran away." He looked to the jury. "I don't know."

Dillingham stepped two paces closer to Peter. "What caliber was the gun?"

"Small-bore," Peter said immediately. "A twenty-two."

Martin chewed the inside of his cheek. Peter had to tell the truth, but did he have to seem so *sure* about it? He sounded like the ammunitions editor for *Concealed Weapons* magazine. What the jury would take from that, Martin feared, was that Peter had fired a lot of different guns.

Dillingham sensed the same thing, and he swooped in for another pass. "You're sure about the caliber?"

"Twenty-two," Peter said again.

"That's the caliber of weapon that killed Garrett Nickel, isn't that right?"

"If you say so."

"That's what the medical examiner has said, isn't it?"

"I object, Your Honor," Martin said. "Mr. Shadd is a witness, not the court stenographer."

The judge nodded. "The caliber of the bullets that struck the victim is in the court record—twenty-two caliber. Let's move on."

Martin had won the objection, but Dillingham had won the point, hammering his most devastating piece of evidence. Martin combed his fingers through his beard, pulling hard at a knot until it gave way. He had anticipated that the gunpowder on Peter's hands would be the heaviest anchor on the defense. But to see it played out stung worse than he had expected.

We're in trouble.

Dillingham checked his notes a moment and then tossed the pad on the table. "Let me just ask about one more point," he said, pausing and looking pensive. "You have admitted that you escaped from prison."

"Yeah, obviously."

"That you robbed your cell mate at gunpoint."

"Like I said."

"That you injected yourself with heroin."

"Yeah."

"And you admit," he shouted, "that you were inside the boathouse when an unidentified victim was murdered and decapitated, and that while in proximity of that brutal killing, you admit you fired a stolen handgun of the same caliber as that which killed Garrett Nickel. You admit all of that, don't you?"

Peter looked to Martin, who could not help him.

"Yeah, I did all that stuff," he squeaked. "But I didn't kill Garrett."

"Of course not," Dillingham cried, mocking him. "When would you have found the time?"

thirty-three

Billy woke with a gasp and looked at his hands.

He could see their outline in the dark. His hands were dry, chapped, not sticky with the blood he had felt in his dream. He rolled over, pulled the pillow over his head, and bit the blanket. The sobs shook him like a seizure, and then suddenly they were gone. His body was exhausted, but Billy was wide-awake.

It was 4:45 A.M. Too late for a sleeping pill. There should be at least one alert juror that day; the defense was expected to finish its presentation. He had an urge for Ovaltine—the toddler's sleep aid. He had slept in jeans, a white-collared dress shirt, socks, and slippers. Not the most comfortable sleepwear, but it saved time when he got up. In the kitchen, Billy warmed milk and scraped hardened Ovaltine from the jar.

He could not live this way forever, stalking Maddox in his sleep, waking in horror, shocked to have clean hands.

I hunt for blood at night. . . . I'm a vampire.

Billy had hoped that if he looked long enough into his own eyes in the mirror, he would see the darkest part of himself and learn if he really could take revenge on Maddox. But he had given up trying to see his own soul. His reflection had told him nothing. He really was a vampire, of sorts. Or worse—what if he was Hamlet?

His thoughts clarified and he realized he didn't need to learn what he was capable of doing; he just needed to decide what to do.

Down the hall, his pop cried out, "Stand like a man!"

What the hell—

Softly, Billy called back, "Pop?"

He listened.

All silent.

Billy turned off the simmering milk and stepped to his father's bedroom. Ear to the door, he listened to the old man snore. It sounded like he was trying to start a chain saw. His father had been talking in his sleep.

Stand like a man?

What did he mean by that? What was dreaming of? His wheelchair? Or me?

Billy stopped at Bo's room and peered in.

The blankets were balled at the foot of the bed, the twin pillows balanced together in a pyramid.

The kid was gone.

Billy pushed open the door, "Bo?"

He clicked on the light. "Bo?" The box that held the boy's Batman costume was on the floor, open and empty.

By the light of a streetlamp outside the window, Billy saw that Bo had pushed his Batman mask up onto his head so that he could use the telescope. The boy's right eye was scrunched tightly shut, his left pressed to the eyepiece of Mr. Metts's telescope in the front room of the funeral parlor beneath the apartment. Bo's toy pistol, a realistic cast-metal model of a .38 revolver, was stuck in his waistband. The heavy toy gun threatened to pull down his pajama bottoms. The telescope was level, aimed across the parade field, toward the sandstone armory.

"Bo."

"Eeee!" the kid shrieked.

He recoiled from the telescope and his little butt hit the floor.

"It's just me, Bo."

Bo nodded. "Mmm." He climbed to his feet. In the excitement, the toy gun had slipped into his pants. He reached down there, fished around a little while, and brought it out.

"What are you doing here?" Billy asked. "Do you know what time it is? What would Mr. Metts say if he caught you down here?"

"Mr. Metts don't mind—he showed me how to use the telescope."

Billy bit his own index finger. He had made the rookie reporter's mistake of asking too many questions, and Bo had taken the politician's escape, answering the one he wanted to.

"What are you looking at?"

Bo pulled the Batman mask back down over his face. "Nothing," he said.

"Maybe I could take a look."

Bo hesitated. "I'm on a mission." The voice behind the mask was suspicious, unsure how much to share.

The plastic Batman face grimaced at Billy. He had seen that tough-guy stare before, from collectors who believed you *could* get blood from a stone, if you squeezed it hard enough and slapped it a few times. Billy squatted to the kid's level. "I won't ruin your mission," he promised. "I could help."

The boy's suspicion evaporated, replaced by hyperactive energy. "You could be Robin!" He pumped his little legs in excitement.

"I don't have a mask."

"Sometimes they don't wear masks, like when they're at home."

Billy saluted. "Okay, boss," he said. "What's our mission?"

With the exhilaration of a sugar rush, Bo reported, "I'm spying on the spy!" He put his eye to the telescope, fiddled with the focus knob, and then stood aside.

Billy put his eye to the scope. The scene across the parade field meant nothing to him at first—a streetlamp illuminating a park bench, three cars parked illegally, two with orange parking tickets on the windshield. He started to ask what to look for.

Then Billy felt a chill. His windpipe tightened, as if from a noose.

In the parked car without a ticket sat a man in a trench coat. Billy recognized the brute with a limp who had tailed him through Federal Hill.

The man was watching Billy's house.

Billy recognized the car, too, a little black Subaru—probably the car that had followed him onto the highway.

"How long has this guy been there?" Billy whispered.

"I been watching him a few days," Bo said. "Since I saw him peeking in Mr. Metts's windows. He's a spy!"

"Is he there every morning?"

"Sometimes he's on the other side of the park."

Billy watched the man sip from a can. "What does he do? Does he just sit there?"

"He's a spy," Bo repeated. "He spies on us."

Billy stood back from the telescope. What to do? Call the cops? Then the man would know they were onto him. Would that be bad?

"Do you think he wants your money?" Bo asked.

"What?" Billy looked into the blue beads shining through Batman's eyeholes. "Why would he want my money?"

Bo kicked at the carpet. "Grandpa says bad men take the money you lose in bets and that's why I don't have a bicycle."

"He said that?" Billy burned with a brief burst of anger.

"I have thirty-seven dollars," the boy confessed. He glanced away, deeper into the funeral home. "I was saving it for somebody else, but you can have it, Billy."

"Bo—" he began, and then fell hushed. Such a gesture of self-sacrifice . . .

In a sudden whoosh of emotion, Billy fell in love with the four-foot stranger who had lived in his house for a year. He hugged the boy—truly held him for the first time since Angie had thrown Billy out.

From his love came rage. Billy seethed over the man sitting in the car across the park, who could be a threat to this little person. He stood, wiped his eyes on his sleeve. "I'm going on a mission," he said. "Gimme your toy gun."

Bo handed it up.

Early in the morning, with the light still dim, the toy could pass as real.

"You're my backup," Billy said.

The kid straightened to attention, stiffened by responsibility.

"Watch through the telescope," Billy said. "If something happens, wake your grandpa."

The morning was cool. Dew beaded on wrought-iron fences. The rising sun glimmered off slick slate roofs on the neighborhood's old Victorians. Billy had slipped out the back door and walked a wide circle around the neighborhood, approaching the black Subaru from behind.

He was going to find out who this guy was. His hand clenched the fake gun. This was dangerous, of course. What if the guy had a real weapon?

It's all in the attitude.

Attitude would make the toy gun real.

Billy looked to the funeral home across the parade field. He imagined Bo in the front window. The kid would be looking at Billy. He nodded and gave a thumbs-up.

The man in the car was reading the paper and drinking Dr Pepper. His window was down.

Billy strode to the car and jammed the toy gun in the man's face.

The man jerked back, eyes wide. He blinked rapidly a moment, then looked up at Billy.

He was older than Billy had expected, maybe sixty. White tuffs sprouted like cotton balls on his knuckles. His hair had been buzzed to a crew cut. His eyes were set deep beneath a high brow. The car was spotless; it might have looked like a rental if not for the plastic Saint Christopher standing ironically on the dash.

"Who the fuck are you?" Billy demanded.

The man said nothing. He calmly folded his paper and laid it on the seat beside him.

"Why have you been following me?"

No answer. Was this guy deaf?

"Tell me who you are or I'll blast your brains all over that nice upholstery."

The man looked away for a moment, tapped his thumb twice on the steering wheel, glanced back to Billy with a frown, and then started his car.

"I'll kill you," Billy bluffed. "I mean it."

Without a word or another glance, he drove away. The license plate was smeared with mud, unreadable.

Billy watched the car disappear. Then he waved to the funeral home so that Bo would know he was okay.

What balls that guy had—to drive away with a gun in his face.

Billy looked at the toy in his hand. Seemed real enough. He looked down the barrel and then slapped his own forehead. "Jesus Christ!" he shrieked.

Bo had corked the gun with a breakfast carrot.

thirty-four

On the first page of his legal pad, Martin wrote the questions for his final witness. On the second page, he jotted notes for the appeal. They were going to lose; Peter was going to be convicted—Martin was sure of it. Dillingham had obliterated Peter at the end of his cross-examination. Maybe Martin hadn't prepared Peter correctly. Maybe it had been a mistake to come forward with the bloody jumpsuit.

Can telling the truth be a mistake? The question, he imagined, would bother his sleep for a long time.

He tossed down his pen and stared at the stucco ceiling in his office. He counted six black ants up there, walking crazy curlicues. Looking around, he noticed three ants on the wall, two on his desk. One had the gall to march across his pad.

In the abstract, Martin was neutral toward ants: He had no love for them, but he didn't mind if they colonized the cracks in the sidewalk. His office, though, was different. He hated them here. Still, he could not kill them. He had a deep-reaching fear—probably irrational, but you never know—that his wife would look into his eyes while they made love and screech, "You have murdered within the animal kingdom!" Such was a sex life with an über-vegan. So he lived with the ants.

Martin rubbed his eyes . . . *Wait a second.*

He popped open his eyeglass case. The spider inside reached up two legs and scratched the air. Martin shooed the spider onto a book-case. "You can stay," he said, "so long as you're catching bugs."

The telephone clanged on Martin's desk.

He waited two rings for Carol to answer it, then remembered he was alone and that Carol was probably on the other end of the line.

"Hello?"

"The judge gave the fifteen-minute warning," Carol said.

"I'll walk right over."

She caught something in his voice. "Marty, you've done your best," she said. "You gave him a fighting chance. And it's not over yet."

"It's over," he replied. "Nobody can find Franklin Flagg, and I'm down to my last witness, whom I'd never dare put on the stand unless the situation was absolutely desperate. Pastor Guy is running for of-fice. He's a loose cannon. Who knows what he's gonna say?"

"What about a hung jury?"

"You bring the rope, I'll hang 'em," he offered. "It's the only way Peter will avoid going down for murder."

"What about the person who sent you the jumpsuit? What if they came forward?"

"Not much chance of that," Martin said, growing more glum. "If they had nothing to hide, they would have just walked the evidence over here."

"Well, at least you can go down like a champ," she said, trying to sound encouraging.

"I've just convinced you that it's hopeless," Martin said. "You're the first person I've persuaded of *anything* since I took this case."

———

Billy's hands still quivered from his encounter that morning with the man in the trench coat.

I threatened to kill him with a carrot.

The only person in the courtroom who looked more nervous was Peter Shadd, who fidgeted, scratched his skin, rubbed his own head—looking like performance art entitled *Nervous Tic.*

Nobody else on the jury seemed to notice Shadd. They had mentally checked out and were only occupying space in the jury box until it was time to vote.

"Mr. Smothers?" the judge said. "You have another witness?"

"Abraham Guy, Your Honor."

The judge nodded to a sheriff, who vanished into the hall to call out, "Abraham Guy!"

After a few moments, the sheriff held the door for a red-faced man on one of those self-balancing scooters. He carried a Bible in one hand and steered the machine with the other. He wore a gray suit, maroon vest, and a bow tie.

A pastor who could be the next governor, entering court on a two-wheel scooter?

That put life back into the jury. He had their attention.

Word of Pastor Guy's testimony had drawn half a dozen political reporters to court. Billy couldn't blame them. There was a time he would have been fascinated by the spectacle of the pastor sparring with Ethan Dillingham in an election preview.

At the witness stand, the pastor stepped off the machine and faced the court clerk.

The empty scooter balanced itself on two wheels, seeming to defy gravity with artificial intelligence. Billy figured everyone in the courtroom, including the judge, was thinking the same thing: *I've got to try one of those.*

"Raise your right hand," the clerk instructed.

The pastor raised his hand. "If you don't mind," he said, "I've brought my own Bible."

The clerk smiled. "We don't use a Bible. You can just swear by your oath."

Pastor Guy turned up his nose. "Nonsense," he said. "If I swear an oath, I use a Bible." He slapped the leather-bound book on the rail with a crackling echo and rested his left hand on it.

Billy stared at the Bible. It was identical to the bloody book he had found in the old boathouse. Pastor Guy's prison ministry must have given all the inmates the same edition.

The clerk put him under oath. The pastor sat and cradled the Bible as he would a baby.

"Good day, Mr. Guy," Martin Smothers began.

The pastor smiled and nodded, projecting the presence of a man too busy to be there but content to do his duty.

"Do you recognize my client?"

The pastor looked to Peter. "I do."

"How do you know Mr. Shadd?"

"I met him through my prison ministry," the pastor said. "He was in the High Security facility, if I remember correctly. We did Bible study, trying to use the Good Word to help us reject wickedness in our lives. And, uh, as the Word tells us, 'If the world hate you, ye know that it hated me before it hated you.' That's the first thing I tell the men in prison when I witness to them."

Martin smiled. "Have you memorized the whole book?"

The pastor chuckled. "If only time would permit," he said, his velvety radio voice projecting through the room. "I encourage my students to memorize the parts of the Holy Book that have the most meaning to them, be they about life, death, the mission of the Savior, and then to carry the tome, always." He smiled.

"How was Peter Shadd as a student?"

Billy watched the pastor's face wrinkle for a split second. He said, "Well, Mr. Shadd didn't have much of a mind for memorization, not like some of my other students."

Martin waited.

But that was it—the whole damn answer.

Peter sucked at Bible class. . . . My case is dead and this guy is shoveling dirt on me.

"Would you say," Martin blurted to fill the silence, "that Mr. Shadd was an attentive student?"

"He tried to be, I'd say."

"So you're saying he took his Bible studies to heart?"

The pastor's face froze in a grimace as he looked to the ceiling for the answer. "I never remember him missing an appointment." He shrugged.

Martin felt a sudden headache, like a power drill in the forehead. "How often," he asked, blinking against the pain, "did you visit with Mr. Shadd?"

"I went to the prison every week," he said. "I generally met with each of the students who sought my guidance each time."

Martin turned to the jury and said, "Every week—that's impressive. You must have felt you were making a difference with these men, considering the hassles of prison security, the paperwork, the body searches—"

"Actually," said the pastor, interrupting, "the correctional officers are quite accustomed to my presence, and they escort me through immediately. I am never inconvenienced in any way. Their way of saying thanks, perhaps." He smiled.

Oh come on! Throw me a crumb!

Over the next hour, Martin dragged bits of usable testimony from Pastor Guy.

Peter had never threatened him.

He had never heard Peter threaten anyone else.

The pastor never feared for his own safety in the unmonitored one-on-one study sessions with Peter.

The examination was hand-to-hand combat with a semihostile witness. The pastor was in no mood to help a smack-addicted prison escapee beat a murder charge on the eve of his first run for governor. How did it play with the jury? Martin couldn't guess.

Throughout his testimony, the pastor sneaked glances at Dillingham, his future opponent in the primary election. Quickly, he would look away. It seemed that Dillingham made him nervous and that the pastor didn't want to meet his eyes unless he had to.

Peter slouched at the defense table, absentmindedly tapping the rubber end of a pencil on a notepad.

He knows, Martin thought in a swirl of guilt. *He knows we're going down.*

thirty-five

Passing under the tall, rounded concrete arch into the Brown University football stadium reminded Billy of when he used to be a sports fan, before he became a gambler and the final score became infinitely more important than how the teams arrived at it. The stadium was more than eighty years old, a throwback to the leather-helmet days when the Ivy League could play with anybody on the gridiron. Hundreds of students had worn their Brown Bears sweat-shirts against the chill on a clear and cool morning.

Hamburger smoke from the concession stand wafted over Billy. Was there any better advertising than the smell of a barbecue? If only his stomach would calm down. Maybe by halftime.

He picked a spot near the forty-yard line, sat on the concrete bench. The old stadium stands, all on one side of the field, were shaped like a smile—high in the middle, sloping down on each side.

The natural grass had still not recovered from a home game in the rain two weeks before; there were patches of dirt here and there, though the field had recently been restriped, the white lines now glowing brightly in the sun. The end zones had been colored deep burgundy, BROWN painted across one and BEARS across the other.

The stadium could hold twenty thousand people; maybe four thousand had come for the game against Cornell.

Knowledgeable hometown fans groaned aloud when the PA announced that offensive tackle Craig Kahn would not play, due to a foot injury.

Billy scanned the crowd for Mia. No luck. With her 335-pound brother hurt, maybe she had stayed home.

For a bunch of smart guys who would need those brains to make a living someday, the Brown players hit hard throughout the game; plastic pads and helmets slapped nosily against one another. But without Craig Kahn, possibly the best offensive lineman in the school's history, the Brown ground game went nowhere, and it seemed the offense was in third-and-long jams all day. Forced to pass against a vicious blitz, Brown's sophomore quarterback chucked three interceptions, two of them returned by the defense for touchdowns.

The local oddsmakers had listed Brown as an eight-point favorite before the game, but the bookies hadn't known about Craig Kahn's weight-lifting accident.

Brown lost the game by ten points, and it could have been worse, except that the Cornell coach was too classy to embarrass the undermanned home team.

Just about everyone left disappointed, except for Billy Povich.

He had won his bet.

The next time Billy saw Walter the collector, he would have Mr. C.'s money, the principal and the interest. No broken face needed.

From the moment he had learned from Mia that her brother was hurt, Billy had an advantage over the sports books. He felt no guilt over using inside knowledge to win the bet—anything can happen in college football, and Brown still could have covered that spread, somehow. Billy had simply bet with the prevailing odds.

He stopped in the men's room and waited to use a urinal behind two Brown alumni moaning about the loss and wondering aloud when Kahn would come back from the injury.

On the bathroom wall, somebody had penned a quote in black Magic Marker.

Everything should be made as simple as possible, but not simpler.
—Albert Einstein

Leave it to Brown students to quote Einstein in men's room graffiti. Whatever happened to dirty limericks? Or the bathroom dating advice: "For a good time, call . . ."

The Einstein quote reminded Billy of something—he had seen some other high-minded graffiti recently. . . . Where had that been?

The walk home was about two miles, through the redbrick Brown campus, past Colonial-era homes with cobblestone walks and steps made from Westerly granite still striped from where the holes had been pounded by hand to split the rock in the quarry, maybe a hundred years ago. Billy hiked past the courthouse, a brick castle of gables jutting every which way, pink stone columns, and a four-faced clock tower. The courthouse was built into a hill so steep that the back entrance was on the fifth floor. He had been coming to the court every day but had never studied the building. Probably because he was always late, always exhausted from having worked all night.

He walked through downtown, past the high-rise hotels—one built during the Jazz Age, one trying to look like it had been—and then under Route 95. Bums had piled boxes and foam mattresses against a bridge abutment. He walked past industrial buildings, a 1970s-style concrete apartment tower that polluted the Providence skyline with its squat, flat ugliness. To his left, the modern police station, with its prowlike atrium, looked like a giant block of masonry that had been rammed by a glass ocean liner.

Billy heard an argument, half in English, half in Spanish. He was almost home. Home used to feel safe. Billy looked around for the black Subaru and the man in the trench coat.

A funeral was under way at Metts & Sons on the first floor. Billy couldn't use the stairs until it was over. He dropped onto a park bench in the parade field, his back to his house, and watched two men, probably a couple, exercising two dogs in the field. They tied their leashes together and let them go. If the dogs—a yellow Lab and a fat black mutt—had worked together, they could have run free. But the Lab wanted to run left, the mutt to the right. Billy watched the dogs yank each other around, and laughed.

They reminded Billy of Peter Shadd and the prison break. Had the three convicts worked together, they might have made it to Canada. But Garrett Nickel persuaded Peter to betray Larry Horne, and the plan began to crumble. Somebody obviously betrayed Nickel. The testimony never did reveal who had helped Garrett with the car, which had never been found.

Ah! Billy remembered something. The construction site down by the docks—that was where he had seen some thoughtful graffiti, when the jury went there by bus. He remembered the quote—"he that believeth shall not make haste."

Must be from the Bible, Billy figured, though he did not recognize it.

With an hour to kill before he could get into his apartment, Billy walked back toward downtown, went into an Internet coffee shop with free access while you sipped. He had eight dollars in his pocket. He bought a venti iced decaf caramel vanilla–hazelnut mocha latte with whole milk and sprinkled cardamom—because the drink cost exactly eight dollars, which seemed like some kind of sign.

On the café's computer, he ran a general Internet search for an on-line electronic Bible. There were dozens of them. He found the King James Version and then typed the quote, word for word, from the construction site into the Bible's search feature. Instantly, the computer brought him the correct verse in the Book of the Prophet Isaiah: "Therefore thus saith the Lord God, Behold, I lay in Zion for a foundation a stone, a tried stone, a precious corner stone, a sure foundation: he that believeth shall not make haste."

Hmmm, so somebody had painted the last part of a long verse. Billy was pleased with himself for figuring out where the quote had been taken from. He sipped his eight-dollar drink and recalled how beautifully rendered the graffiti letters had been on the building.

Then he remembered the way Martin Smothers had described Garrett Nickel in court: Nickel had been a graffiti artist of great reputation before he graduated to violent crime. He had met his own violent end at that construction site by the waterfront, where Billy had seen the snippet from the Bible.

He read the full verse again.

Inspiration clocked him across the head.

"Phone!" he blurted to the barista, a birch white college kid with a shaved head.

"Dude?"

"Telephone," Billy said. "You have one here?"

The barista stared blankly at Billy for a few seconds. "Local?"

"Yes, local call. Just gimme the phone."

The barista reached under the counter and handed Billy the cordless.

Billy dialed Mia's cell phone.

She answered, saying, "Has to be Billy."

"How'd you know?"

"Caller ID. A coffee shop on the West Side. Who else?"

"Where are you?"

"Hanging with my brother," she said. "He's bummed because Brown lost to Cornell. Did you hear about that?"

"Twenty-two to twelve," Billy said. "Brown ran the ball like eleven old ladies."

"Hey!" she scolded, and laughed.

"Meet me tonight."

She teased him with a giggle and then said, "Meet you for what?"

Billy turned his back to the barista and walked across the café. "I have a crazy idea that I know what Garrett Nickel did with J.R.'s head."

"What!"

"Do you have any tools?"

thirty-six

Some talent-starved tagger had recently sprayed "Cheryl is a slut!" in sky blue over the fragment of biblical verse on the wall. The fresh graffiti was drippy and ugly, and it seemed much more like vandalism than the Scripture in elegant letters beneath it.

The night was overcast and dark, and a chill mist had just begun to fall. In the distance, rumbling, clanking cranes unloaded another cargo ship. Billy panned the flashlight over the construction site, the painted wall, and then across the street, where Garrett Nickel had staggered, shot and dying, and plunged into the water.

Mia read the Bible quote out loud. "I don't know what it means," she said. "We still have so many questions."

"Yeah," Billy agreed. "Where's this Cheryl?"

She laughed and smacked his arm.

"We know Garrett Nickel was here the night he escaped," Billy said, turning serious. "This is where he went into the water, so this building is the last thing Nickel saw before the bottom of the stream. I checked some archived photos at the paper. Back then, the construction was not as far along as it is now."

Mia wrinkled her nose at the abandoned jumble of cinder block and rusting steel. "It's not even half-done now," she said.

"Money problems. Happens all the time," Billy said. "Anyway, Pastor Guy testified at trial yesterday—the defense had called him as a character witness, not that he helped them much. The pastor said he did one-on-one Bible studies with Peter Shadd, which means he probably studied one-on-one with Garrett Nickel, too."

"Makes sense."

"There has been a lot of testimony about Garrett quoting the Bible from memory," Billy said. "He did it all the time, just like the pastor."

"I never understood how some killers seem so reverent."

Billy thought about his own reverence, during his trips to confession. He felt his face redden and was glad for the darkness.

"We know Garrett Nickel's criminal record began with graffiti," Billy continued. "Supposedly, he had a talent for it. Whoever painted *this* had talent, wouldn't you say?"

"I'd prefer some separation between the characters, to make it easier to read."

"I'd prefer to look at Henri Matisse, but this is pretty good," Billy said. "I think Garrett Nickel painted it just before he was killed."

"I'm with you," she said. "What's it mean?"

"It comes from Isaiah, from a verse that speaks metaphorically about a foundation, a cornerstone," Billy explained. "And when I read that, I realized that this building has a cornerstone. If you build something from steel and concrete, you expect it to last, so you have a little gathering and install a ceremonial cornerstone with the date chipped into it. You entomb a copy of that day's newspaper and some other trinkets behind the cornerstone, for some future race to dig up two hundred years from now."

"Like a time capsule," she said.

Billy took from his pocket a square torn from a newspaper. "This ran in my paper a day before Garrett Nickel escaped prison," he said. "I looked it up after I called you today."

The clip was from the newspaper's business page—the paper had published a photograph of six well-groomed executives, looking goofy in business suits and hard hats, standing around an unfinished wall of cinder block. The photo caption confirmed the event that had taken place: "Cornerstone laid at waterfront office building."

"That photo was taken here," Billy said.

Mia read the caption and then said, "They were going to close up the cornerstone permanently that weekend," she said.

"They did close it up," Billy confirmed. "But it was open the night Garrett Nickel decapitated your friend J.R. and ran off with the head."

Mia nodded, understanding. She looked intently at Billy and said, "I've got my dad's old tools in the car."

The ceremonial cornerstone was a pink granite plaque about the size of a traffic sign and one inch thick. The date and the names of two dozen corporate executives had been chiseled into it. The stone was at the far back corner of the building, which was fine with Billy, since he never liked to destroy private property under a streetlight. He ran his finger along the edge where the slab had been cemented in place. Rain fell, light and fine, and it was not so cold now that Billy had gotten used to it.

He tapped a nine-pound sledgehammer on the stone. "Holy shit, that's loud," he said. "And that was only a test."

"At least it sounds hollow," said Mia.

"That's loud enough to wake Garrett Nickel from the fuckin' stream."

She laughed and looked at him sweetly. "I wish you were funny more often. You have a real sense of humor—I've seen it the last couple times we talked. Why do you keep it hidden?"

Billy pulled on work gloves.

"Haven't felt funny since Maddox killed my wife," he said. He looked to see if his bluntness had shocked her. She didn't seem shocked. "I laugh at stuff when I'm distracted." He smiled. "I've felt funnier around you, but I haven't been myself for thirteen months."

"That's not a *long* time," she said softly, "but isn't it a respectful amount to mourn?"

Billy rocked the hammer like a pendulum, getting the feel for its weight and balance.

"I'm not mourning," he confessed. "I'm thinking that this stone . . . is Maddox's head."

He swung the hammer in a wide arc and crashed it into the slab.

Wham!

The blow echoed like a gunshot. A crack appeared in the center of the stone and zigzagged to the top.

Mia covered her ears. "Holy shit! We're gonna get caught."

Billy gestured to the cargo ship. "So much noise down there, nobody lives around here," he said. "So there's nobody to call the cops."

Her thoughts were elsewhere. "You sound so *sure* that you know what happened in that car," she said.

Billy choked up a few inches on the hammer. "The cops say they lost the original police report. That makes it sure enough for me."

He swung.

Wham!

When the bang had echoed and died, Billy pulled off a glove and ran a finger along the crack. "This won't take long."

Mia asked, "What would you do with the proof about the cause of that crash? Would you hate Charles Maddox even more? Or would knowing that you're right allow you to forgive him?"

"I am right."

Wham!

"You're so positive Maddox is evil—yet, as you said, there's no proof. Do you hate him for the crash? Or for shacking up with your ex?"

Billy pressed his lips tightly together to stop himself from cursing. He swung the hammer three times. *Wham! Wham! Wham!*

He stopped, panting. He confessed in a low, hoarse voice, "I can't accept that she could have loved him, too. Not after me. I don't accept that the grandest emotion in the universe is so . . . temporary."

He wiped his face on a glove. The stiff leather scratched his cheek. He looked off toward the bay. The sprinkling had stopped and the air smelled like wet asphalt.

"You find it inconceivable that a woman could love two men," she said.

Billy glanced at her as he swung. The hammer's steel head smashed against the stone. The slab shattered into chunks that crumbled to the ground, revealing a dark hole in the wall.

"You got it," she cried.

Billy flung the hammer away and dropped to his knees. He aimed the light into the hole. The compartment behind the ceremonial slab was half-filled with sand. "Hold the light," Billy told her. "I'll dig."

He wormed his shoulders into the hole. The sand was cool and loosely packed, very dry.

Within a minute, Billy pulled out a plastic bag. Parts of it were stiff with dried blood.

From its size and its weight, they knew what was inside and saw no need to open it.

"When Garrett Nickel painted that message about the cornerstone," Mia asked grimly, "was he reminding himself where he had hidden the head?"

"After hearing about Nickel in court, my guess is he painted that because it made him feel clever," Billy said.

"But why bring it here? Why take such a risk?"

Billy set the bag down and reached back inside the hole. He found a piece of stiff cardboard. He brought it into the light.

A photograph.

Mia glanced at it and confirmed who it was. "That's J.R."

"Are you sure?"

"I chased him from back alleys to abandoned houses all over this city. That's definitely the guy who called himself J.R."

"Because I could swear—" The hairs on Billy's neck waved on their own, like hundreds of little creatures that had just had a fright.

"What?"

"This guy looks like a younger version of Pastor Abraham Guy."

She stared at the photo. "I never saw the pastor before."

"Who ever sees people from the radio? But I'm telling you, the resemblance is striking. This guy could be his son."

Mia slapped a hand over her mouth. She blurted, "He called himself J.R.! Billy, can you see? J.R. stands for *junior.*"

They stared at the photograph.

"I should have figured it out," Billy whispered. "For Chrissake, *I'm* a junior."

thirty-seven

The white van turned up Martin's street at 6:00 A.M., right when it was supposed to be there.

Waiting on the sidewalk, Martin Smothers suddenly felt hollow in his gut. If he'd whistled, he might have echoed on the inside, like a cave.

Should I be doing this?

He remembered the call that had awakened him: a woman's voice. She had wanted to meet. She knew of the bloody jumpsuit that had arrived anonymously at Martin's office, and that it had come by way of FedEx.

Nobody beside the attorney general and the judge knew how that box had arrived.

She sent it. . . . What else could it be?

The van slowed. Martin saw a young woman at the wheel. Spiky hair, freaky-looking silver piercings, tattoos, friendly smile.

The van stopped.

Martin hesitated a moment and then got in.

He slammed the door and the van drove off.

From the back of the truck, a man said, "Good morning, Mr. Smothers."

Martin whirled, blinked, then slapped his cheek lightly. "William Povich?" he said, nearly in a shriek. "What the hell! Ohmigod! I can't be talking to you. You're a juror." He clutched his own head. "I could get thrown off the fucking bar."

Martin looked to the young woman for help. Her eyes were on the road.

"There's some stuff you need to know," Povich said. "C'mon back here, out of sight."

For the next twenty seconds, Martin seriously considered throwing himself from the van.

The van needed shocks. It squeaked over bumps. Martin sat cross-legged over the rear axel, on the dusty metal bed, with no care for his linen suit. He sipped a Dunkin' Donuts dark roast they had bought him at a drive-through. He tried not to think about professional ethics. Legal and moral were not always the same, he reminded himself. If he helped an innocent man beat a bad rap, wouldn't that be moral?

"So Pastor Guy helped plan the prison break with Garrett Nickel?" Martin said, summing up some of what he had been told.

"Nickel must have been planning the escape a long time," Povich said. "But he needed help on the street, once outside the prison."

"He needed a car."

"And regular clothes, too. And money."

"Okay," Martin said, "but how did they arrange it?"

"The pastor met alone with Garrett Nickel every week in Bible study. You remember Larry Horne's testimony about Garrett having cocaine in his Bible? If I were a betting man—and God knows, I am—I'd wager that the pastor was supplying the drugs, hiding them in his own Bible. When the two of them got together, they just switched books. All those prison Bibles are the identical edition."

"This is nutty," Martin said, though he wanted to hear more.

"Just before he was killed, J.R. had been shooting off his mouth about coming into money—a lot of it, more than any homeless drunk could make with bottle deposits."

"Blackmail?"

Povich spread his hands. "Why not? Let's say that somewhere along the road, Pastor Guy made his own deposit—which turned into the son he never wanted. Maybe he paid off the mother to keep it quiet. He put the kid out of his mind. But imagine—on the eve of his run for governor, some smelly homeless guy shows up claiming to be his son, and looking for cash."

This crazy theory was becoming too much for Martin. "Who would believe it?" he scoffed. "Just deny it, dismiss the guy for what he is—a crazy fuckin' bum—and get on with the campaign."

Povich reached into his back pocket, drew out a photograph, and gave it to Martin. "This," he said, "was J.R."

Martin studied the picture. "Wow," he said. The man in the frame needed a shave, a shower, a barber, and a dentist. But the eyes were Pastor Guy's. The chin, the shape of the head. He whistled. "This could be persuasive."

"Imagine this guy on the front page, pictured next to Pastor Guy," Povich said. "That would give the pastor a lot of grief, probably derail his campaign."

Martin flicked his finger on the photo. "So what happened to this guy? Why did Garrett kill him?"

"I'm guessing," Povich said, "that in exchange for the coke, some cash, and the getaway car, Garrett Nickel agreed to use his underworld sources to find where J.R. spent his nights, and then track him down, kill him, and make sure the body was unrecognizable."

Martin frowned. "Taking the head would certainly accomplish *that*."

"But the pastor didn't want witnesses," Povich said. "Especially one like Nickel, who would have skinned his own mother for ten cents and a roll of Certs."

"He'd have done it for half that."

"So the pastor double-crossed Garrett, and shot him," Povich said. "Peter Shadd got pinned with the crime. It's the perfect resolution for the pastor—so long as Peter is convicted and there are no loose ends, or open investigations."

Martin twirled a lock of beard in his fingers and considered what Povich had alleged. A terrible thought struck him. "Alec Black!" he cried.

"Your best juror," Povich confirmed. "It was obvious Alec would never vote to convict. The pastor had to get rid of him."

"Can't be," Martin insisted. "Alec left a suicide note—I saw it."

"Handwritten? Or typed?"

Martin stroked his beard as he called up the memory. Alec's note had been simple—too much pressure in his life . . . considered himself a failure—pretty standard stuff. "Holy Jesus—it was typed," he suddenly shouted.

Povich nodded. "Planted on him."

Martin inhaled deeply and thought more about Povich's theory. He wanted to ask how one juror had become so involved—and why— but he thought better of it. Martin had already danced a jig upon the code of ethics.

What Povich had outlined sounded possible, but . . .

"You're hesitant," Povich guessed. "I would be, too. That's why

I'm giving you the photograph to keep, and I'm going to give you this . . ."

He dragged something heavy inside a ratty, balled-up plastic bag and set it in front of Martin.

"How we found this," Povich said, "is a story by itself."

thirty-eight

Billy felt brittle, having skipped a night's sleep on Saturday, but alert, almost hyper, as if the jury box might not be able to contain him.

Pastor Guy returned to court that morning in a blue pinstriped suit, gray vest, red bow tie. He scootered slowly to the witness box.

He was to face cross-examination from Dillingham, and news of that political spectacle had filled the gallery with reporters, who days ago could not have been forced, bribed, or tricked into caring about Peter Shadd and his trial. With the reporters sat political operatives and old hacks, who had not yet committed to any gubernatorial campaign. The clash between Dillingham and Pastor Guy was like a public audition. The victor would have the better choice of hacks.

Once the pastor was in place at the witness stand, the judge reminded him, "You are still under oath."

"Those in service of the Word are under the oath of truth at all times, Your Honor," the pastor said with a friendly smile.

The judge asked Martin Smothers, "Anything more in direct examination?"

Billy clenched his fists. How would Martin expose the pastor?

Martin half-stood. "Nothing further." He sat.

What the—

Billy tried to catch Martin's eye. The defense lawyer turned a page in his legal pad and made some casual scribbles. Billy stared through Martin's skull, demanding by way of telepathy that Martin look up. Had he gone chicken after Billy and Mia dropped him off? Had it been a mistake to trust him? To give him the photo . . . and the head?

Dillingham pushed slowly from the table. His chair scraped on the floor. Reporters in the gallery pressed their ballpoints to paper in anticipation. There was melodrama in the stilted way Dillingham rose to his feet. He stood without notes before a bare wooden table so shiny that he could have shaved in front of it, and then he greeted the witness. "Good morning, pastor."

"Mr. Dillingham," the pastor replied as a greeting.

"How well did you know Garrett Nickel?"

The question seemed to strike the pastor like a gust of wind, pushing him against the back of his seat. He leaned forward again. "Can't say *well*," he responded.

"What *can* you say?"

"Um, I don't—" He glanced to the reporters in the gallery, seemed to find his voice, and announced with confidence, "I ministered to every man in that cell block. That's why I was called to testify."

"How much time did you spend alone with Garrett Nickel?"

The pastor huffed. "I don't see what that has to do with the matter at hand. Are you going to ask me about Peter Shadd?"

"How was your relationship with Garrett Nickel?"

"I tried to be his spiritual mentor, but—uh, uh—he was a hard case."

"Are you running for governor?"

Reporters shot one another urgent glances and scribbled madly.

The judge cleared his throat and held out a hand to stop the testimony. He asked, "Any objection, Mr. Smothers?"

"No, sir," Martin said without looking up.

The pastor stared, slack-jawed, at Martin for a moment, then shut his trap, glared at Dillingham, and crossed his arms. "Is that what this is about?" he asked. "Fine, then, yes, I'm running, Mr. Dillingham. Are you?"

The prosecutor plowed ahead: "Do you have any children?"

The pastor's lips bent into an ironic smile. "Every person who finds their path through my preaching is my child," he said. "But I have none of the biological kind."

Dillingham leaned forward and pressed his fists onto the prosecutor's table. "Have you ever *fathered* any children?"

"No,—"

Pastor Guy froze. In an instant, he paled, then licked his lips and blinked with his whole face.

He suspects Dillingham knows the truth, Billy thought.

The pastor looked to a man in the gallery, a brooding young guy Billy had *seen* in the courtroom before but had never *noticed.* The young guy's face showed anger and worry. He gave the pastor the most minuscule shrug. Billy looked around—had anybody else seen the shrug?

"No," the pastor repeated. "I'm married to my Bible."

Dillingham rubbed his hand lightly over the glossy table. He asked firmly, "Did you ever give Garrett Nickel cocaine?"

"*What?*"

Pastor Guy looked to Martin, perhaps for an objection. The defense lawyer seemed engrossed in his notes.

Dillingham waited for the answer.

"That's ridiculous," the pastor charged. "How dare you?"

"It's a yes or no question," Dillingham said.

"No—certainly not!"

Dillingham suddenly thundered in a voice booming in echo: "Because his Bible is in evidence and our tests show cocaine!"

The pastor shrank from him. "I don't know anything about that."

"You gave him that Bible."

"I gave them all Bibles." Pastor Guy glanced helplessly to the judge.

"Did you know the man who called himself J.R.? The man Garrett Nickel killed and beheaded in the boathouse on the night he escaped? Did you know that man?"

The pastor raised an arm, as if to ward off Dillingham's attacks. He said, "I don't know what you're talking about."

Seething, the prosecutor demanded through gritted teeth, "Was that man your son?"

Reporters gasped.

"This attack," the pastor wheezed, "on my character!"

"Was he blackmailing you?"

"Whom do you mean?"

"Was he threatening to expose himself as your bastard son—"

"Absurd!"

"—whom you abandoned to poverty and homelessness, while you grew rich telling others how they ought to live," Dillingham shouted. "Did you see him as a threat to your dreams of political power?"

The pastor glared at Dillingham and then looked past him, again to the man in the gallery.

Dillingham didn't wait for the answer. He badgered: "Did you persuade Garrett Nickel to use his underworld contacts to track this man down? Did you help Garrett Nickel escape from prison, in exchange for killing this man—in exchange for *killing your son*?"

"What the f—" exclaimed a reporter in the gallery. He caught himself before the word was out, and quietly apologized. Nobody blamed him.

The courtroom fell silent. Nobody dared flinch.

The pastor looked around. Everyone else looked at him. He

tugged on his jacket, cleared his throat. "All of this," he shouted desperately to the corners of the room, "is a lie!"

He let the words echo and fade.

"A despicable lie," the pastor roared, "perpetrated by my political opponent, who has just proven by these attacks that he is unfit for public office." He stabbed his finger toward Dillingham. "People warned me that politics is nasty, but I never expected *this*."

The pastor rose in his chair. He cheeks reddened.

"These lies will backfire upon you," the pastor swore. "These reporters, in the back of the room—they've heard it. They'll write about this *mockery*. The entire state will see you're unfit to be governor." He fiddled with his bow tie. "You'll see."

Dillingham nodded to a man in the gallery.

The man stood at attention. He wore a white knit shirt and white pants.

The prosecutor gestured to the man. "This is Michael," he explained in an introduction. "He's a DNA specialist at the Department of Health. He can clear up this controversy."

"Your Honor," the pastor pleaded.

"The paternity test is not painful," Dillingham insisted. "All you need do is swipe a cotton swab inside your cheek to provide the sample."

The pastor combed his hands through sweat-matted hair. "I'll not participate in this political game," he said.

"Your Honor," Dillingham said pleasantly, "I have two motions to file. The first is a motion to dismiss the murder charge against Mr. Shadd, due to new evidence—pending the results of my second motion."

"Mm-hm," the judge said. "Go on."

"The second is a motion to compel Abraham Guy to provide DNA for testing."

"Goddamn!" The pastor cried toward the gallery. "Victor! Help me! Help me!"

A sheriff appeared at the pastor's side. The pastor fell back onto his chair, seemingly in a daze.

The pastor's brooding accomplice in the gallery rose to leave, but he walked into a hand the size of an oven mitt, belonging to a body-builder in a sheriff's uniform. "You'll be staying," the sheriff told him.

The reporters had behaved long enough; they couldn't stand it anymore.

"Pastor Guy!" one yelled. "Did you do it?"

"Will you submit to the test?"

"How did you help them escape?"

Others shouted questions at Dillingham, at Martin Smothers, at Peter Shadd.

The judge pounded the gavel, but to no effect. Sheriff's deputies plunged into the gallery to restore order, while pleading for help on their radios.

Martin Smothers ignored the chaos. He shook hands with Peter, shot a glance to the jury box, met eyes with Billy, looked away, and flashed a covert thumbs-up.

thirty-nine

Billy sensed Mia next to him at the monkey cage. For a minute, she said nothing. They watched a dozen cotton-top tamarin, which were inside a glass case the size of a two-story elevator shaft. The little primates, with dark faces and Einstein's haircut, hurled themselves in perpetual motion, bouncing from shelves to the branches of an artificial tree, then to the floor, and then to the shelves again.

"I haven't been to the zoo in years," Mia said. She held a bag under Billy's nose. "Licorice? It's old. I got it from a machine."

Billy took a piece of candy and kept watch on the monkeys. "I'm trying to learn the rules of this game they're playing," he told her. "Notice the guys on the shelf—I think they're on the bench until somebody fouls out. It seems the premise of the game is that these little guys hurl themselves at one another, one at a time. The target monkey must jump out of the way before somebody crashes into him.

"Look—there!" he said, pointing. "It looks choreographed, but I can't figure out how they know whose turn it is."

She laughed, and warned him, "Don't bet on a game until you know the rules."

They watched the bouncing monkeys for a few minutes and ate licorice.

Mia said finally, "I read that Peter Shadd got three extra years for his escape."

Billy shrugged. "He deserved that much—but he still might have a life someday."

"Pastor Guy and his assistant, Victor Henshaw, won't be so lucky."

"Not after four murders," he agreed.

"My police sources tell me the pastor is blaming Victor for the murders of Alec Black and that ex-con, Franklin Flagg—who turned up in the morgue as a former John Doe who was practically atomized by a high-speed train in South County."

"Victor must have been monitoring the trial and hadn't liked how it was going," Billy said.

"The pastor has offered to testify against Victor, but that won't help him much," she said. "Henshaw is blaming Pastor Guy for arranging the murder of J.R., and then double-crossing Garrett Nickel and shooting him in the back."

"Nice couple of guys, eh? No wonder they went into politics together."

"Mmm," she agreed. "Did you call Martin Smothers back?"

Billy tore off a chunk of licorice. "Yeah, he offered me a job," he said. "Is this candy stale?"

"A job?" she squealed.

"Investigator," he confirmed. "I'd have to wait six months before taking it, so it wouldn't look suspicious after the trial, but it's an interesting offer."

"What did you tell him?"

"To ask again in six months."

They watched the monkeys in silence for another minute.

She asked him, "Do you still wonder if a woman can love two men?"

He looked at her. She stared back with a narrow-eyed seriousness that surprised him. "Is that why you wanted to meet today?"

She reached up and stroked his face. Then she took four sheets of white paper, folded into quarters, from her purse. "I got this for you," she said. "You're not going to like it."

Billy laughed. "Then what kind of gift is that?"

She lifted her chin. A sparkle of light descended the ladder of rings in her ear. "A police accident report—an original."

Billy's hand drew over his heart. "Angie?" he whispered.

"It's the proof you wanted."

He could barely speak. "What does it prove?"

She tucked the papers into his waistband and then slid a hand over his chest and behind his head. She told him, "It proves that two men can love the same woman." She pulled Billy within range, kissed him briefly. Then she left him there, alone.

He parked the van at the bottom of the hill, at a streetlight still burning after dawn. The night had been cloudy, and the air had stayed warm. Billy sweat into his shirt as he hiked the hill leading toward Charlie Maddox's house.

Two cars passed. He did not try to hide from them.

Billy lost himself in the tap of his own feet on the concrete. He wondered about fate. Was it destiny that he had been called for the jury? That he had met Mia in a boathouse? He pushed logic to its limit: What if Pastor Guy had never shot Garrett Nickel? Would Billy have ever confirmed the truth?

Maddox's house was a cream Tudor, with a front yard of cedar chips and pachysandra. The kitchen light was on. *Good,* Billy thought, *he's home and I won't have to wait.*

Suddenly, a little black car flew past Billy, bounced onto the sidewalk, and scraped to a stop.

What the hell—

A big-shouldered man in a cabdriver's cap exploded from the car, coming at Billy.

He's the one following me.

Billy stepped back. "Who the hell—"

Whack!

Billy clutched his jaw and went down like a corpse.

The man threw his cap to the ground. Billy covered up for a beating.

But the man only reached down and patted his shoulder. "Forgive me, my son."

That voice . . .

"Father Capricchio?"

The priest said, "I'm here to save your soul, Billy."

"I think you broke my fucking jaw."

"Oh nonsense," the priest said, blessing himself. "You're speaking with it, aren't you?" He pulled Billy to his feet.

"You've been spying on me, following me around."

"I haven't slept in a week," the priest admitted. His eyes were translucent blue, like Bo's eyes. "I was so worried—I can't let you kill him, Billy."

A smile spread over Billy's face. "You figured out what trial I was on and tracked me down to my house." He pointed at the padre. "You broke your vow of the confessional! You acted on something I said in the booth."

"Shhhh!"

"Well, I'll be damned."

"Not if I can help it," the priest said. He hiked up his pants. Tears gathered in his eyes. "Now are you going to get in the car, or must I rough you up some more?"

Billy stared at him. The priest sank into a wrestler's crouch. He was ready to fight for Billy's soul—to fight until they both were bloody. He had been stalking Billy, watching him, making sure he went nowhere near Maddox.

Billy was awed.

He fell to the ground, hugged the priest around the knees, and let a tear drip.

"I'm not here to kill him, Father," Billy confessed. "I was wrong—a friend found the proof."

"What? But then—the officer *wasn't* drunk in the crash?"

"Who knows?" Billy said. "The cops didn't test Maddox that night because *he wasn't driving.*" He sighed. "Angie was."

"Oh, dear Jesus."

"Maddox persuaded his buddies to help him take the rap, as the driver who had screwed up. That's why the police report was rewritten."

Father Capricchio patted Billy's head. "He sacrificed his own reputation to save hers."

The priest held Billy a minute, then pushed him roughly away. He put his hands on his wide hips. "Then why the heck are you here?"

"My boy wants his mom's cat," Billy said. "Maddox has it."

"Are you here to steal it?"

"I'm here to ask for it," Billy said. "If he says no, then I steal." He grinned.

The priest picked up his cap, punched it back into shape, and snapped it over his head. "Tell me about it tonight—in confession."